TOO CRAZY TO QUIT

"This is McKendree. You can kill my friends. You can kill me, too. But the great white race is awakening at last. My blood will fertilize the nation, and more defenders will rise up from the earth to crush you. . . ."

McKay brought the big V-450 to a stop fifty meters from the fortified bunker. "All right," he announced, "this is your big chance to throw in the towel. Otherwise we're gonna have to crack down here."

The response was a sheet of fire.

McKay lit the night with the .50 caliber and then put the pedal to the metal. Mobile One plowed into the house. Wood splintered. Broken studs scraped at the hull like the fingernails of dying men. He dozed the house from one end to the other, getting a crazy-quilt impression of curtains and furniture and bodies whirling away. McKay hit the far wall with an end-of-the-world crash. . . .

THE GUARDIANS series
from Jove

THE GUARDIANS
DEVIL'S DEAL

RICHARD AUSTIN

JOVE BOOKS, NEW YORK

THE GUARDIANS: DEVIL'S DEAL

A Jove Book/published by arrangement with the author

PRINTING HISTORY
Jove edition/December 1989

ISBN: 0-515-10192-3

PRINTED IN THE UNITED STATES OF AMERICA

10 9 8 7 6 5 4 3 2 1

For Michael Weaver:
The Standard Guardians Party Mix
—for hospitality
and friendship
and all like that

PROLOGUE ─────────────────

Summer came hot and hard to Wyoming when it came at all, but winter had stayed late this year, as it had the year before. It had something to do with the War, Eduardo knew. It had been all over the television, even before it happened. The *norteamericanos* figured it would freeze the whole world, but that hadn't happened. It just went to show how little the *gringo* understood about life.

Summer had arrived at the homestead at last. But the wind that blew down out of the Gros Ventre range carried ice like a razor's edge. Turning up the sheepskin-lined collar of his Levi jacket, Eduardo was grateful for that cold wind. The day wouldn't get really hot until ten o'clock, and he had work to do.

The sun hadn't climbed out from behind the Wind River range when he rode out from the trailer propped on blocks that he shared with his family. The tip of Gros Ventre Peak glowed like a candle flame.

He rode the range he had staked for himself, checking the cattle he and his brothers-in-law had just herded down from their winter pasture. He followed the boundary through spruce stands and meadows of brief winter-stiff grass, checking the two strands of barbed wire for breaks. The wire was to keep valuable stock from straying too far, not to keep anybody out. It wasn't the way things were done in Mexico; everything was much more involved here in the north, even two years after the Third World War. Life was more casual in Mexico, and he could still see the good in that; no question. But he had put Mexico behind him. Even if not entirely by choice.

There had been a rainstorm two nights before, accompanied by lightning that threatened to set the sky on fire and thunder that made the earth shake like a quake in the Valley of Mexico. Ofi and Fela had wept in fear and clung to their mother. Chona had comforted them, assured them there was nothing to fear, and in the light of the alcohol lamp only Eduardo could see the tremors around her set mouth that proved what he knew already, that the brave front was a lie. His wife had always dreaded thunder herself.

As he suspected, the wire was broken in several places by fallen limbs. In one place a looming dead tree had been split off by a lightning strike and crashed through the wire.

He spent several hours restringing the wire by hand, carefully splicing it where needed with sixteen-gauge wire from a roll tied to his saddle—baling wire, salvaged from hay bales. It was not the habit of the Mexican peasant to let anything go to waste. A useful trait in the stricken, strange world they lived in now, which once had been the home of plenty.

The sun was high when he finished, and hot, as he'd known it would be. He took off the red rolled handkerchief he'd been wearing as a headband and wrung it out on the silvered bole of a tree that had fallen victim to another ferocious storm long before. He cursed himself for a fool; had he thought to ask yesterday he might have had the help of Chona's brothers. But he had set out on this task by impulse this morning. The stinging of sweat in an open cut on his hand, where the backlash had caught him after a splice failed to hold, reproved him for his carelessness.

He drank from the U.S. Army surplus canteen slung from the horn of his high-cantled saddle—a family heirloom, hand tooled and chased in silver, one of few possessions he'd gotten out of Chihuahua with—and mounted his scrubby dun gelding. A huge mug of steaming coffee, preferably with a shot of trade whiskey in it, would restore him, and afterward a solid breakfast of *chorizo* and eggs and beans, all smothered in chili and cheese, with some good gooey *gringo* pastries on the side; he didn't share the odd preoccupation *norteamericanos* had with trimming one's diet down to nothing.

The Americans had tried to hide from any hint of risk, before the War. Safety was all they talked about, it seemed. Now most of them were dead. It didn't surprise him.

He wiped his mouth with the back of one hand. When he had restoppered the canteen he raised his head and saw smoke trailing into the sky to the north.

A thin drool of white, looking drawn-in where it crossed a distant cumulus jumble. As he watched it swelled and blackened.

North. A faint popping reached his ears.

"Chona!" he shouted. He threw himself across the saddle. Already sensing something wrong, the dun sidestepped and rolled its eyes.

He spurred hard for the ranch-house trailer, not sparing the gelding on slopes. Once its unshod hooves slipped on loose shale in a streambed and they almost went down, but the horse managed to keep its feet and stagger into a run again.

The trailer was a long white box at the head of a clearing, with fir trees pressing close behind, clinging to a steepening slope. The popping had swelled and hardened into sounds like hammering on a corrugated tin roof, echoing inside his head, almost as loud as the desperate drumming of his pulse. It was dying away as he broke through the trees on the clearing's southwest edge.

The horses were screaming and hurling themselves into the wire mesh that was strung around salvaged railroad ties to form a corral. He saw them first. Then he saw flames hurling themselves out the windows of the trailer, hot updrafts blowing up tattered blue awnings that hadn't yet taken fire. Then the men with hoods on their heads and guns in their hands.

Then he saw his wife. María Ernestina. Plump but still prett*/*, with a face that managed to be both delicate and robust in that curious Indian way. Kneeling with only the cheap fabric of her skirt to protect her knees from the hard-packed earth in front of the trailer.

"Chona!" he screamed. She raised her face. It was enameled with tears. Their eyes met across seventy meters.

The muzzle of the short black assault rifle was almost touching the gray-dusted roll of black hair at the nape of her neck when it went off.

He screamed again, a cry without words like a wild wounded animal's. He ripped the old Winchester .30-30 from its scabbard fixed to the front rigging ring by his right knee.

He had already made his last mistake, he knew. He snapped up the rifle and fired at the man who had shot Chona. He saw him drop as the dun reared, frantically pumped the lever of his Winchester.

The hooded men returned fire from among the makeshift outbuildings, nasty high-pitched cracking of full-automatic fire cut across by the heavy door-slam of a single heavy-caliber shot. Eduardo felt stinging impacts in arm, thigh, and chest.

Brief pain was instantly replaced with cold leaden numbness. He was falling, the horse falling beneath him. He felt a tearing wrench as the animal's weight jerked his right hip from its socket.

The rifle had fallen. It lay in a clump of grass, tantalizing centimeters beyond his reach. He strained for it, ignoring a sensation that was more being cut off from his own body than pain.

As if from a hundred miles away he heard a fresh flurry of firing. Black dirt spurted before his eyes. His outstretched hand spewed blood from a sudden stigma.

Brass-knuckle blows rolled him over. His vision blurred, washed away.

He lay on his back, feeling his heart kicking spastically in his chest like the dying horse thrashing in the dirt by his side. He heard no sound. It was as if his ears were packed with earth.

Blinking brought sight reluctantly back to his left eye. The sky was high and hurting-brilliant overhead. Far above an eagle circled placidly, unaware or disdainful of the violence below.

He had not made a mistake after all, he realized. *Chona, I am coming now.*

The eagle became a flying crucifix, black silhouette against white cloud. He felt his soul soar to meet it.

CHAPTER
ONE —————————————————————————

"How goes the war effort, Mr. Chairman?" the sleek blond man asked the television set in the anonymous apartment. Outside the city lay hidden under blackness. Night didn't mean bright lights in Chicago anymore.

The image on the screen was that of a man defying gravity on the downslope of his middle years. He wore a burgundy dressing gown around a powerful chest, open at the throat to reveal a thatch of graying hair. His head was large, hair heavy and brown and streaked at the temples with gray, slicked back from a bluff of forehead; it gave the impression at once of being immaculately groomed and being barely under control. The beard surrounding the full-lipped mouth was much the same.

"Quite well. The Pan-Turanians became badly disorganized over the winter. We're preparing a massive spring offensive. Their logistics were poor, their hygiene worse, and they've been splintering into factions along ethnic and religious lines. Not"—the lips smiled—"without assistance from our operatives."

The blond man narrowed long sea green eyes. "I should be there."

The bearded man chuckled and shook his head. "Jacquin, whom you personally trained, has the situation well in hand. Iskander Bey is in for some markedly unpleasant surprises when we make our move.'' Bushy brows swept low. ''Meanwhile, you should be where I choose to employ you, and I choose to employ you precisely where you are.''

The craggy face brightened again, as if clouds had drifted past the sun. ''But surely my favorite son did not insist on speaking with me personally—much to the wounded dignity of the so-lovely Nathalie Frechette, who continues to hide her light under a bushel of dowdiness—merely to satisfy your curiosity about the war effort.'' *Son* was a figure of speech; the blond man was a Georgian, for example, and the man on the screen Ukrainian, though both spoke Russian with a cultured Moscow accent.

''That's right. As of now our tenuous truce with the Guardians appears to remain in effect. I need to know if it should continue to do so.''

''They want your assistance for the final phase?''

The blond man hesitated, nodded. ''I want to know if they should receive it.''

The big man twined fingers in his beard. The rings on them belied their blunt strength. ''They should.''

''But, Chairman Maximov—''

Yevgeny Maximov, chairman and sole ruler of the Federated States of Europe, raised one finger. ''Do not mistake me, Vanya. I have not grown soft. But neither have I abandoned my intention to conquer the territory once known as the United States of America. I prefer to capture it as intact as possible. Am I clear?''

''Indeed.''

''And after you have helped them to succeed, should they be naïve enough to expect advance notice of the dissolution of the entente the late Colonel Morrigan forced upon us, that's hardly our fault, is it?

''A very good evening to you, Colonel.''

''I don't like it,'' Sonny Jim said.

''You don't have to like it,'' Jenner said. ''Just got to sit it out.''

It was an appropriate kind of location: an ammo-storage bunker, WWII vintage, forgotten on the outskirts of Vicksburg where there was nothing much but trailer courts, used-car lots, and swampy tributaries of the Yazoo. The area hadn't amounted to much even before the Third World War, and property values hadn't appreciated much since then. Nonetheless, the weather maps of William Morrigan—who preferred to go by the handle Marcus Aurelius—showed the prevailing winds were right to disperse the nerve gas, stowed in the bunker in neat yellow and black canisters, right over the densest concentrations of the bustling survivor community that had gotten established in the river-junction city.

It was stone uncomfortable in here, humid and still and close, rank with mildew and sweat. Even in the hour before dawn the bunker was a hothouse where tensions grew like mushrooms. Sonny Jim still didn't know what the fuck he'd done to piss the old man off enough to ship his ass down here. Morrigan even had the balls to claim it was an *honor*.

He turned away from the steel door with a disgusted gesture. "We haven't heard from Chicago in three days."

"M.A. had a lot goin' down," Rosetti said, not looking up from his scarfed skin mag. They were primo trade items; good porn had been pretty damn hard to come by even before the War, what with national censorship and all. Not *scarce*; prohibition never worked that way. But hard to come by. The light of the pair of alcohol lamps wasn't great for reading, but Rosetti was probably not reading any fine print. "He was arranging for the Motor City Madman to kiss his skinny ass big time, last we heard, in case it slipped your alleged mind."

Sonny Jim ripped the magazine away, held it up for examination, dropped it on the cement floor. "You're disgusting. How can you stand to look as such filth?"

"Easy."

Sonny Jim paced and pummeled the air with his big red hands. "Don't you remember what was supposed to happen if we didn't hear from Chicago?" He drew his forefinger across his throat. "We're supposed to lay down a little law."

"Fuck *me*," Rosetti said, retrieving his magazine. "He's all ready to gas ten thousand wool hats and here he's worked up about me looking at pictures of young ladies I'm sure are sincerely in love with one another."

"Will you all kindly shut the fuck up?" asked the heavy voice of Boothe the radioman from the shadowed recesses of the bunker. "I'm getting some kinda funny interference."

Somebody knocked on the door.

There was much silence. Sonny Jim clutched at his chest. He had on cammie pants and a sweat-soaked OD tee shirt with tufts of red hair sticking out the front of the neck. "Shit! I'm out of uniform."

"You figure this is a snap inspection?" Rosetti asked skeptically. "I mean, we're only eight hundred miles from Chi. Maybe M.A. decided to pop down, pass out a few demerits before breakfast."

"Don't laugh, okay?" Boothe murmured. "Wouldn't put it past him."

"Fuck, fuck." Rosetti went back to the door, stuffing his tee shirt back into his waistband.

With a minimum of motion Jenner had picked up his H&K 5.56-millimeter assault rifle and chambered a round. "Why don't you see who it is?"

Sonny Jim fidgeted some more, checked the Beretta service pistol in his hip holster—it hadn't fallen out, sure enough—and slid back the steel shutter covering the peephole.

"It's some old nigger," he said, sliding the judas shut and turning away.

"Say *what*?" demanded Boothe, whose albedo was low enough for him to take that remark personally.

"Um," Sonny Jim said. He opened the peephole.

"Got me a mess of crawdads," the old black man said. He had a gray moustache and an abbreviated salt-and-pepper Afro with a striped railroad cap propped on top of it. He spoke with one of those Deep South black accents that Sonny Jim, Chicago born and bred, could barely make out; sounded like he was trying to talk through a mouthful of Gummi Bears.

"Say what?" Sonny Jim said. He recoiled from the viewport; the old bastard's moustache looked *matted* somehow. Who the fuck knew what kind of horrible post-Holocaust cruds he might be suffering from? Some of the things the nesters came down with in Chicago . . . He shuddered.

" 'Dads. Got me a mess of crawdads. Nice an' fresh. Boil 'em up with some spices, they mighty good eating."

He had a wooden dolly wheeled onto the bunker's cement apron beside him, with an oil drum full of murky water on it. He picked a pair of peeled twigs off the drum's rim, dipped them into the water, brought out a dripping, squirming green crustacean chopstick-style.

"Jesus! What's *that*?"

"Crayfish," said Jenner quietly.

"They're just like shrimp, fuckwit," Rosetti added helpfully. "Haven't you ever seen a shrimp before?"

"Not that wasn't boiled."

"You boil these, just like the man said," Boothe said. He hit his receiver with a broad thick hand. "Damn, satellite link's gone fuzzy and now the landline's dead. After the goddam electro-magnetic pulse took out so much of the electronics in the War you can't rely on anything. I could do with some fresh food; these freeze-dry rats are making my skin turn gray."

"Didn't we used to have a sentry?" Rosetti asked. Jenner's mouth tightened and he turned back to the door.

The old guy had his face mushed up against the peephole and was rolling his eyes around at the cots and stacked supplies. There was nothing much secret in view; the other five men of the bunker's complement were sacked out behind a partition, and the nerve gas cans were stashed in a separate bunker connected by a tunnel that could be made airtight at a moment's notice.

"Yeah," he said, "Mister Rourke. He said I could bring my 'dads on up here. Said he hoped you-all would buy 'em. I just catched 'em this morning."

Jenner's knife-slit mouth got even tighter. "What the fuck. Let's take a look."

Looking doubtful, Sonny Jim turned the bolt and slid it back—no high-tech electric locks down in this Southern rathole, not like the Citadel. Fuck Morrigan anyway; he'd been promising them they were about to run the whole Disunited States, just a couple days before, and now they were hearing jack shit—

"Here y'go, son," the antique spade said, handing something to Sonny Jim. By reflex he reached out for it—a readiness to take what was offered was a common trait among Morrigan's heroes.

It was a fucking *crayfish*. Hard and slimy and writhing in a really gross way. It promptly bit him at the base of his thumb.

"Shit!" he screamed, voice breaking like an adolescent's. He whipped his hand up and down and the damned thing went ricocheting back into the bunker, to howls of laughter from Sonny Jim's alleged buddies.

He turned around to thump the jig a few times to teach him how to talk to a Morrigan man. The crusty old fuck had his hands stuck into that cruddy-looking water to the elbows, root-ing around.

Funny, Sonny Jim thought, *he's sure got a smooth neck for an old codger—*

"Got somethin' else for y'all," the black man said, dumping a wet mass on the bunker floor at Sonny Jim's feet. He shied back, frowned at it. It looked like a plastic bag wrapped around with gross wet weeds. There was something like an aluminum can inside.

No, by God, it was a stun grenade. With a sliver of metal beside it, like the pin—

He opened his mouth to scream.

The world went white.

"Whoo-*ee*," the lean troopie in the fatigue hat called from the peephole. "Get a load of *this*. There's a blond bimbo out here, and she must be six feet tall!"

"What the fuck, over?" the CO said.

"I hope that's just what she's got in mind!"

It was an old, smelly basement in an unreconstructed section of downtown San Antonio. What it had been aboveground no-body was too sure of; urban renewal had planed it off even before the Lackland blast, so that the main effect of the One-Day War had been to prevent construction of a government-subsidized apartment for the upper middle class.

Before mounting the steps to the sunken doorway the CO did a quick visual check to make sure there were no obvious military impedimenta lying around in plain view. Not that it really mat-tered; if you wanted to walk around in cammies with automatic weapons hanging off you, these Texicans regarded that as strictly your business, unless you started pointing the things at people, in which case it was strictly your funeral. These Republic of Texas morons really had no sense of how to discipline their pop-ulation; they were just begging for what William Morrigan had to offer, if only they knew it.

Still, M.A.'s explicit instructions had been to avoid calling attention to themselves. So they played the roles of scavengers working over unreclaimed ruins. Even these easygoing Texican doofs would probably find reason to object to somebody storing enough nerve gas in their spare room to scour everything inside the Interstate 410 belt of life.

Witkowski was bending down to peer out the peephole. His tongue was practically hanging out of his head.

"Ah *know* it's early," the CO heard one of your exaggerated West Texas deb voices say. He had to admit it brought to mind something he'd read in a book once, that with Texan coeds the question wasn't whether they gave head but how well. "Ah'm just tryin' to do a li'l business, sugar. It *is* the oldest profession, after all. Here, I'll show you—"

"Out of the way, Witkowski." He pushed the troopie to one side and bent down to look for himself.

He found himself staring down the barrels of two of the most gorgeous tits he had seen in his entire life.

He jerked his head back, wondering if he was hallucinating. Witkowski gaped at him, started to bend back to the peephole. The CO shouldered him aside.

They were still there. Satin-skinned and firm as breasts that big so rarely are. The nipples were pink, standing proudly out from daintily goosefleshed aureoles.

Their owner took a step back. She was everything Witkowski had said: even without the spike heels she would have topped six feet, with honey blond hair gathered into pigtails framing a high-cheekboned Scandinavian face and her boobs hanging out of a slinky dress that had to have been scarfed from Neiman-Marcus. A combination of country-girl innocence and *Hustler* challenge: fantasy made flesh.

"You like 'em?" she was saying, shaking her shoulders. Her nipples traced figure eights in the crisp predawn air. "Believe me, sugar, they're only appetizers."

"Uh," the CO said, "well."

"What's going on?" Townsend called from below. "Trouble?"

"Not exactly."

The CO was feeling a familiar stirring in the regions aft of his fly. They'd been cooped up in this hole a mighty long time, waiting to back M.A.'s big play. With their commo link to Chicago down—again—the men were getting tense and bored. The phrase *a tonic for the troops* suggested itself.

Not to mention a tonic for the boss, the CO thought. *Rank doth have its privileges.* It was part of what M.A.'s revolution was about, in fact.

He worked the bolt. "Come on in, darling," he said, opening the door. "My name's Martin."

She smiled sweetly. She was beautiful enough for the cover of *Cosmo*.

"Then we'll know what to write on your tombstone, honey," she said, "if you make even the least little noise."

She brought her right hand around from behind her back. What it held actually managed to draw his attention from those fantastic boobs.

Heckler & Koch MP5 machine pistols with integral silencers have that effect on some people.

CHAPTER
TWO ———————————————————

The wind hunted along the slope of Green Mountain, carrying cold along with it. Overhead the stars were bright and hard as diamond drill bits.

They didn't spill much light on the front foothills of the Rockies. But it was enough for the miracle of high-temperature superconductor technology that was the scope on Casey Wilson's rifle. He tracked it along the low grass-covered hummock at the base of the hill—why they called the thing a *mountain*, when there were *real* mountains shouldering into the early-morning sky right behind, was a mystery to him—until he caught a glimpse of his target.

What with the wave of defense-research contracts that had come flooding out of the District of Columbia with the election of hard-line hawk William ("Wild Bill") Lowell as president, there were parts of the country where you couldn't walk fifty meters without straying up against a top-security area. That was especially true in Denver and environs. Denver had always been a company town for the U.S. government, since the Second World War at least.

A few klicks to the east, for example, sprawled the Denver Federal Center; not even military connected, it was a stronghold of the IRS and the largest civilian governmental compound in

the U.S. Right now it belonged to the forces of the Reverend
Nathan Bedford Forrest Smith's Church of the New Dispensa-
tion, plague decimated but still hanging tough, but the point
remained that it had been Fed originally.

The facility down at the base of the lumpy cone misnamed
Green Mountain, hidden by a swell of ridge from the rest of the
suburb of Lakewood, had been one of innumerable satellites of
the Rocky Mountain Arsenal laid down after Wild Bill's inau-
guration. It was ideal for the use to which it was currently being
put. The locals knew there were Big Secrets there, and were
accustomed to steering clear.

There had been no particular attempt to conceal the cameras
covering the entrance to the subterranean facility. With the ambient light–enhancing feature of the scope on-line, Casey had
little trouble spotting the white plastic oblong, a third of a meter
long, from his vantage point in a clump of crumbly red rock
four hundred meters away.

He watched it for a moment. It didn't track. He wasn't surprised. From its look it had a multiple switchable optic array,
which was a fancy way of saying it was actually three digital
video pickups built into one that could cover better than ninety
degrees without moving.

Guardians training taught you a lot of stuff like that.

He cracked the bolt of his rifle, slid it back with the gentle
authority of a lover. It was a retrograde sort of piece, a real
contrast to the Star Wars scope: a bolt action with a heavy barrel,
built on an ancient Remington 700 in .308 caliber, adapted to
take a twenty round NATO magazine. A California kid, way
progressive as a general thing, Casey was a true reactionary in
this area: he felt a semiauto defeated the purpose of a sniper's rifle. You couldn't miss fast enough to catch up, as Billy
McKay always said about full-auto fire, and besides, even with
modern technology you couldn't make a semiautomatic rifle with
the kind of excruciating nail-head accuracy of a fine bolt gun.

And nothing short of the theoretical max was worthy of Casey
Wilson.

On that last mission over Syria he'd made his fifth and final
kill of the sortie with just three twenty-millimeter rounds to the
cockpit of a MiG-29: max range and plenty of angle-off. That
Fulcrum had just snap-rolled onto its back and gone right into
the ground.

This particular target was reminiscent of the old days in one good particular, he reflected as he took a special round from the breast pocket of his camouflaged coveralls. He would be shooting at a machine rather than a person. Not that that would last, of course.

He slipped the needle-nosed round into the chamber, carefully closed the bolt. It was a loaded-down round; without the supersonic *crack* of a full-powered load headed downrange the big rifle made no more sound than knuckles cracking.

The wind blew laterally. There were all kinds of fancy functions built into the scope to compensate for that. He didn't bring them up. He didn't need them; at this range he didn't need more than iron sights for a target that size, once he had it spotted.

He settled the barrel into its sandbag prop, welded his cheek to the fiberglass stock, drew in a deep breath, released it halfway, and squeezed the trigger.

Recoil was light, bringing the heavy suppressor-mounted barrel up only a few degrees. When it settled back down the camera was in the center of the vision field. It had a little black hole in its housing now, just behind the gleaming compound eye. He spoke a word—or rather, he went through the motions; the minute microphone taped to his larynx read subvocalized speech so that he didn't have to talk out loud.

There was an interval of shadow motion downslope.

While it occurred he took out a second powered-down cartridge and chambered it. In the scenario in his head he might have call for one more totally suppressed shot; then he might as well start burning the full loads in the box magazine. They made enough sound to warn alert listeners that caps were being busted, but were muffled enough by the suppressor to make it impossible to localize their source.

Minutes passed. He waited, settled comfortably in a meditation state that kept him ready to respond instantly when anything happened. In time something did.

Diffuse gray was beginning to stain the sky behind Casey when light spilled out of one end of the bunker. He already had the rifle pointed in that direction; all it took was to ease himself into firing position behind it and look through the scope.

As a high-tech warrior himself, he knew how prone all those marvelous technotoys were to malfunction. This was probably not the first time one of the security cameras had gone out since

Morrigan's people had occupied the place. It was annoyingly common, if not routine. Nothing to call down an alert about.

They hadn't gotten all the way complacent, though, sad to say. The technician who emerged with a lineman's belt at his waist turned to secure the door. He couldn't be permitted to do that.

Incredibly, one of his comrades opened the door all the way to find out what had become of him. Casey had just had time to click the magazine the rest of the way into the well and work the bolt again. So the second man got to discover firsthand what had happened to his buddy.

As coolly as if he were tying his shoes, Casey chambered another round. The Freehold strike team hit the still-unsealed door, tossing stun grenades inside and following them with shotguns and submachine guns blazing. His job was over now, if things went as planned.

But a Guardian never took anything for granted.

The East Coast had not been a lucky place to be during the brief global misunderstanding the survivors fondly knew as the One-Day War. For all the bullshit both sides had generated in advance of the actual event, purely civilian targets had the lowest possible priorities; each contestant was interested first and foremost in hitting the other's missile farms and bomber bases, and anything else was pretty incidental.

But the Soviet Union, which failed to invade Poland in 1980, which was the latest in a long succession of countries to lose a war of conquest in Afghanistan, and which started the thermonuclear ball rolling because it couldn't keep a full-scale war in Western Europe supplied for longer than a hundred and seventy hours, had itself a Big Notion. The Soviet war planners actually believed the USSR was going to fight a protracted conventional war in the aftermath of a nuclear spasm. So over the howled protests of the rocket forces they got a number of warheads aimed at "strategic" targets, strikes designed to damage America's ability to resist the grand conquest. Not a lot. If they were going to try to conquer the West they wanted to damage the physical plant as little as possible; some of the older hands remembered the Stalinist days of wooden gears in tractors. Just to weaken the opposition.

As it happened neither superpower had survived the exchange.

But the dose of reality came too late to do the vast industrial and transportation complex of the Bos-Wash Corridor any good.

Still, some had made it through the bombings and the epidemics and famines that followed. Eventually refugees and others began to filter into the blasted cities in search of rich troves of *scarf*, salvageable goods. Thermonuclear war was a lot harder on human beings than on their possessions.

It was a bank in Trenton. Not a glass Bauhaus box, or one of the later designs that attempted to relieve the cubical grimness of the Bauhaus plague with often bizarre whimsy. It was built in the days when the dollar was solid and banks were expected to be too. It had survived the warheads and the liquid propane firestorm they had ignited pretty much unscathed. The subsequent riots had passed it by; these were the nineties, after all, and looters were far too sophisticated to waste calories liberating pink and blue New Dollar notes; they hadn't been worth all that much *before* the balloon went up.

Unobtrusive. Hardened. Easily defensible. *Ideal*.

Well, almost.

It had been a dance studio in Trenton. It was on the second story above one of the city's oldest financial institutions; the floors were thick enough that not even the tightest-sphinctered banker could hear enough of even the most elephantine *jetés* to object.

Standard issue post-War derelict litter was scattered along one wall that used to be mirrored before some of the more recent occupants found time weighing heavy on their hands. There was a circular scorch spang in the center of the hardwood floor where somebody had built a fire. The windows were rectangles of spoiled salmon and curdled milk sky.

Objects that looked like big overturned flowerpots had been arranged in a weird pattern on the floor. A pre-War district attorney of the crusading type would probably have read Satanic ritual significance into the design. He wouldn't have been that far wrong.

The black dude had a big peace sign painted across the front of his Kevlar, ceramic, and steel assault vest. A gas mask hung around his skinny neck. Human fingerbones dangled from his ears.

His eyes glittered in the sort of light as he raised his head to look across the array of inverted flowerpots.

"Shee-it," he whispered reverently, "I ain't never blown no bank before." Outside some squatter's rooster crowed.

Tom Rogers, formerly Lieutenant Thomas Rogers, U.S. Army Special Forces, motioned him back to join the rest of the wildly garbed Tide Camp team in the shadows well clear of the pattern of shaped charges.

"It ain't all it's cracked up to be," he said, and snapped open the cover of the initiator.

The Commune of Seattle consisted of typical bourgeois naïfs playing at revolution. That was how Colonel Ivan Vesensky, formerly of the KGB, saw them, anyway. They wouldn't have loved him either.

But he didn't have to love them to save them; he had his orders. The late and notably unlamented William Morrigan had managed to infiltrate into Seattle some of the cache of nerve gas his equally unmourned scientific adviser, Dr. Magnus Cromartie, had turned him on to. Inside the city, Vesensky still had available at short notice covert assets he'd cultivated before the War, and Maximov's concern over Morrigan's scheme to wreak postmortem vengeance on the country he coveted was great enough for him to burn them up.

So now he was crouched on a mound that still showed signs of expensive landscaping, with the early-hours breeze off Puget Sound stirring tall pine trees at his back. The mansion in the upwardly mobile suburb of Richmond Highlands didn't look much like a mansion, which was probably why it hadn't been collectivized. It was an earth-sheltered home dug into a hillside, very very eco-conscious; the granola collectivists who ran Seattle these days seemed too inclined to enjoy the sort of resource-intensive bourgeois pleasures they denied the proletarians to go for dwelling in an upscale hobbit hole.

But the place wasn't going to waste. This detachment of Marcus Aurelius's praetorians knew how to live well, at least.

Too well, in all probability. The body of the sole sentry sprawled next to a redwood bench nearby. Vesensky had removed him by the simple expedient of shooting him in the head with a silenced pistol. He had never much gone for the sort of elaborate hand-to-hand sentry neutralization techniques they used to devote centerfolds to in *Soldier of Fortune*. Especially when his left and master forearm was locked in a plastic mesh cast. One of Morrigan's bodyguards who'd stayed at home had broken it for him during the short, sweet fight for the Citadel.

He shot almost as perfectly with his right hand as his left, fortunately.

He signaled his men forward. A trio of unreconstructed Stalinists—in *America*, for God's sake, the country really was decadent—slipped forward, dressed like him in black, ski masks over their faces, Kalashnikovs from a cache Spetsnaz had optimistically hidden on Cape Flattery in their hands. The others were hidden in the woods and on the grounds, a few watching for Seattle patrols, the rest covering the exits. These were all in the front. Marvelous things, earth-berm houses: no back doors.

He walked in a crouch to a housing that stuck out of the apparent hillside like a gable. At rest, he could hear the hum of a fan inside, running off a solar accumulator. It was a type of heat and air exchanger, called an economizer, that provided ventilation for the airtight structure.

He undid the Velcro fastener of his belt pouch and took out a small torpedo-shaped container. It looked like a bottle of spray cologne. He unscrewed a cap and sprayed a quick white mist in front of the intake. Then he stuck the bottle back in his belt and waddled to the front of the concealed building, unslinging a silenced MP5 right-handed.

They could have turned the tables on Morrigan's merry men, hauled some of the nerve gas they'd liberated from the Citadel out here and piped it down the burrow. But nerve gas was tricky stuff. Vesensky had heard too many horror stories during his own military training and later to trust *anybody's* NBC protective gear. Besides, Maximov's whole idea was to *avoid* releasing the stuff in the land of which he would be king.

Luckily, there was an easier way.

Coming up through the soles of his Chinese slippers, Vesensky felt a high-frequency vibration. It seemed to rise and fall in cycles. Just like an alarm. He braced the butt of the machine pistol against his thigh and cocked the weapon with his right hand, then deftly caught the pistol grip again before it could fall.

Along with the nerve gas canisters, Morrigan's men had taken along a standard type of contamination detector. As quick acting as the gas was, the things wouldn't be much help if there was an accidental release, but apparently having them made the boys feel better. The spray bottle contained a harmless ester whipped up by biochemist Suzette Nguyen during two nights of frantic preparation for the simultaneous raids on Morrigan's hidden nerve gas dumps. The contam sensors, however, would think it anything but harmless.

Is that screaming I hear? It was probably just imagination.

The door blew open as though somebody'd slapped an X-charge to it. A man fell out of it, went scrambling across the cedar-bark front yard on all fours with his shirttails flapping around his butt. Vesensky gave him a short burst. He rolled over and over, coughing up blood.

He could hear screams now, no question at all. There was a commotion right underfoot, and three more men burst into the cool air, disarmed and dressed only in skivvies. A fusillade of Kalashnikov fire hit them like a mobile wall.

There were procedures to follow in the event of a contamination alert. Stickler for discipline that he was, Marcus Aurelius Morrigan would have insisted his minions be drilled in them. But to the best of these boys' knowledge M.A. was thousands of kilometers away—and the VX cans were up close and personal.

Three more men ran out into the gunfire they almost certainly knew was waiting for them. A marvelous thing was panic, too.

He waved his MP5 above his head. Time for the loyal Stalinists to go into the house to dig out the foes too shrewd, stubborn, or befuddled to have been flushed by the phony alarm.

And time likewise for Colonel Ivan Vesensky, now of the Federated States of Europe, to pull his patented disappearing act, before the Guardians got back to Chicago and discovered the homecoming present he'd left them.

CHAPTER
THREE ───────────────────────

A millisecond before the Close Assault Weapons System bucked and roared, Sam Sloan ducked back around the doorway. *How do I get myself into these situations?* he asked himself. His breathing roared in his respirator hood.

He winced and hugged his Galil/M203 combo to his chest as 000 pellets rattled around him in the cement stairwell. His bulky armor kept them from doing more than stinging here and there.

It was all his fault. He was the one who had teased Morrigan's data base into spitting out the locations of the secret installations with which the Citadel's mad master planned to blackmail America into submission. That had set this bad craziness in motion, and was the proximate cause of his being here, pinned down in the hallway of what used to be a small but very cutting-edge Palo Alto microprocessor firm.

Of course, the *real* trouble had started when he volunteered to be a Guardian. Everything followed from that. Inevitable, like.

Something clattered on the floor at his feet. He glanced down and almost made the mistake of staring at it.

A stun grenade. Just like the ones hung at his belt. Just in time he turned his head and shut his eyes.

They were supposed to have all the advantages. He was bundled up like the Sta-Puft Marshmallow Man in heavy assault armor. He had the best in modern gear and communications, including protection against varied chemical and biological nastinesses that incidentally also served to cut down the disorienting effects of flash-bang bombs. The rest of the strike force did too, courtesy of the scavenger/trader network set up by Israeli-born economist Dr. Jacob Morgenstern. Not that it was so surprising that Morgenstern could wangle access to such paraphernalia. He *was* the Guardians' boss, after all.

Unfortunately, the bad guys had all the good stuff too. Like the CAWS super-shotgun Sloan had just managed to elude. The buckshot wouldn't get through his armor, but the odds were the gunner also had depleted uranium slugs that would burn right on through the steel ceramic inserts in his vest.

Like the stun grenade. Which went flash, and also bang.

There was a doctrine used in employing those things. The bad guy knew it as well as Sloan. Which was a lick on *him*.

When he popped around the corner with his CAWS leveled from the hip, Sam Sloan was already tightening his finger on the trigger of the M203 grenade launcher slung under the barrel of his assault rifle. The multiple projectile round that vomited out of the stubby barrel made it an even bigger shotgun than the CAWS. A mass of double-aught punched a hole the size of a one-pound coffee can right through the middle of the defender and he just went flying.

Sloan followed his MP charge out into the open, hurled himself to the floor, firing the Galil flat out. Two more troopies had been trotting behind the first, M16s at port arms. One of them turned and took off like an Olympic sprinter, disappearing into a work area that opened up at the far end of the corridor. The other probably wanted to do the same, but was too busy rolling around clutching his shattered shin to do much sprinting.

A second swaddled figure flopped ungainly down beside Sam Sloan. "What it is?" a muffled voice asked.

"About time you got here, Idaho."

"Better late than never. Ran into some new friends on the ground floor. How many of these dudes are supposed to be in here, anyway?"

"Ten seemed to be the usual number."

The hooded head shook. "Seen that many already. What're we waiting for? They might be getting ready to blow the gas."

"Right." As one, the two men jumped up and ran.

The stocky man put his hard hat back on thick silver-gray hair brushed carefully back from his face and took a deep breath. *"Sauget,"* he said, with mock satisfaction.

McKay squinted into the stink that the early sunlight seemed to be squeezing out of the ground. "That what you call that smell?"

"In a manner of speaking. It's what they call the suburb."

All McKay knew was that it was like a piece of Old New Jersey across the river from St. Louis. "They quit pumping the pollutants two years ago, and it still smells like this?" he said, sticking a cigar in his face.

"Takes a while for it to wear off. Chemicals seep into the soil." He grabbed McKay's brawny arm as the former marine and current head of the Guardians prepared to strike a match. "Not so fast, big fella, or we'll be watching this show from orbit."

"Oh, yeah." To be safe he took the cigar out of his mouth and stuck it back into what he hoped was a pocket, beneath the bulky white suit he was wearing. "How're we doing with the preparations?"

"Pumps are going, hoses are in place," Max Weber said, scratching his moustache with his thumb. He was a self-educated engineer turned gentleman terrorist during last year's fight against the FSE's army of occupation. Tom Rogers had run across him while roaming the country raising general hell as a prelude to springing President Jeff MacGregor from Heartland. He was straw boss of the team of local talent that had turned out to help McKay. "This should work, if you discount details like a really major chance of dying."

McKay shrugged. "Hey. Those are just the kind of odds I like."

The engineer cocked a skeptical eyebrow. Well, it sounded idiotic to McKay too, but he felt like he had to say something.

He didn't think much of this scheme, either, to tell the goddam truth. It wasn't *his* fault his plane, of all the ones Washington had turned out for this mission, had developed engine trouble and been forced to emergency land on Interstate 55 in the middle of fucking Illinois. Not even that long a delay.

Just long enough for the boys holed up in a bunker that was part of a former gasoline-additive plant to discover that their buddies scattered across the country were coming into some serious hurt all at the same time.

A man who called himself Marcus Aurelius undoubtedly expected his men to do or die without question. Fat fucking chance; McKay could have told him. Standing orders were to vent the gas at the first sign of trouble. The boys in the bunker realized what their lives were worth if they did that. Instead they wanted to negotiate—and held a good chunk of the Mississippi Valley hostage.

"Message for Billy McKay," a female voice said behind his right ear. "Are you in?"

"Funny," he said for his larynx mike to relay back to the Volkswagen commo van. "Put 'em on."

"McKay? Gates, Vicksburg."

Staff Sergeant—now Lieutenant by presidential decree—Horatio Gates had started out with the United States Army fighting the Russians in Europe, wound up serving under the Federated States after USAREUR commanding general Mark Shaw had recognized the authority of Yevgeny Maximov. He'd come back to the States as part of an Effsee expedition to seize a secret facility called Starshine, part of the shadowy Blueprint for Renewal which was the one prize Maximov most wanted to grab out of the ruins of America. The Guardians had thwarted the FSE plan. Gates and his men, who had been told by the Effsees that the U.S. no longer existed, had surrendered after the defeat of the expeditionary force and sworn allegiance to President MacGregor.

"Yeah? How'd it go?"

"All secure now, McKay. Had one boy wanted to be a hero, started firing blind after I popped a stun grenade on him. I tipped over an oil drum full of crawdaddies, the water knocked the legs out from under him, and that was that."

"Hm," said McKay.

"Now all I got to do is get this God damned shoe polish out of my hair. Say, I hear you up in my old stomping grounds. How's East St. Louis these days?"

"Smells like shit."

"Ho. You must be in Sauget."

He was laughing when he broke the connection. Instantly Janey in the commo van was back, talking through the bone-conduction phone taped to McKay's mastoid process.

'' 'Nother call incoming, Lieutenant. You must be a popular kind of guy.''

You couldn't have told that from the next voice; McKay could almost see the icicles hanging off the West Texas drawl.

"This is Eklund. We got the nest in San Antone all cleared out. You wanted us to let you-all know." Marla Eklund, major in the armed forces of the Republic of Texas and former state women's bodybuilding champion, had been Billy McKay's semi-sort-of-live-in squeeze for a while in Texas, until she had discovered him tangled up with a naked teenager who happened to be the youngest daughter of the president of the Republic. She hadn't calmed down enough yet to listen to an explanation. Not that he had too many that were going to sound real convincing.

"Right," McKay said. All business, yep, yep.

"Eklund out."

Before that connection went McKay could have sworn he heard another Texican voice in the background say, "With all due respect, Major, hadn't you better tuck your tits back in? They're distractin' the troops."

"No," he said aloud. "I do not want to know. No way do I want to know."

Weber cleared his throat meaningfully. McKay caught himself with his cigar halfway to his lips.

"Uh, yeah."

A skinny, leggy brunette with curly dark hair spilling out from under her Fritz helmet came trotting up, snapped off a comic-opera salute to McKay, and draped herself on Weber's shoulder.

"Everything's ready, *sir*," she said, batting huge dark eyes sarcastically at McKay.

"Thanks, Joy," Weber said, sending her on her way with a friendly slap on the taut fanny of her cammie pants.

"Is your whole staff nineteen-year-old sex kittens?"

"Most of 'em. Joy's twenty-two, though."

McKay shook his head. "Well, I guess it's time to go talk to our little friends."

"Sure you want to play it this way?"

"Only way I know."

"You always sound like a beer commercial? Well, it's your funeral, fella." He solemnly shook McKay's hand and retreated behind an earth bank.

McKay stooped to pick up his hood and a battery-powered

megaphone. Joints popped. He had gone *mano-a-mano* with Morrigan's outsized chief of security during the final fight for the Citadel. It was a testimony to just how badly he'd fucked the so-called major up that Llewellyn had come in a distant second— or dead last, depending. Until he got some real live rest, McKay was going to feel the contest actually came out third, second, and No Award.

He walked slowly across a field of bare earth. His boots squelched, and fumes seemed to shimmer up out of the dirt. It was hot as hell inside the suit; sweat poured from his armpits and tickled its way down his aching ribs. This was going to be a long day.

Even though the odds were outstanding it was going to be over before too much more time has passed on the clock.

"Hold it. That's far enough," a voice cracked from a loud-speaker on a pole at one end of the bunker. McKay kept walking. "Hey, you stupid fuck, stop right there or we let the gas go."

Fifteen meters from the bunker McKay stopped.

"What do you want, dipshit?"

McKay took his cigar out again, secured the front of his suit, and put the cigar in his mouth before answering. "Just wanted to give you boys one last chance to surrender," he said. He liked the way that sounded; vintage Dirty Harry.

The loudspeaker laughed at him. "Say, that's good. You got a very good sense of humor. You want us out of here, you do what we say, you got that? We want to talk to the president."

"Can't talk to the president. How about talking to Jesus?"

"What? You some kind of crazy man? What are you talking about?"

"Your gas. I'm talking your fucking VX."

"What about it?"

"Funny thing," he said, "heat neutralizes it."

He dropped his hood over his face and struck a match. Two hundred and fifty thousand liters of number 6 fuel oil flashed off with a mighty *whoomp.*

"Don't come no closer." He had a headband and a wild look. His eyes seemed to stand right out of his grimy face.

Sam Sloan heard the crackling. It seemed to be all around, like the noise of a waterfall close up. He couldn't smell the smoke through his respirator, of course, but he could feel the floor growing warm beneath the soles of his combat boots.

If we can just draw this little melodrama out a bit longer, he thought, *the floor'll give way and the gas will be broken down by the flames.*

Of course, we'll all go up with it. Every plan has its downside.

"Let's be reasonable," he said, taking a step forward.

"*Fuck* reasonable!" The soldier brandished what looked like a black remote-control unit for a VCR in the thick air between them.

"You know what this is?"

Sloan cast a glance sideways at Idaho. The Californian held his M16 across his chest, warily ready.

"I think I can make an educated guess."

"It's a deadman switch. If I take my thumb off, *these* go." He swept his free hand around the room.

Aside from worktables topped in hard black rubber everything seemed to have been stripped from the lab long since. But a few things had been added fairly recently. Like the silent rows of nerve gas containers, gleaming black and yellow like hornet soldiers. Det cord bundles connected them, looped loosely neck to neck.

"If you shoot me, my thumb comes off, and all the charges fastened to the caps of these pressurized bottles blow: *poof.* Then it's bye-bye, Bay Area." He turned his right hand empty palm up and worked his fingers back and forth. "So c'mon, shoot me. Make my day."

There's always somebody who never gets the message, and the troopie Sam had missed out in the hall was the one for today. Or maybe assorted stresses had fractured his mind. One way or another he suddenly popped up from behind an abandoned worktable and triggered a long burst from the hip.

Idaho grunted and went down. Sloan dove behind another workstation.

"*Knock it off, you stupid piece of shit!*" the man with the electrical detonator shrieked. "If you put a hole in one of these cans we're all fucked, you simple bastard."

The man lowered his piece and his chin. "Oh," he said.

Idaho shot him. Had the assault team been wearing only Kevlar, the high-velocity 5.56-millimeter rounds might have punched through it at this range, or at the very least imparted enough energy to crack ribs and possibly stop his heart. But because today's mission called more for straight-ahead action than endurance or agility, their monkey suits had these neat composite steel and ceramic inserts inside. The shots hadn't done much more than knock the breath out of Idaho and punch him off his feet.

"You fucker!" the man with the detonator screamed. He aimed the device at Idaho as if he were trying to fast-forward past him. "You killed him! You killed Fritz!"

"Yeah, well, he made me mad," Idaho said. He kept his rifle pointed carefully away from the man.

"Where are you? Where's the other one?"

Well, I'm out of his line of sight, Sloan thought. He came up with a stubby little trashcan-shaped grenade from his belt. Normally he wore a vest of the forty-millimeter rounds, but today he would have had to wear it either under the armored apron, which wouldn't be practical, or over it, in which case if he took a shot to the chest he stood a chance of dying a lot less pleasant death than if he weren't wearing any armor at all, what with all the nasty white phosphorus grenades he carried. The flakes *clung*, and burned hot enough to melt steel . . . like the inserts in his armor apron.

He confirmed with a quick touch that it had an ogive projectile on the end; he didn't care what identifying color combination body and head bore, as long as it wasn't a flat-tipped multiple projectile round. The thing wasn't supposed to go off anyway. He shoved it into the spout of the launcher and pulled it shut as quietly as he could.

The man with the detonator was keeping himself pretty occupied with the sound of his own voice anyway. "Where? Where is he?" he was screaming, looming over the supine Idaho and all but prodding him with the M16 he'd recovered from his fallen buddy.

"I think he's over there," Sloan heard Idaho say.

He took a deep breath and stuck his head out. Sure enough, Idaho was pointing off in the opposite direction. The troopie had his head obediently turned in that direction.

Sloan poked his weapon into the clear and sighted. This was going to be mainly an instinct shot. *Now we'll see if McKay's right, that I can't hack it when I don't have a few thousand tons of guided-missile cruiser around me. . . .*

The man started to turn. From the corner of his eye he saw the rifle poking at him.

"Yah, shoot! See what good it—"

The high-low propulsion charge thumped like a giant door closing. The high-explosive dual-purpose grenade struck him on the hand, smashed it, shattered the crystal in the remote detonator, then hurtled past in a shower of blood and fragments of plastic and bone to bury itself in the cinderblock wall—still centimeters short of the ten-meter free flight required to arm its warhead.

Sam had an upward firing angle; he wasn't endangering the nerve gas cans. He let the man have half a magazine, on general principles.

Joy swallowed slowly. Her china-fine face had gone green under its sprinkling of freckles. It didn't make a pretty composition in the orange hellglare of the inferno raging scant meters in front of them.

"McKay—" she whispered.

Max Weber stuck his head cautiously out from behind the embankment, shook it. "Son of a bitch had to play it his own damn way."

A figure appeared in the midst of hell, a man-shaped outline of darker flame. It moved quite casually for a man who was burning to death. Almost jauntily, in fact.

A moment, and the flames parted like a curtain. An enormous white form strolled out.

"I'll be God damned," a muffled voice declared. Gauntleted hands lifted off the white hood to reveal the head of Billy McKay, with its close-cropped blond hair plastered flat down by sweat. He spit out the mouthpiece of a Scott air-pack. "This oil-rig fire-fighter suit really works! I've wanted to do this Red Adair shit all my life."

He took the broken-off stub of his cigar from his mouth, turned around, and stuck it into the wall of flames.

Just far enough to light it.

CHAPTER
FOUR ———————————————————

He had only the greatest respect for the Guardians. Really he did.

But there were times in every professional's life when he had to swallow his personal likes and dislikes. The Japanese had a phrase for it: *giri* over *ninjō*. *Ninjō* meant "human feelings," *giri* meant "honor." All cut and dried. He'd always admired the Japanese.

Had the Guardians been in the Citadel he doubted he would have been able to get inside. He was good. One of the best. But he knew his limitations. He prided himself on that. The Guardians were the best, no question.

Really a pity that they had to die.

He left the lights on in the briefing theater. He was wearing the perfect camouflage of the postindustrial age: serviceman's coveralls. With even the cream of the Detroiter complement that had formed the backbone of the force that had attacked the Citadel gone—off, like the Guardians themselves, digging out and neutralizing piecemeal the legacy "Marcus Aurelius" had tried to leave America—there was nobody on hand with enough on the ball to think of scrutinizing him.

Besides, if anybody gave him serious trouble . . . He smiled. He had ways of dealing with those situations.

31

One thing was sure: William Morrigan had known how to do well for himself. When the One-Day War went down America was in the process of becoming an ever more pyramidal society, and the Citadel had originally been built as an urban-center enclave for the managerial class, the bureaucrats in charge of planning and administration: the layer just below the top of the heap. The Citadel came equipped with everything the American New Class required: luxury apartments with government subsidized rent, offices, weight rooms, swimming pools, aerobics floor, restaurants, even a small shopping center. Everything to ensure they didn't actually have to mingle with the teeming masses of the hive they planned to rule.

The operative guessed the briefing chamber must have been meant for high-level teleconferences, complete with two-way video, live action and real time. That was certainly what it was going to be used for after the Guardians returned. There was a major flap brewing in Washington. A crisis that spelled both danger and opportunity for the interests he served.

Which of course were the interests of America.

The theater was a powder blue room with gently tiered rows of seats mounting toward the back wall. There were assorted modules of furniture that could be moved into the front of the room, ranging from a simple lectern to a curved podium capable of seating half a dozen. At the moment there was nothing at all to distract attention from the main event, which was the front wall of the theater itself. From waist height almost to the sloping acoustic ceiling it was one giant flat-screen TV display, computer driven so that it could be split up into an almost infinite variety of images and windows.

From waist level down the wall was control console. The operative—he thought of himself that way when he was on a job; names had no place in his line of work—the operative knelt before this and began to unfasten the cover.

It had been Hoped—always with a capital letter when it was people on that level who were doing the hoping—that the renegade KGB agent Vesensky would do the reasonable thing, i.e., turn on the Guardians and liquidate them. *There* was a *mésalliance*, a marriage truly made in hell. While it made optimum sense for Vesensky's master Maximov to make the alliance in the first place, it made no sense at all for it to continue one nanosecond after the threat that necessitated it was contained.

But Vesensky showed no signs of coming through. The powers that would be had grown impatient. So the operative was dispatched to Chicago to take advantage of a rare window of vulnerability: the intersection at a fixed point in the not-too-distant future of the Guardians and a known location that was, for the moment, inadequately secured.

The console cover gave trouble. Something was holding it besides the screws. He opened his satchel, rummaged for a tool. It was fortunate nobody had seriously challenged him; the three Claymore mines inside were not part of any service tech's standard tool kit.

Unless, he thought with a thin amused smile, the tech was in his line of service.

With help from a folding prybar with a plastic-coated tip, the console cover began to come away. It was almost as if someone had tried to make the console as hard to service as possible. It couldn't possibly be a design feature; there was a Japanese corporate logo on the front of the unit, it wasn't the slapdash American stuff protectionist laws forced the common herd to get along with.

He looked inside, saw strings of some adhesive pulling like taffy. The sort of thing designed to keep the casually curious you sometimes ran into in a technophile age from dissecting the thing out of hand. He'd used similar props himself, as a sort of front-line defense, with the *serious* tamper-proofing waiting in case—

—*in case*—

He turned to run. The shockwave front of fifty kilos of high explosive going off at once was a good deal quicker.

It was a two-engine pusher with a white bone of canard in its nose. Red highway flares picked out what was allegedly an intact runway from the vast flat patch of blackness that was O'Hare. Back during the ill-fated FSE occupation of America—the big one, not the later battalion-sized effort that had deposited Horatio Gates and his buddies down in the coon-ass swamps of Louisiana—Chicago had been a major concentration point for the Expeditionary Force. As such it drew a lot of attention from Tom Rogers when he was traveling around the country like the Johnny Appleseed of guerrilla resistance. Cratering the runways had been a major pastime for Tommy and his happy helpers.

Supposedly the good guys held the airport for the moment,

and equally supposedly they had marked off enough clear strips to bring down safely the aircraft returning from various compass points. All the same, McKay was glad he wasn't the pilot. He was a lot less glad he'd insisted on riding up front in the copilot's chair.

The wheels kissed pavement once, twice, three times, with that high nails-on-blackboard keen. There was a final bump, and the wheels were rolling smooth. The flares formed unbroken ruby laser lines to left and right.

"Whew," the pilot said, braking the plane with flaps and the odd sharply curved props. "Never thought we'd make it. This strip looks like the hind end of the moon in daylight."

"Thanks a whole hell of a lot for telling me," McKay said, and lit his cigar. The pilot had declared he'd put him off the plane if he lit the rope in flight. Fine. Let him try *now*.

A strand of flares crossed their path. Following the instructions radioed to them on approach the pilot turned right. The plane taxied across a highway overpass. McKay glanced down. There were still cars stalled down there, humps dimly visible in the starlight, like so many circus elephants stricken with simultaneous infarcts.

Tom Rogers was already waiting beside the darkened Air Canada terminal with his arms crossed and his bag by his feet. McKay was beat, utterly wrung out and ready for a stretch of R&R after the events of the last few weeks. But if you told Tommy right this very instant to toss his bag into another airplane and fly off to Thailand to raise a rebellion against its crackpot self-proclaimed king he'd do it without changing a square centimeter of that stone face of his. And as soon as his bootsoles touched down in the dust of the Korat Plateau he'd be keen and quick as if he'd rested a month.

He nodded. "Billy." His voice was soft as the warm Midwestern wind.

"Yo. How'd it go?"

Shrug. "No problem."

The reports McKay had heard indicated the Trenton bank had been almost as tough to take down as Sam Sloan's target in California, where there were more than twice as many bad guys stationed than anticipated. But for Tom Rogers a savage gun, grenade, and knife duel at bad-breath range was "no problem." More like a light aerobic workout.

"What about you, Billy?" Rogers asked politely. "How was St. Louis? Looks like you got a little sun."

"Yeah." Actually, he'd stood too close to the damn fire after he took his hood off, and a shift of the wind had damned near singed his eyebrows off. He'd been light-headed running around in that damn inferno suit; it had gotten hotter inside that thing than he realized while he was wading through the flames he'd ignited. He'd put it off to exhilaration.

They stood in silence as the white wedge-shaped plane that had delivered McKay turned and taxied away for takeoff. Eventually they heard a heavy thrum of engines and a larger craft swept past them, not showing lights.

It returned five minutes later, the funny high-wing flying boat-like silhouette of a de Havilland Canada Ranger, big brother to the famed Twin Otter. It stuck out a sidewise tongue of ramp that Casey and Sam presently walked down.

"Where're the brass bands and dancing girls?" Sloan asked.

"Nesters ate 'em."

Sloan swallowed. Strange things crawled out of the urban rubble after dark. Not mutants from a made-for-videocassette-release Holocaust drama; any creature born of radiation-damaged genes would almost certainly be born dead. But the sort of two-legged creatures that scuttled from the light when you turned over the rock hopefully labeled *civilization*.

"Angie says hi," Casey Wilson offered. Angela Connoly was Casey's significant other in Colorado, the closest thing to a leader the high-tech anarchists of the Freehold would admit to. She was also the daughter of Dr. Marguerite Connoly, chief adviser to President MacGregor and longtime sparring partner to the Guardians.

"Yeah," McKay said. "Any more news from Vesensky?"

Sloan shook his head. "Last report we got indicated he and his strike team were still trying to dodge the Seattle authorities. He'll make it back as best he can."

"Huh."

The Ranger jock wandered over while some of Tom's indigenous assets refueled his ship from bladders they'd borrowed from the Effsees and squirreled away somewhere. He had a saltwater tan, wavy hair so blond it looked white, and sunglasses. McKay had absolutely no idea where Washington had gotten *him*.

The mixed force of Detroiter infantry and local irregulars who had secured the runways for tonight fired up the engines of their convoy of makeshift armored cars. They were impatient for the plane to be on its way again so they could start the run back into the Loop. Nobody ruled the Chicago night.

"Say," he said, "what are our chances of getting to use some of these airplanes for our next gig? It'd save us a shitload of driving time."

The pilot looked at him as if he'd flashed his wing-wang. "No *way*," he said. "Do you have any idea what it *costs* to run these things?"

"What the fuck, over?" McKay popped the top of the armored van and poked his big upper body out into the wind off the lake.

"Looks as if we haven't had all the excitement, man," Casey said over the communicators.

The lights were on all over the Citadel compound, big halogen jobs that ate up power cranked out of alcohol- and methane-fueled generators so greedily that even Morrigan, who took tribute from every settled survivor in the greater Chicago area, could hardly afford to burn them. They revealed as clearly as daylight just how much damage the attack several days before had done.

There might have been another attack in progress, the way people were running around inside the razor-tape tangles. There were thick hoses strung across the yuppie brick courtyard, and smoke poured from the larger of the two towers Siamese-twinned by a skyway above the street.

The open machine-gun-mounted car behind stopped. Casey stood up with his hands on the rollbar like a kid, and even Tom's forehead was creased. The side door of McKay's van opened and Sloan stepped out.

"What's happening?" Sloan asked.

"Damn," the scarfaced van driver said. She hit the dashboard with the base of her fist. "Thought the radio was fucked up again."

A soldier came running from the gate, holding a Fritz on his head with one hand. Three ribbons in the Motor City Madman's colors had been tied around the scoop-shaped Kevlar helmet, identifying him as a Detroiter.

"What's going on here, troop?" McKay demanded.

The squaddie saluted. His face was smudged with soot.

"Sorry, sir. We had our communications temporarily knocked out. Good to see you back, sir. Congratulations on your successful mission, if I may be so bold, sir."

"You may," McKay said. "Now *what the fuck is going on*?"

His bellow almost blew the kid's helmet off. "Exp-p-plosion, sir! In the main briefing theater. They think it's sabotage."

"Sabotage, huh?" McKay looked at the thick gray snakes of smoke twining out of the lobby.

"Fire's under control, sir. They built this one pretty fireproof."

"Yeah." McKay looked at the other three Guardians. "So now, can somebody tell me why I have this feeling we've seen the last of Comrade Vesensky for a while?"

CHAPTER
FIVE ———————————————————

"Oh, Jesus," Billy McKay groaned. "Not Mexicans *again*."

"Billy!" Sam Sloan exclaimed.

"Not exactly," Dr. Jacob Morgenstern said from the lower left-hand corner of the screen in the subterranean vault. William Morrigan had planned to fort himself up here with his mistress, pre-War sex goddess Merith Tobias, while his hidden outposts unleashed their gas on a recalcitrant America. It was a wall-sized TV, but it was a more modest wall than the one in the late, great briefing theater. It was equipped for two-way video; signals were routed through the complex's main communications center.

"Or, to be more precise, not exclusively. This is Eduardo Velez."

He referred to the image that occupied the majority of the screen. It was a man's face, dark by heredity and exposure to sunlight, round without suggesting fat. There was an impressive sweep of moustache. The eyes seemed sunken, the lower lids dark, as if from fatigue.

"Does the name ring any bells, gentlemen?"

It didn't.

"He was a leader of the Popular Party of the North, a political movement hostile to the Mexican PRI, which you will recall ruled the country until shortly before the Third World War. As you may also recall, the PRI did not surrender power with conspicuous grace. Velez was forced to flee to the United States shortly before Enrique Córdoba acceded to the presidency of Mexico. Because the American government was going through one of its periodic spells of believing the PRI to be sympathetic to the communists, Velez was granted political asylum, and has remained in the U.S. since.''

"Excuse me, sir," Sam Sloan said hesitantly, "but it was my understanding that President Córdoba's coalition government liberalized the country and permitted a number of political refugees to return.''

"True. You however demonstrate your lack of understanding of the nature of that coalition, Commander. Disgraced though the PRI was, certain of its remnants had to be included in the coalition, and likewise there were certain parties too firmly entrenched to be dislodged without precipitating the sort of crisis Córdoba in fact managed to avert until his assassination—which, by the way, our latest intelligence would seem to indicate was engineered and in all probability carried out by Colonel Ivan Vesensky.''

McKay grunted. *Figures.* Overnight they had received word that the KGB turncoat and the tag end of his strike force had been besieged in a farmhouse south of Seattle by local authorities. The house had mysteriously caught fire, the way houses with armed fugitives in them always seemed to do during police sieges before the War. There were no survivors.

Billy McKay truly believed their longtime adversary and short-term ally was dead. He also believed in Santa Claus, the Easter Bunny, and that the Feds were about to win the war on drugs when the One-Day War canceled all accounts. If there was one thing life had taught him, it was that the choppers are *never* on their way.

"Among the entrenched powers was one Apolinar Morales, head of the Federal Security Directorate. He had a personal grudge against Velez, and a notoriously lengthy memory. He's an old friend of yours, though you never met him in person, to the best of my knowledge. He goes by the nickname *la Araña,* the Spider.''

"Urk," Sloan said. "I can see why he stayed.''

During their brief vacation in Mexico the Guardians had managed to carve themselves an immortal niche on Mexico's chief secret policeman's shit list. Last they'd heard from him was when a hit team he'd sent had tried to gun down McKay on a San Antonio street shortly before the Guardians left for Chicago.

"Velez settled in southwestern Wyoming. He was subsequently involved in a dispute between Mexican squatters and the forest service.

"He was murdered, along with his family, three days ago."

McKay scratched his heavy chin. "So what's the big deal? Our pal Spiderman managed to make one stick. Hired himself a better class of killer."

"La Araña was forced into exile in Central America after you broke up the Cristero movement. He was known to have operatives in place in Texas; it was simple enough for him to set your botched assassination in motion, even though he was deposed. On the other hand, he would have found it difficult to mount a similar initiative into Wyoming, separated as he was from his power base. There is also the consideration that Morales made no hostile moves against Velez after he fled Chihuahua."

"Maybe we pissed him off enough—"

"*If* you will indulge me?" Morgenstern raised a gray eyebrow.

McKay shut up. There were very few men alive who could shut him down like that. Morgenstern's friend Major Crenna, who'd conceived of both the Guardians and Project Blueprint, had been that way too.

Velez's picture was replaced by that of a middle-aged Asian man. "This is Minh Ngo Bai. He was prominent in the Vietnamese community that began to spring up in Fort Collins, Colorado, in the early 1990s. Increasing economic hardship brought a good deal of resentment to bear on hardworking Asian immigrants all over the country; Minh was involved in a number of incidents. Colorado authorities attempted to blame much of the trouble on his encouragement of the Vietnamese to defend themselves.

"After the Third World War the region received heavy fallout from groundbursts on the Warren Air Force Base missile complex. Minh led a number of Vietnamese back into the area once the fallout began to die down, accepting the increased risk of health effects as a trade-off for the opportunity to stake a claim on reclaimed land.

"He was assassinated two weeks ago."

A third face appeared: an obviously heavyset black man, wearing spectacles with incongruously tiny round lenses perched to either side of a broad, broken-looking nose. "Filbert Nightingale. Murdered in Casper.

"Frank Ed Yellow Bull. Shot and seriously wounded in his trailer near Garryowen, not far from Little Bighorn, on the Crow Indian Reservation in Montana.

"Miranda Baxa. Died three days after being shot at the Philippine refugee camp northwest of Rapid City."

As he recited the names new pictures appeared on the screen with dates and places overwritten at the bottom. When he was finished the screen showed twelve faces, all brown or black.

"In all, there have been a dozen attacks on prominent members of ethnic survivor communities in the northern Rockies region in the last three months. All but two of those have been fatal, and in the cases of Yellow Bull and Singh it wasn't for lack of effort on the part of their assailants. Even though Washington sent out a team of specialists, Singh is expected to be paralyzed for life."

The Guardians exchanged a look. Things were changing; not so long ago Washington was a battlefield for rubble-running gangs. Now they were shipping high-powered medical teams to the hinterlands, not to mention providing air transport for the mop-up of Morrigan's holdouts.

"Look, Doc, not to be disrespectful or nothing—" McKay began.

"Why do you always find it necessary to preface your insubordinate statements in that way, Lieutenant? Do you think that I won't notice?"

"Uh, no. Anyway, Doctor, how does this Bing Singh or whatever his name is rate? I mean, if *I* got *my* a— uh, leg shot off, would Washington ship out a lot of high-powered witch doctors to kiss it and make it better?"

"The president is taking a substantial personal interest in this case," Morgenstern said.

McKay pouched out his mouth and scoured his tongue between his lower lip and teeth. Evasion wasn't Dr. J's usual style.

Two new pictures replaced the dozen. Full-face and profile

shots of an apparently Caucasian man in his late thirties or early
forties. They were the sort of portraits usually labeled at the
bottom with the subject's Social Security number. It was hard
to make out much detail from them. The face seemed to consist
entirely of angry, brushy shelves of brow, a mashed kind of
nose, and masses of tangled black beard and hair.

The eyes stood right out, though. An intense electric blue.
They seemed to burn out from the black undergrowth like arc
lights.

"What the hell?" McKay grunted. "They been hitting ethnic
Neanderthals, too?"

"This is Reuben McKendree." The image switched to an obvious news photo of a tall, powerfully built man with neat hair
and beard dressed in a dove gray business suit and leg irons
being led through some kind of public-building corridor by an
elbow—both hands were out of sight behind the broad back, and
it was no great leap to infer handcuffs. The man bore a passing
resemblance to Big Ben Davidson.

Only the eyes, blue and piercing, connected him to the pre-
vious shots.

"This is McKendree after his arraignment in federal court in
Cheyenne, Wyoming, on charges of possession of automatic
weapons, two years before the One-Day War. He was, and still
seems to be, the head of a radical white-supremacist group called
White Action!

"Washington believes he, and White Action!, are responsible
for the recent wave of assassinations."

To emphasize the point a map of what had been the continen-
tal U.S. appeared on-screen, with Wyoming appearing in orange
against the blue of the rest of the country. Yellow dots repre-
sented the places the attacks had taken place. They clustered in
and around the state like fireflies.

"What I don't quite get, Doctor," Sam Sloan said, slipping
into his Missouri-farm-boy voice, as he sometimes did when he
wasn't too sure of himself—addressing Jacob Morgenstern, for
example, "is if they had hold of this McKendree character, why'd
they ever let him go?"

"The investigation was apparently quashed. Charges were dismissed." McKay looked at Sloan and made a face. "McKendree
was under fairly close scrutiny by federal investigators at the
time of the One-Day War. He had spent the months since his

release ensconced in a retreat owned by White Action! in the Absaroka range east of Yellowstone''—a winking white point of light appeared in the upper left-hand corner of the state—''publishing a newsletter called *Action!* and preparing for what he thought was the inevitable approach of Armageddon.''

Casey chuckled. Everybody turned to look at him. ''I guess, like, nobody's wrong *all* the time.''

McKay scowled. ''Case, you're a major flake. You know that, don't you?'' He turned back to the screen. ''So what's all this got to do with us, Doctor?''

''Washington wants you to bring these assassinations to a halt.''

''Not to be disre— aw, fuck it. This ain't in our job description, Doctor,'' McKay said. ''We're supposed to be looking for pieces of the Blueprint for Renewal, not chasing peckerwoods around the mountains.''

''I agree with you, Lieutenant. However, the president has expressed a personal desire that you handle this.''

''What about the Wyoming state authorities?'' Tom Rogers asked. ''I understand their state government's started to get its act together since the Effsees left.''

''President MacGregor feels this is an appropriate opportunity to demonstrate the returning authority of the federal government.''

McKay started to crack his knuckles, thought better of it. He'd busted the second knuckle of his left hand on the face of Morrigan's chief of security. It hadn't had much time to heal.

''I can get into that, anyway, Doc. We go, we kick ass, we take names. Nothing to it.''

Morgenstern's image was back on the screen. He looked vaguely disapproving, but then that was pretty much the rest state for his tanned and aquiline face.

''I urge you not to become overconfident, no matter what kind of an overmatch this appears to be. I'm downloading a complete dossier on McKendree; he's not a wise man to underestimate.

''Nor should you entertain any idea that you're simply being sent out to assassinate someone. Your brief is to find out who is behind these murders and bring the responsible party or parties to justice. It is by no means established that McKendree is involved.''

"Doesn't seem as if there's much room for doubt, Doctor," Sam Sloan drawled.

"Perhaps not. Nonetheless, you are to take no action as long as any doubt remains."

McKay looked at Sloan. Sam looked back. They weren't in accord any too often. In some ways they were polar opposites, the dark, soft-spoken Sloan, long-distance runner, something of a technocrat, who could switch at will between aw-shucks country boy and Annapolis-honed ice and elegance, and blond city boy McKay with his linebacker's build, his beer and cigars, and his tendency to live life as hard and loud as possible. McKay thought Sam Sloan was a black-shoe navy pantywaist and liberal wimp, and Sloan thought McKay was a typical bullet-headed right-wing marine. But on this they were in complete agreement: their status as Guardians gave them the maximum room for flexibility and initiative. If they felt they had to act they would, and if that meant they had to answer to harsh taskmaster Morgenstern—or to Jeffrey MacGregor—so be it. Nobody had become a Guardian who was afraid to take responsibility for his own actions.

"So what's on the agenda?" McKay asked.

"Your first task will be to establish liaison with Wyoming governor Greenwell. . . ."

CHAPTER
SIX ————————————————————

"If I leave you with no other impression, gentlemen," Karl Greenwell said, "permit me to impress on you what a thoroughly dangerous individual Reuben McKendree is."

"We're Guardians, Governor," Billy McKay said. "We don't scare easy."

Greenwell's black eyebrows pulled together and down over hazel eyes. He didn't exactly match McKay's notion of what a Western governor should look like. He was young—early forties, their data said—and looked younger. An inch or two under six feet, he had an athletic build that suggested aerobic workouts more than heavy work outdoors. His hair was almost blue-black, cut in a stiff, straight brush above a high forehead. The most striking thing about him was the extreme pallor of his skin—not unhealthy, it had a sort of clear sheen to it and you could see blue-looking veins near the surface. But it was almost typing-paper white. For all of that McKay knew Greenwell had a reputation as a New Age kind of outdoorsman, big on hiking and horseback riding—which was about all McKay did know about the man.

Maybe he used a lot of sunscreen.

"You of course familiarized yourself with McKendree's record on the trip here?"

Even though he didn't normally think of himself as a sensitive kind of guy—probably because he wasn't—Billy McKay caught more than a hint of implication that they probably *hadn't*.

It was not going to be easy for him to like Governor Greenwell.

The trip had gone without particular incident. The Guardians were not your normal troop, who had to be rotated out of the firing line after a couple weeks or a month of action or go down as psychological casualties. The single most important trait that had led to each of them being chosen for the most elite unit ever assembled from the American military was that combination of mental, physical, and moral resiliency. The Guardians *thrived* on a diet of constant action, constant danger, constant stress.

It said so right here in their job description.

So they'd set out the day after their conference with Dr. Morgenstern—less than thirty-six hours after the last of them touched down at O'Hare on their return from the Morrigan mopping up.

They left the Citadel under the command of one of Tom Rogers's alums, an incredibly tall, lean black woman who called herself Ice. The top Detroit field commander, Ugandan-born Terry Achemba, had led the strike on Morrigan's nest in Detroit proper and stayed at home to debrief his boss, the Motor City Madman. But the Detroiter infantry company that had helped take the Citadel stayed behind, supported by one of the pair of field-expedient gunboats that had accompanied them.

McKay for one had felt misgivings about the situation they were leaving behind them. Something was going to have to get done here sooner or later about the Madman and the tidy little empire he was carving himself out of the north-central and Midwestern states. He was pretty up-front about regarding President MacGregor as a peer rather than as a superior authority. That was not a situation that could be permitted to continue, and McKay's gut told him that the sooner that business got taken care of the better it was going to be.

But McKay came from a long line of marines, and the tradition said, if they told you to saddle up and go, you saddled up and went. He didn't make policy and that was how he thought it should be. He was content to accept the authority of MacGregor and Morgenstern, even if he did reserve the right to a degree of flexibility in the field.

Of course, Morgenstern had not seemed entirely comfortable with this job—whatever else the Guardians were, they weren't cops. And McKay did *not* accept the authority of Dr. Maggie Connoly, whose plump little hand he thought he detected in this assignment. She had small use for the Guardians, and the feeling was mutual.

The only person who seemed really sorry to see them leave Chicago was Suzette Nguyen, the Vietnamese-born biochemist assigned by none other than Yevgeny Maximov his own bad self to help them break Morrigan. She had been a royal pain in the ass from the get-go, even though she was a foxy one: she was an FSE hard-liner who thought the Guardians were typical American roughneck bandits.

Events had turned her head around to the extent that she chose to remain in the not-so-United States after Morrigan's captive squeeze blew his brainpan mostly empty. Apparently Ivan Vesensky had given his approval to her resignation, or at least a pledge of noninterference.

On the other hand, Vesensky was not a man whose word you wanted to rely on implicitly. After an unnamed intruder—who was going to remain that way, since post-Holocaust forensic science wasn't up to identifying a critter that crispy—had inadvertently tripped the trap Vesensky had left his beloved comrades in arms the Guardians, Nguyen had been acting insecure. In fact McKay got the impression the blast had scared the scientist right into Sam Sloan's bed the night before they left—not that that would have taken much.

Four days later they were in John F. Kennedy City, the makeshift capital of the state of Wyoming.

"I know everybody seems to think this McKendree's some kind of maximum badass," McKay said, helping himself to some more water. That was the kind of hospitality they had here in the Wooden Palace: the only thing they served that he was going to put in his mouth was *water*. "Himself included."

"It makes no sense to minimize the threat posed by someone like McKendree," said Governor Greenwell's chief adviser, who sat propped on the sill of a double-paned window looking out over a field of wildflowers toward the slate blue heights of the Bighorn Mountains. "The man's a menace. You've seen the indictments: assault, firearms violations, threatening federal officers.''

"I notice he wasn't convicted on too many of them," remarked Sam Sloan. He sat in a heavy wooden chair near the governor's desk, which like the Sloan chair, all the visible fittings in the room, and indeed the palace itself was made entirely of natural products of Wyoming and vicinity. He was drinking some of the herbal tea Greenwell had offered and McKay had shied away from.

Dr. Nicholas Brant's mobile mouth writhed. "A reflection on the scandalous state of justice in the country before the War. Mother knows what kind of influence he used to get out of that federal indictment. Of course, William Lowell's Justice Department could hardly be expected to pursue *right-wing* criminals with any ardor.'' The expression on the thin, small face, which seemed in some danger of being overwhelmed by the butte of forehead thrusting out of thinning sandy hair above it, suggested his words smelled to him of sewage.

" 'Mother?' " Casey asked. He was folded into a chair with his own cup of tea and his Genesis tour cap tucked discreetly between his butt and the chair's arm.

"Earth, of course," Brant said, as if Casey were last in his special-ed class.

"Yeah. Of course." Casey Wilson shed sarcasm like a duck's ass shed water.

"I notice he was a union organizer in the logging camps at one time," Sloan said tentatively. "Did he have a change of heart at some point?"

Brant pushed square wire-rimmed glasses up his narrow nose. "I don't know how the truly *aware* can continue their reflexive support of unions. In the latter half century many of them have been positively retrogressive in their outlooks. Particularly on environmental matters."

"Oh," Sloan said. McKay waited for him to say more, but he didn't. He seemed off-balance, which wasn't his general style.

The problem was, Brant had been some kind of big environmentalist wheel before the War, and had written a ton of books. McKay hadn't read any of them, of course, but he gathered Sloan had. That was one of those things about being an intellectual like Sam: just having an Authority around cut your nuts right off. Not for the first time, McKay was glad *he* wasn't a goddam intellectual.

"We certainly appreciate President MacGregor's solicitude," the governor said. "Still, I must say I feel confident we could have handled the situation without your assistance."

"Minimizing the threat posed by this dude McKendree, Governor?" McKay asked. He tossed off the last of his water, grimaced, set the cup down on the counter. "So when do we get started?"

Stiff grass crackled beneath their boots as they walked away from the sprawling all-wooden statehouse. The sky was blue and wide and pale. Thin clouds were drawn across it in streaks. Wind rustled hungrily in the trees several hundred meters upslope.

JFK City spread out around the palace. The new state capital had a shantytown air, a collection of longhouse-style public buildings and residential log cabins and rude plank shacks scattered down a gradual incline. Aside from a cinderblock building beside the paved state road that obviously used to be a gas station, there was no sign that the area had been settled before the One-Day War.

Their escort was walking along with his big balding head drawn down between narrow shoulders and the tails of his tan suit coat flapping in the breeze. Nicholas Brant paused to take a hand from his pocket and point at a crew at work on some kind of barnlike building two hundred meters away.

"Look there. That is the new Department of Education building. That's how the statehouse was built."

"The Wooden Palace?" McKay asked.

Brant squinted at him sidelong. "Who called it that?"

"Somebody we talked to on the way in."

Brant eyed him a moment longer. "We don't encourage such disparaging remarks. Let it pass. More important that you should see what we're about here: voluntary, collective action at work, in concert with nature. If America is going to be rebuilt, that's how it will have to be. Our Mother won't permit the same mistakes to be made again."

"Don't say 'if,' " McKay rumbled, taking out an Indonesian cigar and biting off the end.

"If that's all voluntary," Sloan asked, "what are the guards with the guns doing?"

"Certain antisocial elements resent being called on to fulfill their voluntary labor obligation. They're inclined to make trouble."

"Like, why do you call it 'voluntary'?" Casey asked.

"The people collectively desire to do this work. Therefore it's voluntary. To allow the individual to selfishly override the desires of the majority is antidemocratic."

McKay turned to Sloan and winched up an eyebrow. "Um," Sloan said.

Brant set off walking down the slope again, as if not caring whether the Guardians followed or not. They did.

It was a long, low bunkhouse with a pitched roof built virtually in the shadow of what the locals were not supposed to call the Wooden Palace. A carved wooden sign announced, "Special Investigative Division, Wyoming Department of Public Safety. Edward J. Shelton Barracks."

"Who was Edward J. Shelton?" McKay asked, following Brant up onto the shadowed porch.

"A Wyoming highway patrolman killed in a battle with the Federated States of Europe Expeditionary Force."

"Didn't know you had a lot of fights with the Effsees in these parts," McKay said.

Brant's lips pinched. "I'm certain there were a good many sacrifices in that conflict of which you are unaware."

"Yeah."

Brant led them into the cool gloom inside. They stood blinking, waiting for their eyes to adjust from the bright daylight outside. There was a foyer with framed photographs on the walls. Beyond was what looked like a cross between a Western bunkhouse and the basic-training barracks all four Guardians were all too familiar with.

"What are we waiting for, Dr. Brant?" Sam Sloan asked.

"Governor Greenwell has personally selected a team to work with you on this case. They're out on an exercise at this moment, but I expect them back shortly. The SID are the elite of our highway patrol; these men are the *crème de la crème*."

"We don't need help, Doctor," McKay said.

"You do not know the terrain, Lieutenant," Brant said, with the air of a man whose patience had started to get weak and watery. "Also, as I believe you pointed out to your own superiors, you are not investigators. These men are expert investigators, and this is their country. Nor are they simply policemen; all of them have seen a substantial amount of combat."

McKay frowned, lifted his head. "What the hell's *that*?" It was a sound like a lot of people whacking on a table with heavily padded bats, briskly but not too hard.

From the front of the building came loud, shuddering snorts and funny chuckling sounds. McKay walked to the front door, his hand going to the Pachmayr grips of his combat-modified .45. Not because instinct told him he was going to need it, but because after the Holocaust anything you couldn't identify right away—and a lot you could—was potential trouble.

There were a bunch of men out in front of the barracks. Wearing cammies and long arms slung, they were swinging down to the beaten earth from—

"Horses? What the hell are they doing on horses?"

"Appropriate technology, as applied to police work. Welcome to the New West, Lieutenant McKay."

CHAPTER
SEVEN

"Snorting beast," the lanky towhead observed, dipping into a drawstring pouch of granola. "Never make it."

"We've been through this part of the world, man," Casey Wilson assured him over his shoulder from the driver's seat. "She can take it."

The res road had washed out, in the torrential rains that immediately followed the One-Day War over much of the Northern Hemisphere in lieu of the much-touted nuclear winter, to judge by the road's condition. Diesel growling mightily, the ten-metric-ton armored car the Guardians variously called Mobile One and home was churning its way up the bank of the coulee that had grown across the highway.

When a Detroiter recon party under the command of the inevitable Terry Achemba had hauled their asses out of a jam in Cleveland—or captured them, depending on point of view—Mobile One had accompanied the Guardians to the Motor City. For obvious reasons it had been left behind when they went to Chicago in the guise of a Detroit detachment slugged to safeguard Merith Tobias, the tribute Morrigan demanded of the Motor City Madman as token of his submission. It had remained under guard in Detroit.

While they were off doing their things in various parts of the country the Madman had, at their request, shipped the car to Chicago for them. It had not been tampered with by Detroiter technicians. That was obvious from the fact that it still existed; *anybody* trying to get past the safeguards Tom Rogers had installed in it was on the fast track to the afterlife.

It could have been the Madman was simply an honorable man. Billy McKay might be Mother Teresa.

More likely, the Madman, who was a pretty shrewd son of a bitch—he'd been America's most popular professional wrestler before the War—had known perfectly well what would happen if his techs got too curious about the car. Mobile One was a marvel in its own way: a Cadillac Gage Super Commando V-450, privately developed descendant of the very successful V-150, equipped with all kinds of goodies like advanced amphibious capabilities and nuclear/biological/chemical hazard protection, topped off by a one-man turret mounting a .50-caliber machine gun in parallel with an Mk-19 automatic 40-millimeter grenade launcher. Additionally, it mounted the fanciest state-of-the-art technogimmickry Project Blueprint had been able to locate, from an onboard system that would have been designated a supercomputer a decade before to the systems it controlled, communications and sensing and navigation. Finally, conformal storage compartments within the foamed steel and titanium alloy hull were packed astonishingly full of survival gear and firepower in sundry forms.

So Mobile One was a testament to how much death could come in how small a package. But there wasn't really that much wrapped up in it that an emperor, even a comparatively small-time one like the Madman, couldn't get his hands on elsewhere. When the Pan-Turanians crashed into Europe like a seismic sea wave, the Effsee Expeditionary Force had left tons of matériel where it lay—and before that a lot of their gear had changed hands involuntarily. Even if the salvaged or liberated stuff wasn't as compact or nifty it could produce pretty much the same effects as anything he could have pried out of Mobile One.

So the Madman decided to save himself some technicians, and the efforts of filling in a crater somewhere, and earn a little cheap goodwill from official representatives of the U.S. government. *Shrewd.*

McKay hoped they weren't going to have to kill him.

One way or another, that lay in the future. The present was the

Crow reservation in southeastern Montana, which the Guardians were crossing on their way to collect testimony from Frank Ed Yellow Bull.

"Huh," the man with the white-blond hair sniffed. "Technofreaks. You'll see."

"This is all a waste of time, you know," his partner said in that bored preppie voice of his. The two sat across from each other in fold-down seats just aft of the turret root.

Billy McKay turned his attention out the forward vision block. The landscape was rolling prairie of high grass waving in the wind, with white thunderheads piling impossibly high above. The West always got to him. There was just too *much* of it.

Better looking out at a too-big sky than sitting in back with their cheerful and cooperative guests. It was supposed to be Sam Sloan's go in the electronic systems operator's seat up next to the driver, but McKay had pulled rank. Anything but having to look at those two.

It was all a waste of time. Both Nicholas Brant and SID team leader Sawtelle took a lot of trouble to explain that to them before they ever left JFK City.

"We know it's McKendree," Sawtelle said, standing in the foyer of their Red Rider meets Rambo bunkhouse. He was a tall, knuckly kind of man, with red hair and a freckled face and olive green eyes that were ten years older than the rest of him. "You don't have to go chasing down witnesses."

"Do you have fresh evidence?" Sam Sloan had asked. "It still seemed up in the air when we left."

"Never up in the air," said the tanned man who came in after Sawtelle with a pair of Scott bicycling goggles pushed up onto his impossibly blond hair. "It's McKendree."

"What Ski Bob said," Sawtelle said.

Sloan wrapped his face around that earnest, gee-help-me-with-this Phil Donahue smile of his. "But how do you know?"

"We're cops," Sawtelle said. "I had eight years with the DEA. We *know*."

"Hey, that's great," McKay said. "But we got our orders."

" *'We got our orders,' "* he heard somebody say in a mincing mocking whisper behind him. He didn't turn around.

"We had to delay going after him while we waited for you," the medium-sized preppie-looking type with straight brown bangs cutting a corner off his square face said. He'd been introduced as Chip Girard. "Now you want us to wait *longer* while you go haring off to Montana?"

"Yeah," McKay said, "I guess that's about the size of it."

"Typical federal obstructionism," sniffed Nicholas Brant.

"*Mother*fucker," Billy McKay subvocalized as Mobile One groaned its way onto a reasonable facsimile of level ground.

"*Beg pardon, Billy?*" Tommy said from the turret. Their two passengers didn't have the fancy communicators that linked the four Guardians together, so they had no idea what was being said or even that anything was.

"*I got us into this. I should get my head overhauled.*"

His buddies tactfully refrained from comment.

He hadn't wanted to play it this way. He was all ready to go charging up into the hills and drag Big Rube McKendree out by his goddam beard. The concern MacGregor was showing for due process in this thing struck him as bleeding-heart bullshit, and he was sure he could come up with a good-sounding reason why he as field commander chose to dispense with it. Not even Samuel Would-Be Eastern Liberal Sloan, whose heart generally bled as freely as anyone's, would give him any static about it; he seemed to think that a Ku Klux Klown like McKendree deserved anything he got.

But the Guardians were here to show the flag. McKay had gotten a bellyful of locals deciding they could go it their own damned way, in Texas first and then Detroit. He was basically fucked if he was going to let these granola-munching Wyoming pissants jack him around. If they thought they were going to hustle the Guardians into racing straight off after McKendree, then the Guardians were by God going to Montana first. By the book, yes *sir*.

Oh well. At least I don't have to worry about Dr. J ripping me a new asshole. Yet.

Brant, speaking for the governor, had insisted that the Guardians take a couple of SID men with them to Montana. "If you're going to indulge in amateur police work," he said, "at least you must have professionals to back you up." He was definitely one of Billy McKay's favorite people, all right.

So Sergeant Robert ("Ski Bob") Malinowski and Patrolman Chip Girard were riding along to the Crow reservation and complaining about the accommodations. The bulk of the Team—that was apparently the only designation they had, the Team—had remained behind. "In case McKendree tries something while you're . . . distracted," as Brant put it.

Billy McKay still wished he'd gone ahead and asked just what the hell an eco-freak writer with a concave chest knew about police work. But the SID squaddies did give him the impression of knowing their shit, and they accepted Brant's authority without rolling their eyes, which was way the hell more than they did for the Guardians. Besides, he didn't want to get a lecture from Tom Rogers about hearts and minds. He *hated* getting lectured about hearts and minds.

He glanced back over his shoulder. Ski Bob and Girard had their heads together in front of Sam Sloan, muttering to each other. Ski Bob caught McKay's eye and shook his head.

It's always a pleasure working with professionals, McKay thought. He folded his big arms across his chest as Mobile One rolled onto asphalt again.

The armored vehicle crawled like a green and brown mottled insect across the big objective lenses of the binoculars.

The large man lowered the glasses and watched with unassisted eyes as the car vanished over a ridge. He felt tufts of grass brushing his face, smelled the soil and the coming rain. He heard the buzz of swarming flies and knew the storm would come soon. He was aware of the gray shield-shaped stink bug struggling through buffalo grass beside him on the hilltop where he lay, and a hawk circling high overhead.

Most of all he was aware of where the armored car had come from. Up from the south. Wyoming.

He smiled. Perhaps someone was making matters easier for him.

The car was gone, leaving only the insistent faint farting sound of its engines, scarcely audible under the wind. He slithered back behind the crest of the hill. A bolt-action rifle with a scope attached lay on a sheet of Mylar. He carefully zipped the rifle back into its ripstop case, rolled the Mylar up and strapped it to the side. Then he walked bent-kneed down the backslope to where his paint horse stood tethered and patient, its mouth muffled by a soft cloth.

Deliberately he fastened the rifle case to the saddle. He unwrapped the horse's black and white muzzle, swung into the saddle, and set off at a steady walk.

The horse would never keep pace with the armored car. But there was no hurry.

He knew where the car was going.

CHAPTER
EIGHT ———————————

"You are a stupid man," observed the man who sat rocking in a chair at the foot of the bed. "You let strangers sneak up on you and shoot your house full of holes, and you too."

The man in the bed roared with laughter and slapped thighs covered by OD army blankets.

Sam Sloan swiveled his head on its neck and stared at Billy McKay with wide eyes. McKay shrugged. *How the fuck do I know?*

"Not only are you a foolish, unlucky fellow," the visitor continued, "but your brother is a Crazy Dog Wishing to Die." He clicked his tongue and shook his head. "I don't know what to expect for you, except for bad things."

The injured man shook with laughter, hugging thick arms to the bandages wrapped tightly around his chest.

McKay, Sloan, Ski Bob, and Chip Girard stood there on the rough plank floor with their teeth in their mouths. Outside, cooling metal pings emerged from Mobile One, where Casey and Tom were holding down the fort and scanning the freeks in case interesting radio traffic happened.

Aside from them, the bed, and the chair with the beak-nosed old coot with two thick braids hanging out from beneath a flat-brimmed black hat with a feather stuck in the band rocking in it and hooting up a storm, the only items of furniture were a pot-bellied stove, currently cold, and a curiously dainty bedside table, enameled in chipped and yellowing white, that somebody must have picked up at a junk store or garage sale. McKay wasn't too clear on how frequently garage sales happened on the res. He was a city boy, himself.

Frank Ed Yellow Bull's trailer near Garryowen wasn't a trailer at all, but a regular Abe Lincoln log cabin. McKay wondered what other useful bits of misinformation had crept into their briefings from Washington.

A woman bustled into the one room through the back door. She was small and wiry and had hair the color of a naval destroyer, though she didn't look to be much past her early forties. She was attractive in a hawkish kind of way, and bore a sneaking resemblance to the big dude on the bed.

"You must go now," she said stiffly. "This man is injured. He needs to rest."

The jovial old fuck ratcheted himself up out of the chair, gathered his faded bombardier's jacket closer around his skinny frame. "Yes, I'm going now. Being around an unlucky man is bad luck. Also, he's so ugly he makes my stomach ache."

Nodding cheerfully to the outsiders he tottered out the door into the cloud-diluted sunlight, the heels of his cowboy boots clunking on the floor. The bootsoles were pulling away at the bottoms.

The door closed. The smile washed off the face of the man on the bed. He shot the door the finger.

"What an asshole," he said. "You know, on the whole, a lot of our great and ancient traditions suck. What can I do you gentlemen for?"

For one of about three times since McKay had known him, Sam Sloan was at a loss for words. Ski Bob chewed gum, loudly. Chip looked bored, hands in pockets of his navy blue SID jacket, eyes blank as the windows on a skyscraper behind the mirrored lenses of his shades.

"I'm Billy McKay. We're the Guardians. Washington sent us to talk to you about the attempt on your life. What the fuck was that all about? Excuse me, ma'am."

Sloan sputtered. McKay ignored him. If the team diplomat choked, he sure couldn't complain about anything McKay said.

The woman was bending over the supine man, who settled

back on his pillows with a groan. "You don't seem to have broken your wounds open with your foolishness."

"Don't *you* start on me, Elaine. I got enough shit from Bear Gets Up to last me all week. They didn't name those bastards the Shit Eaters for nothing."

The woman's stern look got sterner. She finished fiddling with the patient and stood up to face the outsiders, very erect.

"I am finished here. I have to go; please excuse me. Please do not let him become too excited. He really is a foolish man; that wasn't just an *i'watkuce* speaking. Good afternoon." She brushed past McKay and out the door the oldster had taken.

Sloan blinked.

The man on the bed laughed. "Please excuse the hell out of everybody; these are tough times down on the res. I'm Frank Ed Yellow Bull, as you've no doubt guessed. And you look like you could use a quick fix of cultural anthropology."

"I think you could say we're a bit perplexed," Sloan confessed.

McKay made a noise. " 'Perplexed'?" he muttered. "What a tool."

Yellow Bull braced his arms, settled himself. His knife-slash of a mouth didn't have much in the way of lips, but what he had went pale. He was obviously hurting bad, but only showing it through purely involuntary reactions. He was a large man who gave the impression of great strength and great force, of being frustrated and thoroughly pissed off at being immobilized like this. His face was big and spare and emphatic, as basic as the bare-bones land outside the log walls of the cabin.

"That was Joe Bear-Gets-Up, a member of my father's clan and a royal pain in the ass. Being in my father's clan makes him *i'watkuce* to me, a joking relative. See, that's one of those old ways some of our people are trying to dredge up again. *I'watkuce* are supposed to mock you, play practical jokes on you. Is that a great idea or fucking what?"

Girard poked his Insect Fear glasses a bit higher on the aristocratic bridge of his nose. "I thought you Crow respected your old ways."

Yellow Bull grunted. "There's a lot *to* respect about the old ways. But I don't believe we need to be—what? Completely uncritical, if you know what I mean.

"Look at it this way: in the old days, we Absaroka used to

think of ourselves as pretty bad asses indeed. The fact was, we were always getting our butts kicked by the Cheyenne and the goddam Lakota—Sioux to you. And you white eyes kicked theirs in turn.''

He shrugged. ''Then again, you boys just got *your* asses kicked, in the One-Day War—''

McKay started to cloud up. Instead he found himself laughing, saying, ''You oughta see the other guy.''

''I *don't* see the other guy, which I reckon I would if he'd come out of it in any better shape. But that's my goddam *point*. From our point of view there's jack shit by way of difference between American faces and Russian faces: they're both white, you know? So your medicine, your white-eyes medicine, obviously leaves something to be desired.

''—Which gets back to what I was saying on the old college lecture circuit before the War, which pissed off just about everybody: that what we Indians want to do—us Crow, anyway—is try to find our own way, taking what we can use from our old ways and your new ways, and winging it when nothing else works.''

He had come off the pillows as he warmed to the subject. Now he grimaced and settled back down. ''So what do you think of all this, anyway?''

''I never heard such a crock of shit in all my life,'' Billy McKay said.

''*Billy,*'' Sam Sloan said, horror-struck.

Yellow Bull's face set like cement, and got very dark. Then a smile cracked through, and he laughed a booming laugh.

''An honest white man. That's a rarity. You got no idea, brother, what a drag it is talking to a lot of uptight honkies who think I'm full of it, and they just sit there and bob their heads up and down like those little dogs people used to put in the back windows of cars, because they would never *dream* of contradicting a real honest-to-God ethnic.

''I don't care if anybody agrees with me, or even if they like me, but I can't stand being patronized. Welcome to my lodge, McKay. What the hell are you drinking?''

''I'd like to help you,'' Frank Ed Yellow Bull said, sipping Old Crow from a decommissioned Welch's grape jelly jar—''our finest Native American crystal,'' as he put it. ''But first of all,

I have no idea in hell who shot me. It was dark. I was here by myself, expecting company. I went to the window—''

He nodded to the windows flanking the cabin's front door. The one to the left was glazed, but the right was covered by an army blanket.

''—just to stand and stare out awhile, and suddenly there was this blinking yellow light and the damn glass blew in. I took two nine-millimeter slugs in the chest and then I hit the floor. Talk about old ways: this cabin—which is an old white-eyes design; I told you we were goddam eclectic—these log walls stop bullets a hell of a lot better than your modern frame-stucco crap.

''Whoever it was out there raked over the front of the place pretty well, but only one round made it through the chinks. But, anyway, I never saw anything but the goddam muzzle flashes.''

Sam Sloan took a drink of his own bourbon. He was reluctant to drink alcohol on duty, but in all truth old-fashioned sipping whiskey was more his style than herbal tea that tasted like a boiled haystack.

''The way you said that implies there's another reason you can't help us.''

''Well, you boys seem to have your hearts set on this dumb peckerwood McKendree being the guilty party. But it wasn't him; no way.''

Sloan looked at McKay and Girard. Ski Bob had wandered outside to look over the camp while various women summoned by of all things a telephone operated by a hand-cranked generator Yellow Bull kept under his bed had brought refreshments and additional chairs from the various shacks, cabins, and trailers that made up the settlement.

''You seem mighty positive about that, Mr. Yellow Bull,'' Sam said.

''Call me Frank. Just don't call me Frank Ed. That's my honest-to-Jesus legal name, but that doesn't mean I have to let people call me that in my own house.''

He tossed off the last of the whiskey, rummaged under the bed, and produced a fresh bottle. He held it up to the afternoon light slanting in through the one good window. It glowed amber.

''Good scarf is getting harder and harder to come by. Pretty soon we'll be reduced to distilling our own, or buying God knows what corrosive substances off traders. You look as if a fish died in your shirt pocket, Mr. Girard; I take it you disapprove of Indians having firewater.''

''I don't think it's wise to foster use of addictive substances,'' Girard said.

''We aren't your resources, Officer. You people down to Wyoming could keep that it mind.''

''So what is all this about your being sure it wasn't McKendree who hit you?'' McKay demanded.

''It wasn't him.''

Chip Girard made a disgusted sound and waved his hand at the air. He stood up, started to the door, stopped just inside.

''You don't care for my opinions any more than my whiskey,'' Yellow Bull said, and coughed. ''Fine. I can handle that.''

''I'm a law enforcement professional,'' Girard said. ''I can't drink on duty. And with all due respect, Mr. Yellow Bull, your opinions are those of a civilian. There's nothing personal about my turning down either one.''

Some kind of bird with a wide wingspan gusted past the window, chasing the bugs that came out in the dusk. Girard recoiled. He turned back to the bed.

''You're lucky to be alive, Mr. Yellow Bull.''

Yellow Bull shrugged, coughed again to cover a grimace. ''Nothing where they got me but muscle, bone, and air. My lungs didn't collapse, and if I don't get an infection I should pull through. My sister has me pumped full of antibiotics—and thank you again, for bringing more of that stuff from Washington—and the rest of the family's got a wound doctor out trying to snooker a vision from the buffalo, which ought to cover all the bases.''

''Your sister?'' Sloan asked.

''Elaine. You met her. Well, maybe you didn't. She's decided to go in for the traditional formality between brother and sister. It's funny; she's got a white-eyes doctor's license, and then she gets all stuck on the old ways in a whole different department. She's like me, I guess, always trying to pick and choose between the new ways and the old.''

He lifted the bottle, stopped it shy of his lips, restoppered it, and stuck it on the table.

''Funny thing is, she and I always fetch up crosswise of each other, when it comes to what we want to keep and what goes in the dumper. Maybe it's not such a bad idea to keep things formal between us. Otherwise we'd fight like owls and magpies."

"But McKendree—" Sloan began.

"—is a very dangerous man," Girard interjected. "You really shouldn't downplay the threat he poses. He might try again."

"You just don't see, do you, Officer? I *know* Rube McKendree. Not personally, I mean, but I met plenty of his kind back when I was in politics, back before I got smart and quit confusing the cause with the cure. Man like that talks tough, oh my, does he ever.

"But gun down a man in the middle of his own lodges? He'd never have the stones."

"Son of a bitch," Billy McKay said.

"There speaks our ever-articulate leader," Sam Sloan said from Mobile One's ESO console.

McKay was lying on an air mattress on the deck aft of the ESO's and driver's seats, with his boots up on a folded-down seat and his close-cropped blond head propped against the turret root, squinting as he tried to read a dossier in the eerie red blackout light inside the armored car's cabin.

"Yellow Bull's sister really is a doctor. Like an M.D."

"Did you think he was lying?" Sloan asked absentmindedly, punching at his keyboard. The onboard computer had a raft of extraordinarily powerful self-test subroutines, but Sloan preferred to run his own spot checks regularly. That kind of attention to detail had been instrumental in saving the cruiser *Winston-Salem* during the Battle of Sidra Gulf, and not incidentally his own personal private ass, back when he was a gunnery officer in the navy.

"Naw. He's a crackpot, but he seems like an honest crackpot. But dig this: his brother, up until the One-Day War, was professor of Western American history at Stanford."

"I wonder what a Crazy Dog Wishing to Die is?" mused Casey Wilson. He had his big sniper's rifle disassembled for maintenance on a sheet of plastic in the rear of the vehicle, between the turret and the engine compartment. It may or may not have needed it; the unit mechanic, he loved to tinker with junk. Also, having been a fighter pilot made him pretty compulsive about checking over anything he planned to trust his life to.

"Who the fuck knows? Or cares?" McKay tossed down the folder full of hardcopy, sat up, began to roll his head on his bull neck to loosen the muscles.

Sloan glanced back at the popping sounds. "If you wouldn't lie like that your neck wouldn't stiffen up that way. Why you won't take care of yourself is beyond me."

"Hey, who died and made you medical officer? The eighties are over, we can wipe our asses with toilet paper without worrying if the fucking dye is gonna raise our chances of getting cancer by a trillionth of one percent. If we're lucky enough to have toilet paper. I listen to you, you'll turn me into a granola muncher like our friends from Kennedy City."

"They're dedicated law enforcement officers."

"Yeah." He stretched his arms and rolled heavy shoulders. "This Yellow Bull seems like a pretty studly dude, even if he is flat on his back. So who'd figure him to have a pencil-neck college professor for a brother?"

Sloan dropped his lightweight headset on the console and swiveled his chair.

"You know, it's genetics, McKay, now that you mention it. Us intellectual pencil-neck types really do tend to breed true. Just like outsized jocks with pea-sized brains—"

"*Billy,*" Tom Rogers's voice said behind his ear. The ex–Green Beret was on watch up atop the one-man turret. The Guardians weren't as confident as Frank Ed Yellow Bull that the bad guys had just given up trying to kill him.

McKay sighed. He had a lot of voices nagging him from inside his skull—just aft of where their bone-conduction phones piped the sound in, in fact—about what was wrong with this mission and what could get worse. They were really being asked to fly blind, and there was nothing to do but do it.

It was a goddam shame Tommy had interrupted. A good fight right about now could really clear the air.

"Readin' you, Tom. What you got?"

"*Chip's coming over from the trailer.*"

Mobile One was a bit cramped for five people to sack out in— one was always on watch, naturally—but fortunately some generous soul among Yellow Bull's followers had agreed to vacate his or her trailer for the night so the two Wyoming troopies could bunk there. That arrangement suited everyone just fine; there wasn't much love lost between the Guardians and the Special

Investigative Department of the Wyoming Highway Patrol, or at least these two representatives of it.

McKay got up off the deck. Yellow Bull was a good host. He'd had his people lay on a hell of a spread for his visitors: chicken, rabbit, venison, various fresh veggies, canned beets—well, even McKay could appreciate the gesture of sharing precious scarfed canned goods with honored guests, even though he'd always *hated* beets. After dinner Ski Bob and Chip had wanted to go off and poke around a bit on their own. McKay hadn't pressed the point. They were *Guardians*, damn it, not homicide dicks. The Wyoming team really were the pros on this terrain, even if they didn't have to rub it in so much.

"Maybe they found something useful," he said without much conviction. Mobile One's hatch stood open to the cool evening air. He went and stood in it.

Chip Girard was walking toward the car with his hands in his jacket pockets. Without his shades on he looked a lot younger. McKay was surprised he didn't wear them at night, too. Maybe that was only traffic cops.

Girard was in the center of the yellow parallelogram of kerosene lamplight Yellow Bull's good window painted on the packed earth, when he suddenly dropped to his knees. His eyes met McKay's. They were very wide. Startled, like.

Then he toppled face forward to the ground.

CHAPTER
NINE

The sound of the shot beat Girard to the ground, if only by a millisecond. McKay went belly down in the dirt an instant later, .45 in hand.

"Sloan, get the car fired up. Tom, are the guns back together? Casey—"

"I saw the muzzle flash, Billy," Casey reported from on top of the car. "Ridgeline, two eighty-five radial, range three hundred approximate."

"Got it, Billy," Tom replied calmly. From behind him McKay heard the whine of electric motors tracking the turret to the northwest.

One's engine kicked in. "What's happening?" Sloan asked.

"Sniper. Girard's down. Casey, get down from there and get into cover. Tom, give that ridge three forty mike-mikes."

"McKay, you can't!" Sloan exclaimed. "There may be—"

"Fuck *may be*. What there *is* is a sniper up there."

The Mk-19 thundered. Seasoned combat grunt though he was, McKay always forgot how *loud* the things could be. The sound seemed to press him down into the hard-packed dirt, made his eardrums bulge inward despite the protective plugs the Guardians wore constantly whenever they weren't asleep. The muzzle exhaust was a touch of dragon's breath on the back of his neck.

71

Recoil made the big car rock on its massive suspension. Flashes punched three big white holes in the night: two High Explosive, Dual Purpose grenades and one white phosphorus. Standard Guardians party mix. If the sniper was still up on that hill it would definitely spoil his day.

But McKay knew in his gut the sniper *wasn't* still on the ridge. Anybody who could make that shot—three hundred meters, dead dark, wind blowing cross-range, moving target, one round, one hit—would not be. You didn't have to be Casey Wilson to do it, but it helped. It wasn't your usual duffer who used to drive up in the hills in his Bronco to bust caps and six-packs with all his good buddies back in the days when deer hunting was still legal, that was for damn sure.

If it wasn't a pro shot, it was sure a top prospect in Triple-A shot. Made by somebody with a clue as to how real sniping was done. The triggerman was gone with the wind. Had been the instant he saw Girard start to go down. McKay had Rogers work over the ridge with forty mike-mike and .50 caliber for a while anyway, just to be sure.

Meanwhile he lay there with his little piddle-ass pistol in hand. He felt foolish. But he didn't put it away.

The people of the little twenty-lodge camp had reacted promptly. All the lights had gone out by the time the roar of the first three-round burst was echoing off along the coulees. They didn't intend to give any bad guys a nicely illuminated target. McKay had the impression men were baling out of the buildings with longarms in hand, but he was concentrating on the ridge, only looking away to avoid screwing up his night vision when another forty-mike-mike burst went home.

Casey was wriggling forward through the dirt to Girard, who had done a great deal of not moving. He popped in and out of the V-450, and was dragging the heavy medical pack with him.

McKay called a halt to the barrage after Tom had burned a belt of each.

"Shall we chase him?" Sloan asked. The only reason McKay heard him was that the words vibrated directly in his skull. He wasn't hearing the external world any too well.

"Negative." A greenie might freak if a Giant Snorting Metal Beast came ripping out in pursuit of him. Somebody who knew his shit would lie in the bottom of a gully somewhere and laugh his ass off. He might do more than laugh, if he had a friendly portable rocket launcher slung across his back. Whether or not McKendree had gotten his hands on an AT before the One-Day War, it sure hadn't been that hard to come by since. The Effsee occupation had seen to that.

A lanky body skidded in the dirt next to his. A beaky adolescent face nodded into his, framed by thick black braids. It was one of Yellow Bull's cousins, Byron Fire Weasel. He had a bolt-action rifle in hand, a compact sporterized British Enfield. This close to Canada .303 made a lot of sense.

"We'll go after him," the kid said. His voice seemed to be coming in from far away. "He won't get away."

"Go for it," McKay said. The kid got up and joined a dozen shadows melting into the surrounding night.

"How's Girard?" Sloan asked.

"Not breathing," Casey said.

"Sloan, take the turret," McKay said. "Tom, go see what you can do." Each Guardian was trained in everybody's specialty, but Tom was the medical officer and none of the rest could come close to him. He could do damn near anything damn well, but as an MO he shone.

"Think they'll catch him?" Sloan asked.

McKay picked himself up, dusted off the fronts of his silvery Guardians coveralls, stuck his Colt back in the Sparks combat holster.

"No fucking way."

Girard didn't make it. The bullet had smashed through the arch of his aorta. With immediate dust-off to the best of pre-War emergency medical treatment, he might have pulled through—might. As it was, they poured liters of artificial blood-replacement into him, and Tom worked him over as enthusiastically as if Girard owed him money. But it was going through the motions.

Sergeant Ski Bob was back within half an hour, snarling at the pair of husky, braided Crow who escorted him to Yellow Bull's cabin. They snarled back.

"We don't need white eyes stumbling around out there getting in our way," the larger one said.

Ski Bob shook himself free. "Amateurs," he said. McKay couldn't tell whether he meant the Indians or the Guardians.

Probably both.

McKay had already been on the horn back to JFK City. Brant was unavailable, off at his ranch somewhere. The state police radio operator had patched him through to the SID barracks, where he had gotten Sawtelle out of bed. He had probably blown any chance he ever had of becoming one of the highway patrol lieutenant's favorite people. And that was *before* Sawtelle found out McKay had lost one of his men for him.

I hold you responsible, Sawtelle had said.

"I hold you responsible," Ski Bob said, as soon as his escorts had gone.

McKay rubbed his chin. He stood near the good window, which had its own blanket tacked over it now. McKay didn't want to give away any more free shots to snipers.

"All right," he said, swinging around to face the highway patrolman. "I'm responsible. This mission's under my command. And your buddy's still dead. Now what?"

Ski Bob stared at him, his snowmelt-pale eyes watering in the thin smoke drooled from the kerosene lantern, whose chimney needed cleaning.

"Now you admit the problem we have with Reuben Mc-Kendree," he said, breaking eye contact with an all but audible snap.

"I got no problem with any Rube McKendree. You Wyoming law enforcement guys do, or think you do, and *I* ain't gonna tell *you* your business. We got a lot of dead ethnics, and now one dead police trooper. And we got nothing resembling a witness. My orders say I need to have some proof before I take any concrete action. What have you given me?"

"What about what Chip gave you?" Ski Bob yelled, suddenly up in McKay's face like a greyhound deciding to challenge a Great Dane for dominance. "He's lying out there in a body bag. *What more do you need for proof?*"

McKay stood his ground, feet planted, shoulders back. "We got a shot out of the dark. Or did you find a card lying out there in a ditch with 'Compliments of Reuben McKendree' engraved on it?"

They heard clapping. Both men snapped their heads around. Sitting up in bed, Frank Ed Yellow Bull slowly applauded.

"This is good," he said. "Really good. Entertainment is not so easy to come by, since there's hardly ever any television except Forrie Smith, and he's too big a fool to stay amusing very long.''

Ski Bob said something under his breath and turned away.

"McKay," Sloan said over the communicator, *"can we talk a moment?"*

McKay glanced at Malinowski. *"Yeah."*

He slipped out of the door, not letting himself stay silhouetted long. Sam Sloan was leaning against the side of the cabin, not far from a long mound lying beneath a sheet of black plastic. Rogers was up on the cabin roof, keeping an eye on things, and Casey was asleep inside Mobile One.

"I couldn't help hearing the debate in there, McKay," Sloan said.

McKay leaned against Mobile One and crossed his arms. "We weren't real quiet, I got to admit."

"McKay, I think Sergeant Malinowski has a point. This McKendree's been proven to be a pretty dangerous character. He's got a string of federal indictments as long as your arm. Why are you denying the truth that's staring you right in the face?"

He pushed off and took a few steps away from McKay. Neither he nor McKay was taking extraordinary precautions against the sniper. If he came back, he came back; they couldn't spend their whole lives hiding under cover.

"There's one possibility I don't really want to face," Sloan continued. "I mean, we don't really have a lot in common, but I certainly do respect you—"

McKay finished unwrapping a cigar, bit off the end. "Spit it out," he said, and did that thing. The cigar he placed between his teeth unlit. Just because he wasn't willing to crawl around all week on his belly like the biggest safety-obsessed Eighties weenie just because there might be Bad Men didn't mean he was going to take extravagant risks for no payoff.

Sloan faced him. "Is it perhaps because you have some kind of twisted sympathy with McKendree's views? You have a fundamentally conservative outlook, and that can certainly lead to—"

McKay's laugh reined him up short. "For such a smart boy you can be real fucking dumb, Sloan. I'd think you'd at least gotten to know me better, last couple of years."

"Well, McKay, listen to yourself talk sometimes. You're not exactly the most tolerant—"

"If you think you're all tolerant, saying that just 'cause I ain't ready to buy into the Big Welfare State I'm a prime candidate to start burning crosses on somebody's lawn, that's fine. I can do without tolerance."

Sloan made a gesture with his hands as if he were trying to hold up an invisible beach ball. "You just don't understand."

"You got that right. I'm a marine. I ain't supposed to understand. I'm just supposed to do. Right now what I'm supposed to *do* is find out who the hell's been offing all these chinks and shit. And if it is Reuben McKendree, just which of us do you think is gonna kick his ass the farther, navy boy?"

"*Billy.*"

"You're right on cue, Casey. Sometimes I think you got an in with the scriptwriter."

"*Radio woke me up, Billy,*" the former fighter jock continued after the slightest pause. "*It was Kennedy City.*"

McKay shut his eyes. He felt the momentary floating sensation that told him fatigue poisons were starting to build up. He wished he could just let himself float away.

"And what good news do you have for me now?"

"*They got a tape from McKendree. He's claiming credit for hitting Patrolman Girard, and he's threatened to assassinate Governor Greenwell.*"

CHAPTER
TEN

"That was quick work," McKay said. "I mean, your man Girard hadn't even gotten cool, and here comes Big Rube claiming credit for taking him down."

Nicholas Brant frowned. He had a thunderous scowl for such a little man. It was all that forehead that did it.

Governor Greenwell stopped pacing the wooden floor of his office and shook his head. His pallor was heavier than ever.

"Don't you see, Lieutenant? Obviously he had this planned in advance." He shuddered. "What kind of a man could lay out such a cold-blooded deed as casually as if he were planning a trip to the Grand Tetons?"

Sitting beneath a photograph of the younger Greenwell shackled to a nuclear sub at Groton, McKay shook his head. There were at least four men in this very room who not only could but *had*. Even Sloan the bleeding heart had calmly discussed things that would make Greenwell's heart *stop*.

Toby Sawtelle just grinned and briefly hit the rewind key. When he came off it the cassette machine growled and said, "—*munist dupe of a State pig. But he's only the first. If Mr. High and Mighty Governor Greenwell doesn't see the light, he could well be next.*

77

"White Action will tolerate no interference. To do so would be treason to the race.

"This is McKendree."

Sam Sloan took a deep breath and let it out, blinking. "Well, that's it. No room for doubt now."

He turned a meaningful look at McKay. His eyes had an owlish look to them; they'd driven right back through the night from Montana. Even for seasoned campaigners there hadn't been much sleep. The sun was shining outside the carefully drawn insulated curtains—all natural fiber, Brant had made sure to point out—but they all felt like the middle of the night after a long, bad day.

McKay kind of pushed one boot off his knee to the floor. He stood up. He stretched. He smiled.

"No, I guess there's not. The time has come to rock and roll."

"The group calling itself White Action!," Toby Sawtelle explained, squatting in the exercise yard on the fringes of JFK City, "is headquartered on an old ranch up in the Absaroka Mountains west of Meeteetse, *here—*"

A tanned hand moved. A red laser dot appeared on the laminated map resting on the beaten-down earth.

"—in the northwestern quadrant of the state. It changed hands a very few years before the War. It was hoped it could be made part of a wilderness area, but Wild Bill Lowell's administration wasn't doling out much money for anything that couldn't be turned to military uses, and the owners weren't interested in selling to the state."

He looked up under his red eyebrows past the rolled-bandanna headband at McKay. "They preferred to sell to a group of white supremacists who wanted a survivalist retreat. A very socially conscious action, don't you think? Just another example of free enterprise in action."

McKay sucked on his cigar. "Look, Sawtelle, it's hot out here. I wanna either kick some ass or get some sleep. Why don't you get to the point?"

Something flickered in through the gauze curtains of McKay's peripheral vision and *chunked* in the hardpan by his foot. The Team hooted laughter.

Maybe fatigue poisons had slowed his reactions, or maybe he was drawing strength from the bottomless well of stubbornness in his Parris Island DI's soul, but he didn't so much as twitch. Just looked down.

A big knife with a black hard-rubber hilt was stuck in the ground a centimeter from his right boot. It was one of those straight-taper two-edged blade things called Arkansas toothpicks. You learned about that sort of dope in Guardians training. He looked up.

There were these two identical yoo-hoos, one called Lew and one called Stew, both wiry, five-ten or -eleven, dark haired, who looked like twins and weren't even related. One was standing there in his jeans and L.L. Bean grinning at McKay in a happy slack-lipped way.

And then the smile slipped off and fell to the ground, because between it and McKay's eyes the three fat white dots that were the combat sights of McKay's .45 had appeared, lined up and aglow in the razor-sharp Western sun.

"Funny joke, Jeffcoat," he said, in the last half second making him as the one who called himself Stew. "Pull it again and I'll kill you. I'm not a fucking dartboard."

Sam reached for his arm as if to pull the gun off-line, thought better of it. "McKay," he said softly, "these are good guys."

"Oh. I didn't know good guys played with knives." He caught the hammer on the fat of his thumb, pressed the trigger, let spring tension ride the gun back up in his fist until the hammer touched gently home.

He kicked the knife toward Jeffcoat. Stew looked daggers at him, naturally enough, then sidled forward and recovered his blade. He wiped it carefully on the leg of his jeans.

Sawtelle just squatted in the dirt, naked but for khaki shorts and tire-soled Mexican sandals, grinning nastily at McKay.

"Well, now that you've shown everybody who's the alpha in this wolf pack, maybe we can get back to the matter at hand. That's what you want, isn't it?"

McKay stuck the piece back in his combat rig.

With a flick of the wrist Sawtelle unrolled a U.S. Geological Survey 1:50,000 map on top of the laminated map of the state. He tossed the laser pointer to the far end to hold it down, went to one knee to bend over the map.

The Guardians clustered around. Floating on the breeze they could hear one of the work gangs listlessly singing "Louie Louie."

"This is the route in. No improved roads past Meeteetse. Survivalist types like their privacy."

"You sound mighty certain of that," Sloan observed.

"We deal with those assholes all the time," said Lewis Polidor, who played Lew to Jeffcoat's Stew. He was supposed to be a big electronics whiz.

"Hoarders," Stew said, cleaning his nails with the point of his knife and shooting McKay sidelong glances. "We can't put up with that kind of selfish shit. People got to share, you know."

The enormous blond trooper introduced as Bubba laughed, *hur-hur*, then winced and rubbed his chest with a hand the size of a hubcap. *Rocket scientist,* McKay thought.

"I know how you like to share that knife," he said to Stew. "How come a cop likes to dick around with knives, anyway?"

"Narcotics detail," said the Team's lone black. An inch or two taller than McKay, he wore a black tee shirt with the sleeves bulged all out of shape by biceps like Georgia hams. "We were on the combat line. War on drugs, you dig?"

"So you stabbed people?" Casey murmured. "Bummer." It was unclear, at least to McKay, whether he objected to a policeman stabbing people or just to such a low-tech approach.

Wham! Something exploded right behind the Guardians.

McKay was eating dirt with his big Colt in both hands. The other Guardians had dropped into a beautiful prone defensive circle, Tom with his basic businesslike .45, Casey with his gigantic Dirty Harry magnum, Sloan with the horrible shiny nickel-plated Python .357 McKay hated so much.

The Team stood around them slapping their knees and laughing like a pack of coyotes.

"What the fuck, over?" McKay demanded, and spit out dirt.

"That's just Dooley," Stew said with malicious satisfaction. "Nothing to be *afraid* of."

McKay looked at Sloan. "Dooley?" Sam said.

Sawtelle jerked his head. A guy built low, like a sack of potatoes, stood in the background with hands stuck in the pockets of his oil-stained blue overalls. He had a California Angels baseball cap crammed down on some long greasy hair with gray strung through it, and a chewable rotating between cheeks covered with what was probably five o'clock shadow last week. He had no shirt beneath his overalls. Looking back at him, McKay caught a stale whiff of grease, human and petrochemical. If he fit the clean-cut Earth-jock profile of the rest of the Team it was hard to see exactly where.

"Dooley's our blaster," Sawtelle explained. "He's also our liaison with Department of Public Safety's intelligence branch."

"Yeah. He looks like an intelligent kind of guy." McKay picked himself up and sorted himself out. "What the hell was that *noise*, Patrolman? You have beans for lunch?"

"Blasting cap. Just testing a new fuse. Get bored, standing around listening to people talk."

"No shit. You people are really *professionals*. I mean, I'm awestruck."

"*Billy,*" Tom subvocalized. McKay waved a hand at him. He knew many demolitions types were maximum flakes.

"The most direct way in," Sawtelle said pointedly, folding his long bare legs again, "is this dirt road that goes around this mountain here, down, then up toward Devers Peak here. It's also the *only* direct route, unless you plan to go in on horseback."

"Or take a dirt bike."

The Team looked at him as if he'd suggested they all take a break to screw their mothers. "You would, wouldn't you?" Lew said primly.

"Nope." He scratched beside his nose with a thumbnail. "Too noisy."

"The big house, here—"

Sawtelle trumped his earlier maps with an aerial photo, computer enhanced for clarity. McKay had seen the things back in Southwest Asia Command, which was to say the Med. He never liked them. He didn't much care to stake his life on what some computer program thought the terrain *ought* to look like.

"—is pretty much McKendree's castle. That's what they call it, in fact: White Castle. Quite the sense of humor these bigots have."

He paused and scanned the faces of his listeners. Only Midwesterner Sam got it. He grimaced. His home region was divided into people who were addicted to White Castle's hamburgerlike substance and people who couldn't stand it. He was in the definitely nonhabituated category.

Seeing his joke didn't go over quite as big as anticipated, Sawtelle shrugged. "Our intelligence says it's hardened, sandbags, concrete reinforcements with loopholes, that sort of thing. Nothing showing, of course.

"These other buildings are mostly frame, some prefab. Everybody lives in them except for McKendree, his bodyguards, bimbos, and chief buttsuckers.''

''How many in the compound?'' Tom Rogers asked.

Sawtelle raised an eyebrow. ''Dooley?''

''DPS Intelligence makes it eighty, ninety. Maybe as many as a hundred, but no more, including kids and grannies.''

'' 'Kids and grannies,' '' Casey echoed. ''You're kidding, man.''

Dooley squirted brown ooze from his mouth. Casey recoiled. ''Heck no. These end-of-the-world types, they believe in having their families with 'em when Armageddon comes to call. 'Cept the ones who hope Missus is home in the suburbs doing the dishes at ground zero.''

''How many can shoot?'' McKay asked.

''Whoo,'' said the final member of the Team, a long drink of water with a cowboy hat and a brick-colored face, and laughed. He answered to Alex. ''All of 'em. They practice all the time. Paramilitary drill, firing practice on targets painted like Jews and jigaboos, whole nine yards.''

''No innocents on the firing line,'' said Ski Bob, who had been hanging on the fringes having as little as possible to do with his former tripmates.

''That makes it easier for us,'' McKay said. He had to remind himself not to get rankled at agreeing with the highway patrol sergeant. *We're on the same side. Just keep repeating that.* ''What's our game plan?''

''So how the hell did you wind up with a name like Elrond?'' McKay asked across the flat wooden bed of the truck. The space between its wooden sides was piled with gear, three of the Team, and Billy McKay.

They'd split from JFK the afternoon before, rolling out past the carved wood sign that said *The New Frontier Starts Here* right after the briefing. Three vehicles, which seemed a poor kind of car-pooling for such environmentally conscious squaddies: Mobile One, the flatbed, and a hyperthyroid pickup that looked like what it really wanted to do in life was have those great big tires rednecks put on their pickups and ride fifteen feet off the ground and be a Monster Car-Crusher Truck. Instead what it did was drag this long trailer with eight entire horses inside, which McKay could still just barely believe. *I mean, horses?*

What with the dubious roads it was eight hours to Devers Peak. They'd spent the night camped on the Powder River with the no-see-'ems making them nuts, and gotten an early start today. They were still undecided on the specifics of their approach to the old Coleman ranch. The Guardians wanted to approach openly in daylight. The Team, perhaps with ingrained narcotics-squad reflex, wanted to make it a predawn raid with zero warning. They figured coming into the target area in mid-afternoon would give them the option to cruise on in or wait for darkness and infiltrate to striking range.

The truck took another massive lurch. The big blond jock didn't change expression. He had an even more spectacularly thick neck than Billy McKay. In fact he was *all 'round* bigger than Billy McKay. He carried an M249 Squad Automatic Weapon with a box magazine of 5.56 plugged into it across his knees. These dudes meant it when they said they were on the firing line.

"My parents were hippies," he said placidly. Bubba had played football at the University of Wyoming. Somehow McKay wasn't surprised.

"Hippies," McKay repeated. Just ahead Mobile One's engine growled in irritation. Sawtelle meant it when he said there were no improved roads up here. "What, were they Scientologists or something?"

Elrond Hughes, d/b/a Bubba, looked blank. It looked like an expression that came real naturally to him. "Scientologists?"

"Yeah. I mean, didn't they have a boss named Elrond or something?"

"Elron, Billy," came Casey's voice over the communicator. He was up front manning the turret of Mobile One and helping ride herd on Sawtelle and Alex, the red-faced shitkicker, who were traveling in the V-450 for reasons of solidarity, or some such shit. *"For L. Ron Hubbard. His real name was Lafayette—"*

"I don't want to know. So what's an Elrond got to do with hippies?" He heard Casey snicker, promised himself he'd make him eat shit later.

The pine trees were putting their heads together above the narrow dirt road, keeping the sun to a dusty, dusky minimum. Ski Bob had his head back and was laughing a superior laugh. Lew Polidor was laughing too, and here came Bubba, only a beat or two late. McKay sat with arms folded across his pecs and did his best imitation of a Rushmore head until they came out of it.

"You don't read much, do you?" Ski Bob asked. McKay grunted. "Elrond was a half-elven hero who lived in Rivendell. Bubba's parents read *Lord of the Rings* too much."

They all laughed again, upturned faces dappled by the tree-spattered sun. Even Bubba joined in, laughing at what goofs his parents were for naming him Elrond.

McKay managed at least a sour grin for how stupid Bubba's parents were for not drowning him in the bathtub when he was five.

Bubba winced and massaged his chest.

"What's the matter with him?" McKay asked.

"Took one in the chest when we were cleanin' out some survivalists a week or so back," Polidor said. "Even with a Kevlar vest, that kinda smarts, you know?"

"Yeah." He did, too.

"Only hurts when I laugh," Bubba said. "Hur-hur. *Ouch.*"

Having made a gesture at comradely conversation, McKay sank back into a sun-warmed stupor while the other three shot general shit about their missions together. They'd been the striking arm of a special anti–organized crime task force before the One-Day War. Business hadn't slacked off any since then; it had gotten if anything brisker, it seemed. There were always survivalist retreats to clean out, a task that the Team seemed to get a particular kick out of. . . . His head slipped back till a wooden slat stopped it, and he let the sunlight falling on his eyelids and the rough road rock him right out from behind his eyes.

He came awake with a start, knowing in his gut something was wrong. Some kind of reports . . . shooting? His hands found his personal weapon beside him, a Maremont M60E3 machine gun with a fifty-round belt in a half-moon box hung off its gleaming black receiver, for all its "lightweight" designation a heavy, hard-hitting, fire-breathing 7.62-millimeter monster that bore the same relationship to Bubba's little mouse-gun SAW as Bubba himself did to skinny Stew, the jiveass with the taste for mumblety-peg.

Stew's counterpart Lew was patting him on the arm, grinning into his face with overlarge teeth.

"Hey, big fella, take it easy. It's only engine trouble."

CHAPTER
ELEVEN ———————————————————

"Shit," McKay said, and slapped the place where a raindrop had struck his cheek as if a yellow jacket had stung him there.

Casey Wilson, Dooley, and Alex Barka were all hanging over the opened front of the stakebed truck like suits of clothes somebody's laid over a rock to dry without remembering to take the occupants out first. Their muttered conversations and occasional breaks to smear grease over their foreheads in the guise of scratching did not suggest men who had a Clue.

" 'Just engine trouble,' " McKay said. "Fucking *great*."

Coming back from a quick whiz in the roadside weeds, Lew finished zipping his cammie pants and laughed. "If you knew what McKendree was like," he said, "you wouldn't be in such a big damn hurry to get to know him."

"You know, I am really sick of hearing what a rough, tough dude this McKendree is," McKay said. "If he really is Superman on angel dust, why the fuck doesn't he run this snake-crotch state?"

"*We* can handle him," Stew Jeffcoat said. "It's you city boys we worry about."

"Hey," Sam Sloan said, walking the rut alongside the defunct truck on his way from petting the horsies. "Who're you calling

a city boy?'' He said it in a joking way, trying to let the air out
of a possible confrontation. He could be a real weenie sometimes.

Alex came swaggering back with his straw cowboy hat pushed
up on his forehead, wiping his hands on a rag. ''Looks like the
fuel pump has gone south.''

''Can you fix it?''

Barka squinted meaningfully up into the sky. The sun shone
hot and bright from the western half of the sky where it was
headed for touchdown in the Absarokas, but its rays slanted in
under really impressive battlements of black cloud from which
the Guardians were periodically getting pissed on, which was
just about the way things were going generally.

''Well, I'm a pretty fair makeshift mechanic, and Dooley can
whip together just about anything with his hands. Stew's good
on your little picayune detail kind of work, though he's mostly
a lock man, and I'd judge your boy Casey knows a thing or two.
All told, we can probably get her back under way in five, six
hours.''

''Six hours? Jesus Christ. It's gonna rain like a mother inside
of an hour.''

''Thirty, forty minutes, more like,'' Alex agreed amiably. He
looked like a narrower Robin Williams who'd been in the sun
too much.

''Shit,'' McKay said. ''Shit, shit, shit.''

''See why we brought horses, McKay?'' Sawtelle asked from
behind him. ''They don't break down.''

''They just bust their legs.''

Sawtelle shrugged. ''Hey. We're still mobile. We have the
animals.''

''You got another truck, too.''

The Team leader shook his head. ''Big one's blocking the
road.''

''Well, for God's sake, push it in the ditch. We're burning
daylight.''

''We don't do things that way in the highway patrol,'' Ski Bob
said. He had his scoped .270 slung with the barrel sticking under
his right arm and his amber goggles on, walking around chewing
on a grass shoot. ''We don't like to rely on that kind of technology, but when we do, we take care of it.''

Alex laughed. "Hey, put it in terms the man can understand. We *signed* for the son of a bitch, all right?"

"We could pull it out without any problem." Casey joined the discussion. "One has a winch."

Sawtelle shook his head. "Sorry."

"Well, for Christ's sake, do we just call it all off and have a picnic here by the side of the road? I thought you people were the ones in a rush to hang McKendree's head on the wall."

Sawtelle raised his face. A few raindrops bounced off his face, making him look like a kid out for a walk through the woods with his slingshot—back when a kid wouldn't have been busted and sent to major therapy for carrying such a lethal weapon, and his parents fined a couple of limbs apiece for neglect.

"We'll work on it for a while. My boys are pretty good at improvisation. If they can't get something together before the clouds blow open, we can always pack it in and go ahead on horseback."

"Christ." McKay stomped a few feet up the road, looked at the clouds, looked at the trees, looked at the undergrowth. There were no good answers hidden anywhere among them, at least not that he could see. "What happens if the peckerwoods decide to go into town for a six-pack?"

"They ain't hardly gonna get past us," Alex pointed out, "and they don't go home without our say-so."

"But what if somebody comes through the woods and spots us?" Casey asked. "They might have, like, patrols."

Say hey. We might make a decent marine out of you yet, McKay thought. "He's right. What happens then?"

Sawtelle looked at his troopies. Everybody shrugged.

"Guess if they spot us and we don't spot them we're blown," Alex said.

"Shit happens," Stew said.

"Great. Just fucking great." McKay went up and stood next to Dooley peering down into the engine compartment. He inhaled and moved a foot or two away, trying not to be conspicuous or anything.

"Can you really fix that thing?"

"In time," Dooley said, scratching the grimy back of his neck, "I can fix anything." He blew a bubble.

"What the fuck is *that*?" McKay asked. "I never saw brown bubble gum before."

"Bubble gum and Red Man chaw, all mixed up," Dooley said, reabsorbing the bubble and spitting brown juice into the ditch, where a tuft of rabbit brush promptly withered and died. "Picked up the trick when I was a catcher in the Angels organization. Made it all the way up to Edmonton in the Pacific Coast League before I realized Triple-A ball was all the higher I'd get."

"Gah," McKay said. It felt as if his tongue had swollen up to fill his mouth. He didn't think he was physically capable of being grossed out anymore. Trust a blaster who was also a burnt-out minor-league catcher to find a way. "Life with you boys is surely interesting. Yes indeed. *Urk.*"

He went back to the confab at the rear of the stakebed.

"Fuck a bunch of hanging around here waiting to get wet and spotted. We're going on. We'll work our way as close as we can and wait for you to catch up. If the rednecks show any sign of spooking we'll just have to move right then."

The Teammates passed a look around. "Wouldn't rightly recommend going in on your own."

"Oh, bullshit. Casey, Sloan—time to saddle up and *go.*"

"You know what?" Sloan said. "Ski Bob had a shot at the next Olympics. He's a real high-powered biathlete. I'd even heard of him, though I didn't make the connection at first."

"Yeah?" said McKay, more bored with lying around in the car listening to the rain thump on the top deck than interested. It was hot and still in the car, even though the shrouded vents were open. "What is it, this biathlete? Never heard of it."

To him it was only a sport if you got to hit somebody. The only reason, say, baseball qualified was the brushback pitch and the hard slide, and they'd been trying to phase those out before the War.

"It's cross-country skiing and marksmanship together in the same event, Billy," said Casey, who was stretched out in the driver's seat with his tour cap pulled down over his eyes.

"So it's like getting a gold medal in being a ski trooper?"

Sloan frowned, thought about it. "I reckon that's about right, yes."

"Shit. Whyn't they have one for being Force RECON? The ten-thousand-meter snoop and poop? Silent sentry removal? And how about a demo event? Tommy and I'd have medals hangin' all over us like pinecones."

"If they had a beer-drinking event you'd sure win a medal, man," Casey said.

McKay sat upright on his air mattress. "What's this? Lieutenant Casey Wilson, former star of the United States Air Force, the man who initially flunked out of Aggressor training for being *too aggressive*—do I understand it that this man has told a *joke*?"

Casey pushed up the bill of his cap. "Hey, I've got a sense of humor." He sounded hurt.

Lightning crashed like an artillery round nearby. The rain rose to a crescendo, for a moment making speech impossible. The three had their communicators squelched so their banter wouldn't distract Tom Rogers, who'd worked his way ahead fifteen hundred meters to a point actually inside the compound, where he could keep an eye on the dwellings.

That had been about the only thing to go right since they pulled away from the Powder River this morning. The rain just ate the noise their burly diesel engine made, enabling them to work much farther along the road than they'd anticipated. And there was nothing to depress a sentry's spirits and alertness like getting good and cold and wet. Not to mention what a storm did to his sensory package: screwed up visibility, filled your ears with white noise and thunder, washed away your sense of smell, turned your skin clammy and numb. Unless you could *taste* an enemy coming you were shit out of luck.

In the best of circumstances sentry-go was not an easy job, even though from the outside it didn't look precisely demanding. It was tough even for trained and seasoned troops—and even if they didn't treat Reuben McKendree with the almost mystical reverence the SID Team held for him, the Guardians did not make the mistake of thinking his kids and grannies and cammie commandos were going to be sad-sack pushovers. A lot of people who had been candy-ass civilians when the balloon went up were veteran troops by now. Life after the Holocaust had that effect on some people. And these bozos *worked* at it.

"Sloan, quit playing with yourself and see if you can raise Colonel Custer and F Troop," McKay said, when talking stopped being a waste of time.

"Good grief, McKay, grow up." But Sloan stirred in his seat, shuffled himself upright, and began scanning the frequencies the Team's communicators were tuned to. It was only about the third time in fifteen minutes, but Sloan didn't complain; he wasn't any less bored than McKay.

"Pony Boy, Pony Boy, this is Turtle One," Sloan said into the microphone of the lightweight headset be wore. "Come in, Pony Boy."

Snap, crackle, pop. McKay always hated commo. The airwaves always sounded like an old cereal commercial.

"—up this ridge—" they thought they heard someone say. The words vanished in a sizzle of lightning and didn't come back.

"Christ," McKay said, for what seemed to be the five hundredth time today. Sister Charles from back at St. Joe's would clean his mouth out with Lysol if she ever caught up with him. St. Joseph's School had vanished along with a sizable chunk of downtown Pittsburgh when a warhead obviously programmed under the influence of nostalgia for the days when the city was a major industrial center popped off half a klick above Schenley Park. McKay figured Sister Charles had probably pulled through, though. It took more than five hundred lousy KT to kill a nun that mean.

"How long ago did those fools quit dicking with their truck and start riding?" he demanded.

"Couple of hours ago," Sloan said distractedly. He was doing this and that to his console, trying to boost the gain on the receiver.

"We didn't leave them all that far back. How the hell long could it take to ride this far?"

"A while, in weather like this. Wait, I think—no. Damn." He glanced back. "They should be coming up with us soon, though."

"Billy."

"Tom? Aw, shit." He fumbled in a reinforced breast pocket of his cammie coveralls, turned his communicator back to *transmit*. "I read you, Tom. Go ahead."

The signals produced by the hand-calculator-sized communicators, powerful though they were, would not actually penetrate Mobile One's armored hide. Instead the internal comm system picked McKay's up and bounced them along via the car's radio.

"Something's happening. Lights have started to come on in the buildings."

"Oh, shit. Think we're spotted?"

"Can't tell, Billy. Seems likely."

"Right. We're on our way." He started up the ladder into the turret. "Fire this puppy up, Case. We be jammin'."

"What about the Team?" Sam Sloan asked.

McKay's voice echoed back down from the turret: "Fuck 'em. It's Miller time."

The road ran like a river. Mobile One's big cleated tires churned up a huge, frothing, muddy wake as the car labored up the grade. Pine branches swept across the turret and upper decks with eerie scratching, squeaking sounds.

"Christ," McKay muttered under his breath, straining to peer out the glass-and-plastic laminate vision blocks of the one-man turret. "It's like going through the world's biggest car wash."

He flipped a switch on the panel beside the receivers of the automatic guns. A screen came alive, a low-light television view of the world outside, piped from a pickup mounted coaxially with the guns.

"Nothin' but branches and rain. Well shit." Through the blocks he could see the gleam of lights six or seven hundred meters away up the flank of the mountain. White Action! had to be running generators; it was tough to get that much juice out of solar accumulators.

"We're coming up on a barrier," Casey reported.

McKay squinted through the vision block. "I see it. Big log with some coils of razor tape thrown over it." Since he was on lookout with nothing to do *but* watch, he was supposed to spot things like that first; Casey had to deal with minor distractions like keeping the ten-tonne mass of Mobile One from slithering right off the road into the close-crowding trees. This wet mud was like oil under the tires.

Oh, well. Casey was a fighter pilot, after all. He was *supposed* to have real strak eyes.

He gave up on the low-light TV, brought up the passive infrared instead. At the same time he increased the gain on a hull-mounted directional mike aimed toward the barrier.

Casey was using LLTV to drive by, plus his own incredibly keen vision. Even through the vision block McKay could see the man on watch at the barrier, straining into the night trying to make out the toadlike blackness snorting and slipping its way inexorably toward him. His face looked like a white balloon bobbing there unsupported in midair. His image glowed on the

IR monitor, red and green where clothing masked some of his body heat, bright yellow where the heat of his face shone out against the rain-chilled air.

With a light push of the pedals McKay traversed the turret left. There was no point in giving the poor fuck cardiac arrest by looming up out of the night pointing two Holland Tunnel-sized gun muzzles at the bridge of his nose. The guy was undoubtedly a crazed pinheaded cross-burning dink-shooting redneck momhumper, but McKay had stood enough cold wet watches to sympathize with the bastard anyway.

A flare of orange caught his eye. A weirdly convulsing blob, off among the trees to the left where a clearing opened away from the road . . .

"Casey," he screamed, *"break right!* Rocket!"

Screen and viewport flared nova white.

CHAPTER
TWELVE —————————————————

The Light Antitank Weapon blew out of a cloud of exhaust flame, trailing a line of white fire behind it.

As he cried warning, McKay had slammed one hand on the switch for the million-candlepower spot mounted in the turret and the other on the bar that fired both guns at once. McKay felt the car accelerate and swerve beneath him even as the weapons' recoil heeled it way over to its starboard side.

Billy McKay had spent a lot of his life in harm's way. Before he ever became a Guardian, he served with the Marine Corps' elite Force RECON in the battlezones of North Africa and the Mideast, then with the shadow warriors of the misleadingly named Studies and Observations Group, Southwest Asia Command, waging a covert campaign of sabotage and assassination against Muslim fanatics and Soviet puppets. After that he'd gone back for another stint in Force RECON before a mission gone totally awry landed him in the hospital bed in Jaffa out of which the one-eyed Major Crenna had recruited him. Since that time he had seen almost two years' interrupted action as boss Guardian.

That kind of experience gave a man an edge. Not just by whetting his senses to a scalpel's fineness. But by giving him the knowledge and the intuition alike to put together circumstance and perception—just a writhing blob of light against the night, body heat seen by an infrared eye—into an instant conviction that death was the press of a firing switch away.

It was just enough.

The rocketeer may have been distracted by the sudden sound-and-light show Billy McKay had unleashed for his benefit. Or Casey's violent maneuver in instanteous response to McKay's warning may have thrown off his aim. Or maybe he just plain *missed*.

But not by much.

The rocket hit the V-450's upper surface just in front of the turret, right on the edge as the car angled away from it into the ditch. The impact triggered its shaped-charge warhead, which went off in a brilliant fan-shaped gush of incandescent gas and sparks that cascaded across the angled armor plate like a volcanic eruption.

McKay's night vision went instantly to hell. He kept goosing the trigger bar, concentrating on the end that fired the .50 solo now. *Those SID pukes were right*, he thought. *These assholes got AT.* That being the case, he wasn't going to burn precious forty mike-mike on a rocket man who had shot his wad. If the guy could prep another LAW with those thumb-sized bullets, one in every five a tracer, plowing up the landscape around his ears, then he had to be wearing a skintight blue suit with a big red *S* on the chest under his K mart cammie shirt and dungarees anyway. If the first ejaculation of high explosive and white death hadn't caught him, which given the way things worked it probably hadn't.

McKay killed the spot. No point in giving the bad guys a beacon to home on. Mobile One wasn't going to be all that hard to spot anyway.

McKay's vision was impaired by this huge purple fan that the explosion seemed to've branded permanently on his retinas, but by the light of the Browning's muzzle flash—only slightly less dazzling than the rocket blast—he saw the lone sentry at the barricade go rabbiting up the road. *Smart man.*

"—Kay, are you all right? Billy, do you hear me?" He became aware of Sloan talking repetitively in his head. Now that he thought about it, the explosion must have momentarily deafened him, aided and abetted by his own artillery. He had no recollection of the missile making any sound at all.

"I'm fine. I don't think the thing got through the hull," and as he said it he knew it hadn't, because if it had, given where it winged the car, Sloan and Casey would probably not be doing a lot of talking to him in this incarnation.

"Did you get him, Billy?" Casey wanted to know. He was navigating the car along the ditch, brushing the occasional pine bole with a splintering crack.

"Probably not. But I don't think we'll be hearing much outta him." Which was a good thing. At this point the trees pressed right up to the road, and while they weren't exactly redwoods there was a definite limit to how far even twenty-two thousand pounds of car was going to bull its way in among them.

"There's definite activity in the compound now, Billy," Tom reported.

He was calm as always: no, "what happened?" or "omigod, are you *all right*?" He'd heard the action; his three buddies all had their communicators turned on now, and he'd put in enough time in the barrel to be able to fill in the blanks. For him this *was* business as usual. *"Shall I fire them up?"*

"Put us back on the road, Casey, and full speed ahead, or whatever you flyboys say. Tom, do it to it. Just scatter some around to get their minds right."

"These people are defending their homes against an armed intruder, McKay," Sloan reminded him.

"Yeah? Well let me remind you, they shot at us first. Besides, I figured you thought nobody like this had any rights you had to respect."

From the loud silence welling up from beneath his feet McKay gathered he'd scored off his buddy and rival, which even in the heat of combat felt good. Those black-shoe navy bastards needed keeping in their place.

"Besides, no worries," McKay said as Mobile One waddled back into the ruts, which were running like rivers. "We got the firepower. If these people are smart they'll do what we say. Nobody has to get hurt."

He could feel Casey beneath him, peering worriedly through vision blocks the wipers couldn't keep clear. "What if they, like, have more LAWs, Billy?"

McKay bit his lip. The kid was beginning to think like a real combat trooper. Which made sense. The *kid* was almost thirty, and had been a Guardian just as long as McKay.

"Um. Right. Which is why you are gonna put on your boonie hat and bail out with your long gun to keep a watch out for bad

guys with rockets. Sloan will drive. This ain't gonna call for any
Unser Brothers shit.''

He half expected some backchat. There was nothing a grunt
liked less than rolling around in the mud, and that was also the
sort of down'n'dirty crap you became a fighter driver to avoid
having to deal with—ever since the Red Baron, who'd blown off
a career in the cavalry for just that reason. But the car came to
an almost instant stop, fishtailing a bit in the loose mud.

Almost everything was cool with Casey. Besides, the kind of
combat grunt he was thinking like was a lot like McKay, who
basically felt an armored fighting vehicle beat walking, and was
dandy for keeping off nuisances like rain and small-caliber projectiles, but that if the rockets started buzzing by on comet tails
of fire they suddenly turned into gigantic targets with a fat, juicy
tank of gasoline dead in the bull's-eye.

The first white flare of a forty-millimeter popped like a flash-
bulb up ahead, the light spiking out through the trees. A moment
later McKay heard the *crunch* of the round. Unless he caught a
bad guy pulling bead on him, Tom was just advertising. They
weren't here to kill people if it wasn't necessary. Not because
McKendree's bunch were Americans too. The years since the
One-Day War had long ago eradicated any inclination on Mc-
Kay's part to cut people any slack just because they were supposed to be countrymen.

The thing was, it was a lot less hassle to frighten the other
guy into keeping his head down than to hammer it down for
him, even if it was also a lot less fun from McKay's perspective.

McKay felt the impact of the side hatch closing. ''We'll give
it sixty seconds. Then move it out, Sloan.''

He wasn't giving Casey much time for all that anal-retentive
crap snipers liked to do about picking a perfect blind and se-
curing avenues of retreat and all—because he wasn't about to
give more budding Rambos time to come sneaking down the
road just twitching with the lust to find out if their contraband
missiles worked the way it said they did in *Soldier of Fortune*.
Casey was basically going to have to haul ass into position and
then wing it, so to speak. Well, fighter pilots were supposed to
be able to improvise.

McKay aimed the turret forward again. He rocked slightly as
Sloan sent the Super Commando rolling up the grade. Flamelight
glowed in blue eerie patches in the trees off to the left as the phos-

phorus flakes burned unaffected by the pouring rain. He was no Ranger Rick, but it stood to reason that the foliage—which was pretty green to start with—just was not going to catch in this downpour. Which was fine with him. He'd never been in a forest fire and didn't need to lose that particular cherry just now.

The crackle of small-arms fire up ahead came through the hull pickups. "What's your status, Tom?"

"They're firing blind. I've been moving around, suppressing them. Should I start firing for effect?"

"Naw. Not unless you see any signs of heavy shit."

"I'm in position," Casey reported, sounding only slightly breathless. *"About three hundred meters from the big house."*

"How much detail is that scope of yours giving you?" Sloan asked.

"Pretty good, man."

"Enough to tell us if the bad guys are pointing a LAW at us?"

"If I'm looking that way, Billy."

Which wasn't the most comforting news. Still, it took a lot of balls to challenge an armored vehicle, even one as comparatively small as Mobile One, at the kind of ranges where a shoulder-fired free-flight rocket like an M72 worked best. Twenty-five to a hundred fifty meters seems awfully close to get to AFV firepower. These White Action! clowns were a lot less likely to have that kind of nuts now that their first crack had fizzled—especially if McKay had been lucky enough to nail the rocketeer.

"Right. Pick up the pace, Sloan."

Gathering speed, the car rolled up a low hill. The trees fell away to either side. McKay wondered if he was just imagining things or the rain was slacking. It was humid as hell in the turret, and he was getting cold.

Despite Tom's good efforts popping forty-millimeter rounds around the ears of the harder-core defenders, a burst of full-auto fire rattled off Mobile One's carapace as they crested the rise. From the rate of fire and tack-hammer timbre McKay guessed it was 5.56. Mobile One could shrug that shit off all night and not even get its paint chipped.

"Stop here," he commanded, shifting his unlit cigar to the rear of his mouth and leaning into the sights. They were shoot-through computer optics, which was a fancy way of saying they would project the image from any of the car's fancy sensors before his eyes, or just get the hell out of the way and let him rely on unassisted vision if that's what he wanted.

The defenders had wised up and shut down the lights. The only illumination was the yellow light of some kind of shack off to one side that was burning fitfully despite the rain, and the firefly flickers of at least a dozen guns bouncing several sizes of leaden chunks off the car. He wasn't seeing much, but he could shoot at muzzle flashes just fine.

"Aren't we silhouetting ourselves?" Sloan asked as he braked the car to a halt. His voice was just a little cracked, as if he were having a flashback to puberty.

"Yeah," McKay said, "but we're such studs we don't *even* care."

"But what if they hit us with another LAW?"

"Then we're dumb fucks, and dead. Gimme a loudspeaker, navy boy."

Sloan was thinking good thoughts, he had to give him that. His instinct was to trust an armored shell implicitly—which was kind of a questionable reflex in these days of guided missiles, even in the surface navy, but had been drilled into him anyway.

"You're on, McKay. Use the intercom."

McKay hit the intercom button on his console with his left thumb. *"Listen up, you people. We're the Guardians. We're official representatives of the United States government. If you hold your fire as of now we'll forget all this felonious assaulting of federal agents you've been getting up to."*

The answer was a burst that jackhammered off the front slope of the turret right in front of McKay's nose. His head jerked reflexively back on its thick neck.

"That's what I hoped you'd say."

There were perhaps twenty houses plus assorted outbuildings, clustered around the White Castle at the crest of a low round hill. That burst had come from the house closest to the Guardians; he'd spotted the muzzle flash. The house looked as if it had been assembled from prefab wooden panels, like the ones produced by the robot factory the Guardians had found in Montana over the winter.

It hadn't been any puny 5.56 burst, either. It was serious shit, 7.62 of some kind—like an FN or Galil, or maybe even a Browning automatic rifle, which had been a popular item to smuggle over the line from Mexico before the War. It could conceivably have been a full-dress machine gun like his Maremont, but he doubted it.

He gave the house a burst of fifty-caliber. Wood splinters flew through the rain. His thumb came off the trigger and immediately flame flared and a single big-caliber round cracked off the front glacis.

"Bastards got some balls," he muttered, not depressing the button that would relay his opinion to the people it was about.

More fire cracked out of the house. "That's it," he announced. "Tom, start taking these fucks down for real. Casey, keep scanning for antitank."

He rammed home the firing bar. The two guns roared, driving Mobile One back on its springs like a running dinosaur trying to stop on a dime. The house blew apart in a series of dazzling multiple explosions, neat as something from a TV movie.

While flaming plank shards were whirling down through the dwindling rain, McKay traversed the turret. Wyoming was officially Friendly Territory, which meant easy access to a couple of resupply caches laid down before the War as preparation for the Guardian project, which meant that they didn't have to worry too much about conserving beans or bullets.

Another jitterbug flame caught his eye; he swung the turret that way, fired a burst from both weapons. A storage building ate death.

"Tom," he said, "where are the bastards holed up?" Just because they had ammo to burn didn't mean he had to burn out the barrels leveling the joint house by house.

"Hottest fire's coming from the castle," Rogers's soft voice said. *"I've dropped HEDP and WP up there, but it don't seem to do much. Otherwise, that house about halfway up on the left seems to be a real nest of them."*

"Yeah," McKay said. Lightning lit the scene a garish instant. The rain was heavier than he thought. He hadn't made out quite what a concentration of muzzle flashes was jabbing out of that house. Or maybe the occupants had been preoccupied with trying to nail Rogers, who had been moving between shots to avoid just that. "I got it now. Drive on, Sloan."

Sam muttered something, probably insubordinate, and goosed the car into motion.

"How fast?"

"Fifteen, twenty kph—just like this."

They rolled down the first rise, across a culvert that spanned a stream that hadn't shown up on any of the maps—a surprise, but no big deal—and then in among the houses. For all his swaggering macho tone McKay felt his nut-sac contract. In among structures the plain grunt with no armor but his skin had all the advantages over the man in the moving tin foxhole. Not even Casey Wilson's *Star Wars* scope could see through walls. An M72 LAW fired from inside a house would probably french-fry the rocketeer and all his buddies with backblast, but the payload would do Mobile One worse.

Oh, well. Fuck it and drive on. He was making a gesture, because it was going to be a shitload easier on everyone concerned if the people in the fortified White Castle just surrendered and didn't make the Guardians dig them out. Vision blocks ringed the turret, and McKay had good peripheral vision.

—Which was showing him the occasional fireball reaching for him from the buildings they passed. The range was so close he imagined he could tell the difference between handgun and long-arm flashes. It gave him a weird feeling.

Instead of replying he centered his sights on the house Rogers had called to his attention. He clicked on his IR eyes and an infrared spot for a quick look. It was a frame stucco like every house in every subdivision in America. The roof sagged at this end. Rogers had obviously done some renovation here.

He did some detail work with the .50, spraying the facade with quick nasty bursts. Whoever was inside was tough enough or stupid enough to hang in there returning fire.

Fifty meters down the dirt road he called Sloan to a stop. *"All right, you assholes,"* he announced, *"this is your big chance to throw in the towel. Otherwise we're gonna have to crack down here."*

The response was a sheet of fire from the house.

There was a lot of shooting going on from the big house, and the occasional brilliant hemisphere of Rogers working it over. Nothing serious, though. McKay began to hope the schmuck by the front gate had been holding the only real anti-tank the peckerwoods had.

"All right, Sammy," he said. "Take us into the master bedroom."

"You want me to drive into the *house*?"

"Full speed ahead."

"You're crazy, McKay."

"That's why I got this chickenshit job. Make it happen, navy boy."

McKay heard mud spatter the hull with machine gun velocity as Sloan put the pedal to the metal. Another lightning stroke showed him the house seeming to rush at them. It seemed to be painted an ugly yellow. There was actually a pane of glass shining in one window here at the end of the house. In the empty space next to it a single face hung like a moon of astonishment.

Darkness returned. McKay lit the night with the .50-caliber, and then they plowed into the house.

Wood splintered. Broken studs scraped at the hull like the fingernails of dying men. McKay got a crazy-quilt impression of curtains and furniture and a couple of bodies whirling away.

Sloan kept it obediently floored. His accuracy had been uncanny: McKay was looking right dead down the hallways toward what was probably the living room. The car was too wide for the hall. Mobile One was crunching interior wall just inboard of either set of tires.

"Don't build these things like they used to," McKay remarked. A couple of men burst from a door to the right. One vanished under the front tire with a despairing scream and a moist crunching *thump*. The other kind of exploded when McKay caught him between the shoulder blades with a pair of seven-hundred-grain slugs.

The big V-450 dozed its way from one end of the house to the other. Through the side blocks McKay saw defenders baling out the windows and doors. A real white American hero was firing them up with, yes, a BAR, kneeling to shoot over the back of a real Goodwill-special sofa. McKay couldn't depress his own bigger, badder Browning enough to nail him. Then the angled snout of Mobile One hit the couch like an icebreaker running down an America's Cup yacht. Couch and hero went crash and splash.

This was the kind of job McKay would rather have a basic psycho like Casey driving. For all that he spent most of his life as the Ultimate Laid-Back California Kid, he was Charley fucking Manson behind the wheel when the shit began to fly. But Sam was driving on as fatalistically as the point man of a *banzai* charge, not swerving, not slowing.

The far wall of the living room loomed up in front of McKay's face, with a pair of camouflage-mottled legs just disappearing out the window. Mobile One hit it with an end-the-world crash and a musical squealing of rending wood.

And stopped.

McKay's forehead ricocheted off the twin receivers. "Shit!" he yelled, bouncing around the inside of the turret. The seat was equipped with a belt, but he wasn't using it. If the car caught an AT round and burned, he wanted to get out in a maximum hurry.

When he got oriented the car was tilted right, growling and bucking in a frustrated frantic way, like a fighting bull trying to hump a brontosaur's leg.

He tried to check the sights, but he *couldn't see.* By muscle memory he cycled through the options: IR, low-light TV, plain visual. Nothing. *Shit, shit, shit.*

He blinked at the sweat in his eyes, dabbed at his face. His fingers came away sticky. He rubbed furiously at his eyes, and his vision reluctantly cleared.

A salty taste trickled into his mouth. *I'm bleeding,* he realized. *Forehead cut.*

"Sam, are you all right?"

"I'm fine."

"Then get us out of here," he said, "because here come the bad guys."

The next house up the hill was maybe fifteen meters away, and dark figures were spilling out of it, running for the armored car. Fanatical motherfuckers. McKay traversed the turret to show them that the moral to the physical was as jack to shit when the physical in question was a fifty-fucking-caliber.

The servos whined peevishly. The turret didn't budge.

"Shit! The roof's fallen in. Sam, back us up."

"I *can't,*" Sloan said. "The damned cheap floor gave way, We're stuck."

McKay opened his mouth to call the wrath of Casey down on these impertinent pussies. And Casey's voice said, *"Billy? Is something wrong?"*

Right on his heels came, *"What's happening?"* from Tom. And McKay realized *neither one could see them.*

Two of the figures paused. Light flickered, flared, glittered on glass: the wicks of Molotov cocktails.

The Team boys would have to approve: this was Appropriate Technology in action. Flaming Death as if People Mattered. Low tech and high lethality.

And that's it for us, thought Billy McKay.

CHAPTER
THIRTEEN ──────────────────────────────

A black figure cocked an arm to throw the comet that blazed at the end of his arm. Triumphant jeers beat off the hull louder than the rain, which was coming in with redoubled fury. It was going to be no goddam help. Even K mart commandos of the woods who wore peaked hoods so they'd fit the points on their heads would know to toss their gasoline bombs in under the *roof*.

Mobile One had done a *really good* job of knocking down the wall; it gaped wide open for five or six feet to either side, offering a fine target.

McKay reached up with his left hand to the latch of the overhead hatch and his right to the rubber grips of his .45. There was no way he was going to get out in time to get a shot off; the odds were better than good he couldn't get out at all, with half the goddam roof lying on the V-450. But he was by Christ going to *try*.

Luminous sleet was falling among the hooting crew outside. Falling *horizontally*. McKay had the latch undone and was pushing up against the weight he'd been afraid to feel holding down the lid when he stopped dead and did another take out the vision block.

One would-be Molotov server was facedown with his makeshift bomb sputtering out its life on the wet grass centimeters from his outstretched hand—make that *her* hand, from the pale head spread on the ground, though some of your nutbag right-wing types had long since started to go in for long hair on guys.

Just as McKay was flashing on the home truth he already knew in the cord of his scrotum—that the glowing sleet raking in parallel to the planet was the one-in-five tracer of a machine gun on full rock and roll—the other Molotail took one and blossomed into yellow hell in the middle of a long overhead lob. It was instant torch time for the boy with the bomb. The two men nearest him got splashed and started to go up. Unlike the Noted Burning Stuntmen of the action/adventure cinema, they had the sense to hit and *roll*, letting the water running free over hard-packed inabsorbent ground douse the flames. The cocktailer was too well alight for those kinds of options, and ran around screaming and flaming instead. His screams pierced the hull like depleted uranium rounds until another gunfire freshet knocked him in a sprawl.

The rest of the campers, no longer so happy, had split in all directions. McKay saw several racing madly for the White Castle in a strobe of lightning.

"Looks like the cavalry's arrived just in time for a rescue, McKay," the voice of Toby Sawtelle said in the back of McKay's head.

"What the hell took you so long?" he rasped.

"Didn't your mother teach you to say thank you?"

"Thank you, sir," piped up Sloan from down below.

"Thanks all to hell. What took you so fucking long?"

"One thing and another. It's not easy riding overland in the dark, in a storm."

"We got here fine. That must be us relying on all this evil Western technology and shit."

Sawtelle laughed. Just what he needed, Sawtelle laughing in the back of his head.

"You should know by now we use modern technology when we need to. But we wash our hands afterwards."

It seemed to McKay that the Team had some kind of slippery standards, but this wasn't the time to debate that, and he didn't give much of a fuck anyway. While Bubba and Ski Bob stayed up in the trees to provide flanking fire with the SAW and sniper's rifle, the rest of the Team moved in forward, pausing to mop up a few pockets of resistance with shotguns and hand grenades. They were viciously efficient as weasels.

"Wow," Casey commented from his own improvised shooter's blind. *"I'm glad I don't have any traffic tickets outstanding in this state."*

Tom snooped and pooped forward, in time to meet up with McKay, who'd finally managed to extricate himself from Mobile One through a side hatch. It turned out that the space between houses here was dead ground relative to the big house, and about time they caught that kind of a break, in McKay's humble opinion.

While Tom covered he went through a brief and noisy house-cleaning exercise with stun grenades and a Smith & Wesson 3000 riot gun, which he executed with textbook precision and would have been impressive as hell if there'd been anybody *in* the goddam house. He emerged to sarcastic applause from Saw-telle, Dozier the Dozer, and Stew or Lew, he couldn't tell which. Their faces were blacked out beneath the waterlogged brims of their boonie hats. The Dozer had a shotgun, the other two wicked-looking little CAR-15 submachine guns, which were really growth-stunted M16s.

"My man Sly Stallone could have done no better," Dozier said.

"Fuckin'-A straight," McKay said.

"Maybe we shoulda brought some mules with us to get the land barge unstuck," said Lew. Or Stew.

The others deployed into a defensive perimeter, keeping a particular eye on the castle, which had fallen quiet. McKay stood out dripping in the rain and gave Sloan confusing and increasingly irritable hand signals until they managed to work the car free of the house. Then he joined Rogers in the house he'd cleared so flawlessly and futilely.

"What's happening?"

Rogers didn't look back from the window. "Nothing since we got here."

"Are you, like, sure *the car's all right, Billy?"* Casey inquired worriedly. He'd offered nervous and useless bits of advice throughout the process of dislodging Mobile One, which hadn't made McKay love him more.

"No," McKay subvocalized, suddenly going taut. *"Now pipe the hell down. I think I hear something."*

He turned, leveling the shotgun from his waist. It was Sawtelle. McKay's RECON-honed senses were amped all the way up, and he just *knew*, from the smell and feel and hints of form in the blackness. *Gestalt*, Sloan called it. You got so you could read it real well, if you hung your ass over the edge of the volcano long enough.

"Shouldn't go sneaking up on people like that," he said.

Sawtelle laughed softly. "Hey. I trust you. You're a professional."

He hunkered down next to Tommy by the window. "So what're you waiting for? You have AT rockets in your Snorting Iron Beast, don't you?"

"So what if we do?" McKay was not reading him at all, at all.

"So they're *primo* bunker busters. You don't think you're going to take that fortress down with your flash-bangs and a scattergun, do you? Or are you planning to run right up and plant a satchel charge in the doorway?"

"Neither," McKay said, tearing down a curtain. "What we do now is call for their surrender. Is this white, do you think? I'd go try to hunt up some bedsheets, but I figure they all got eyeholes cut in 'em."

Sawtelle made an exasperated noise. "You actually think you can negotiate with these fanatics?"

"Beats fuck outta me. All I know is, I don't get paid enough to dig 'em out unless they fuckin' *make* me."

Waving his curtain on the end of its rod, McKay approached the White Castle. His testicles were trying to retract again. Ian Fleming was full of bullshit. You *couldn't* get 'em to go back inside your abdomen, unless you poked them up there with a rifle barrel or something and didn't plan on making use of them again.

Since he wasn't a *total* fool, he was wearing the full assault armor they used on the mop-up of Morrigan's merry men: Hard Corps IV, with all the bells and whistles. It was only moderately heavy, but it was extremely unwieldy, and made him feel like the Michelin Tire Man when he moved, which was why the Guardians didn't routinely climb into the stuff to take care of business. But it did mean it would take something like a .50-caliber to do him substantial bodily harm, at least from the neckline to the knees. It left his head unprotected, but as Sloan had helpfully pointed out, that was a very small target. McKay hadn't been terrifically comforted by that remark, and suspected he ought to pound Sloan for it.

The ground was cleared for forty meters around the big house in all directions. No structures of any sort stood closer, even the garages. A kill-zone if McKay had ever seen one, and he'd seen a bunch. That implied Claymores or their field-expedient equivalent. Which was why McKay carried a megaphone in his other hand. He wasn't getting any closer to the damned castle than the nearest house on the road. He wanted at least the illusion of being able to dive for cover if they popped Claymores on him.

From relatively close up the main house did not look all that well for wear. The stucco had been shot to shit, blasted away in huge patches. Underneath was adobe brick, probably a foot thick and capable of stopping most small-arms rounds. Where larger arms had left their mark he could make out whiter glints of cement in the frequent flashes of lightning. The area around the window to the left of the front door had been thoroughly blasted, revealing that the window was a dummy, masking a firing slit. How the place was ventilated, Christ alone knew. Reuben McKendree was showing every sign of being *seriously* paranoid.

Except of course people really had come to kill him, which went to show he was crazy like a fox. At least in some departments.

"Everybody in position?" he subvocalized. He already knew the answer, since he had asked the same question twice before in the last minute and a half. The acknowledgments came rattling promptly back. The hilltop fortress was surrounded, and since it was at a higher elevation than the besiegers there was virtually no likelihood of their cross-firing each other.

Great. They'll be perfectly poised to recover the body. Nuts.

He stepped forward, brandished his white flag, and raised the loudspeaker.

"All right in there." It was tough competing with the storm, even electronically amplified. He shoved his bellow up a notch. "We've come for Reuben McKendree. We're not leaving without him. You can make it hard, or you can make it easy. The easy way would be to open up and send somebody out to talk—"

White light lanced out of all the firing slits at once.

CHAPTER
FOURTEEN ─────────────────────

It was inertia that saved him.

Reuben McKendree's personal *Führerbunker* was a heavy-weight construct. Even when a whole *lot* of serious high explosives were going off at mostly one and the same time it took a while to get all that mass of cement and adobe into motion.

Not a lot of a while, but enough.

Either White Action! heroes weren't allowed private ownership of cars—that was another thing McKay had noticed about far-right whack groups, that you could hardly tell them from fucking commies most of the time—or the rules said they all had to be parked in one of the big garages. There were no vehicles on the roads or next to any of the houses. McKay had to roll through somebody's overly well irrigated vegetable garden and become one with the wall of the last house before the kill-zone to get any cover at all. A tsunami of hot air, overpressure, and noise rolled over him. He put his hands over his head and did his very best armadillo imitation while waiting for all that stuff the explosion had kicked *up* in the air to come *down*.

It seemed like forever, and then when it arrived it was all too soon. All kinds of crap pounding down on and around him with an avalanche roar that pushed the storm aside. He'd been gang-stomped a couple of times, in his younger, more foolish years—

that sort of thing happened no matter how tough you thought you were, and as a matter of fact the tougher you thought you were, the likelier it was. So anyway, at a couple of points in his career McKay had picked the wrong ten or twenty guys to take on all at once, and hadn't yet gotten a license from the United States government to carry a machine gun, and the experience had been a lot like this. Fist-sized lumps of cement raining down on you weren't all that different from combat boots, at least if you were wearing lots of Kevlar reinforced with metal plates. One piece did bounce off the back of his uppermost hand—his right one, which meant he didn't rebreak the knuckle he'd busted on Llewellyn's jaw, but might mean he'd have two gimped hands for the foreseeable future.

Other than that it wasn't bad, by the standards of having the shit kicked out of you.

Then it was over, and the blissful peace of a raging mountain cloudburst and thunderstorm descended. Gradually McKay became aware of a lot of voices talking in his skull at once. Unfortunately, they weren't signs of delirium.

He raised his head, very cautiously, half afraid it would crumble into dust if he jarred it too hard. It was positively immoral to feel like this without having been on one hell of a drunk in advance.

The house wasn't gone. *That* big a blast probably would have torn McKay apart as if he were a fly caught in the tweezers of a sadistic child, or buried him under a few dozen cubic meters of detritus. It had just sort of raised the upper part of the building up in the air and put it down again, not necessarily where it had gotten it. The White Castle seemed mostly to have fallen in on itself.

"I'm fine," he tried to say. His tongue felt like a roll of sweat socks, and his throat felt as if he'd swallowed a cheese grater. He couldn't have spoken out loud on a bet, but the larynx mike read him loud and clear. "But I think you can write off Rube McKendree."

Then he looked around and noticed the bathtub-sized chunk of angled cement that had punched in the front of the house he'd sheltered against, somewhat less than the length of his arm from where his head had rested. And suddenly he had to sit down.

They hadn't secured the entire settlement, of course, but somehow it felt a whole lot less urgent. Guardians and Team called in their well-soaked snipers, set out a couple of fresh sentries, and carefully urged Mobile One back into the house it had violated, where it wouldn't be such an obvious target. Then they laagered in to wait for daylight.

The storm didn't live out the night. Dawn was clear except for a stratum of adobe-colored clouds that sandwiched the first fat swollen sun of day against the Bighorn range. The morning air had the clarity of fine crystal, and gave everything an edge like broken glass.

The storm had been so violent that morning actually smelled fresh. But as McKay stepped out and stretched he could smell the hints of burned-explosive residue beginning to seep out of the soil, and the bodies were going to get really interesting within minutes of the sun's hitting them.

There were fifteen scattered in and among the houses. There might have been more in the two houses that had burned out despite the storm. What lay in the crater between the collapsed outer walls of the big house they had neither the means nor the inclination to determine with any certainty.

Sam Sloan stood on an island of solid concrete in rubble, staring down into the crater, trying not to think how much like a sphincter it looked. There was a little arm outflung maybe twenty feet from the toes of his boots, child-chubby, that terminated where two blocks of cement had pinched together.

What have we done? he wondered.

He was a thoughtful man, a sensitive man, a reflective man—everything, he knew, that Billy McKay wasn't. But he was also a Guardian. The one thing he wasn't given to questioning was the mission he shared with his three comrades. Until now.

"That's what I call a job well done," said Stew Jeffcoat, dusting his hands against each other. Sloan wondered if he'd been able to bring his beloved knife into play last night. "Those reactionary bastards aren't gonna be blockin' progress anymore."

He's absolutely right, Sloan thought. *So why do I want to slug him?*

Sometimes he was afraid McKay was right, that he really was a wimp. He should be ecstatic at their victory over mad-dog racists he'd despised all his life. He should be appalled by Stew's insensitivity. He couldn't figure out which he really felt.

He turned his back on the crater and the little hand reaching

out for help that was long too late. He walked down among the
deserted houses. His comrades were searching through them for
clues to something or other. The mood he was in now, it made
no sense to him.

There was a wide clear space directly west of the ruined castle, the side away from the road in, where the hill it rested on
fell away toward a valley where the trees took up again and urged
the land back upward into a serious mountain, Devers Peak.
Sloan let his footsteps take him there.

McKay and a couple of the Team were downslope a ways,
examining upright posts with silhouettes painted on pieces of
cardboard hung on them. It looked to Sloan like a pistol range.

McKay was studying a silhouette badly faded by the recent
weather. "How the hell can you tell this is supposed to be a
nigger?" he asked.

Sloan turned right around. He couldn't deal with this right
now.

The ground opened twenty meters to his left and somebody
came flying right at him. He spun, clawing for the fat grips of
his shoulder-holstered Python. And froze.

It was a tall, skinny teenaged girl running at him, arms outstretched, ponytail trailing.

"Get me away from him," she was screaming. "Save me!
I've been kidnapped."

Behind her a bulky male figure was clambering out of the
concealed bolt hole with the Choate pistol grip of a combat
shotgun in his hand. Alex Barka was just trucking down from
the former castle with a cigarette stuck in his red face and his
Beretta nine-millimeter submachine gun slung in front of his
belly. Without ever shifting his liplock on the smoke he grabbed
the SMG, pivoted it, and gave the shotgunner a quick burst.

A hand snapped past Sloan's ear, leveling a pistol at the girl.
She screamed, stopped, threw her hands in front of her face.
Horrified, Sloan saw the tension come into the muscles of the
hand as the finger took in the trigger slack.

He reacted instantaneously, grabbing the hand in both of his in
an aikido hold and flipping its owner onto his back on the ground.
He got a quick look into the face of one of the Lew/Stew twins,
with brown hair hanging in furious eyes, and then the highway
patrolman got a boot in his belly and pitched him over on his
own back in a neat judo throw.

The girl lunged for him, then was caught short and reeled in by a wiry arm, a huge knife with a straight-sided tapering blade pressed under the line of her jaw. That settled the problem of identification; it was Lew Polidor jumping to his feet behind Sloan and pointing his Beretta service auto at Sloan with shaking, white-knuckled hands.

"Interfering with an officer discharging his duty is a felony," Lew screamed.

A multiple metal click from close behind made his eyes swivel around and try to look through the back of his skull.

"So's messing with a duly appointed representative of the U.S. government," McKay said. "Which we are."

"But this is the state of Wyoming! It's our jurisdiction."

"Right," said McKay around the stub of his cigar. "And this is *my* jurisdiction right here: a Colt MkIV Government Model, series 1980. It ain't the most powerful handgun made, but if you give me an ounce of shit I'll give the trigger two pounds of pressure, and you'll never know the difference between it and a forty-four mag. So come on, narc. Make my day."

Sloan had taken advantage of the little side drama to unlimber his own nickel-shiny hand cannon, which he aimed carefully at Stew Jeffcoat's right kneecap. "Let the girl go."

Stew shifted his eyes from his partner to Sloan. The Arkansas toothpick dug a deeper furrow in the smooth skin of the girl's neck. She quivered briefly and then froze, breathing raggedly through widened nostrils.

"Young lady, I hereby arrest you, under the power vested in me by the government of the United States of America. Officer Jeffcoat, you will immediately release the prisoner into the custody of the nearest federal officer, namely me. Or you can forget about dancing the fox-trot anymore."

Jeffcoat's face looked as if it were trying to twist itself inside out. Then he let his breath and the girl go with an explosive sigh.

"Hey," he complained, "I figured she was trying to kamikaze you, you know. She's *one* of them. I was just trying to save you."

"Yeah," Sloan said, pulling himself to one knee and keeping his piece pointed. He didn't know how far ol' Stew could flip that young broadsword, but he didn't intend to give him a chance to demonstrate. "Right."

And then the girl hit him in a flying tackle and wrapped un-believably strong arms around his neck, cutting off his air, and he wondered for a mad moment if Jeffcoat was right all along. That would certainly be a bitch, as McKay would say.

Then, "Save me!" the girl was screeching in his ear. "You've got to get me away from him! *He raped me!*"

CHAPTER
FIFTEEN ―――――――――――――――――――

"Officer Jeffcoat?" Sloan asked, completely confused.

The girl sobbed copiously in the collar of his camouflaged jumpsuit, which had just begun to dry after last night. *"Reuben McKendree."*

"Oh," he said.

Sawtelle came swinging down the slope, wearing a black tee shirt and khaki shorts, with his CAR slung over his shoulder. "What's going on here?"

"Just a misunderstanding," Alex said hurriedly. "I think we got it all straightened out now. We got this young woman here, claims to be a civilian kidnapped by McKendree."

It seemed to Sloan he put an odd emphasis on "civilian." He didn't pay much attention; he was busy trying to tuck away his .357, now that the crisis had apparently passed and it made him feel as if he were standing there with his cock in his hand, and disentangle the girl's arm from his neck.

Sawtelle stood a moment, wrinkling up his forehead and not saying anything. Everybody started lowering their pieces and backing away from each other, looking sheepish.

"Right," Sawtelle said. Glad it's all straightened out." He turned and disappeared over the hill.

"Here," Sloan said, hugging the girl tentatively. "It's all

right." *What an idiotic thing to say,* he thought. *It's clearly* not *all right.*

He and McKay backed her cautiously away from the highway patrolmen, who seemed abruptly uninterested in her or them. They took her to a house that had been secured and sat down around the kitchen table sweeping a stack of assorted hate literature onto the floor.

"What's your name, honey?" Sloan asked.

"Where the hell did she pop out of, is what I want to know," McKay said.

Sloan frowned at him. "First things first. C'mon, what's your name?"

She sniffled, accepted a tissue from Sloan, who was prone to allergies and always carried some, blew her nose.

She seemed liable to occupy herself with that for some moments. Not wanting to put pressure on her after whatever she'd been through, Sloan turned to his chief and said, "Thanks for backing my play, McKay."

Standing with his butt propped on the sink, McKay spat out a tobacco fleck. "Shit," he said, "it's every marine's duty to look after you navy boys like you're our little brother. It's ingrained so we do it automatic like. Even when you do something stupid."

"Um," Sloan said.

"My name's Jessica," she said. "Jessica . . . Turner."

She seemed uncertain, or maybe this was Sloan's day for reading uncertainty into everything people said. He was probably just projecting his own mental state.

"I'm pleased to meet you, Jessica," he said. "I'm Sam Sloan. This is Billy McKay. We're Guardians. That means—"

"I know about you," she said. "I read about you in *Parade.*" She tried a smile on. It seemed to fit very nicely, thank you.

"So what were you doin' in a hole in the ground in the middle of a camp full of armed crazies?" McKay asked. "Seems like a pretty dangerous place for a little girl like you to be."

Sloan kept making frantic *cool-it* gestures, which McKay naturally ignored. But the girl took the question in stride.

"It was supposed to be a hidey-hole. The White Action! people spent a lot of time fortifying the house. But Reuben—Mr. McKendree, that is—he always seemed to think that was kind of funny. He thought it was mostly just a big target, that the kind

of enemies White Action! had would be just as happy to find
them all together in one place where they could all be wiped out
at one time. He said the only real chance of safety lay in con-
cealment. That's why he had these standing orders that if anything bad happened I was supposed to be taken down in one
of the hideouts. He said White Action's enemies'd have weapons
that could knock down walls made of all the cement in the
world.''

Sloan looked at McKay, who shoved out his lower lip, raised
an eyebrow, and cocked his head. McKendree and he had a
similar outlook on war, anyway.

She shrugged. She was at the coltish stage of adolescence,
seemingly all long skinny arms and legs, left bare by cut-off
jeans and an olive drab tee shirt that featured a skull wearing a
green beret and the legend *Kill 'Em All—Let God Sort 'Em Out,*
which combination of words and images was one of the few
things in the world that could piss Tom Rogers off. She had a
narrow head, frizzy red-brown hair pulled back into a ponytail
that emphasized the aquiline cast of her features, the large,
slightly fleshy nose and pouty lips. Her eyes were long and large
and very dark, piercing in her tanned, freckled face. Sam thought
she looked Jewish, and was ashamed at such an essentially big-
oted assessment. She was gawky with the kind of gawkiness that
can turn to striking beauty overnight somewhere in the mid to
late teens.

''I guess he was right.'' She leaned forward with her hands
on the heavy wooden table, eyes and lips glistening. ''How'd
you do it? Did you have some kind of superweapon?''

The subject made Sam distinctly uncomfortable. ''Uh, what
were you doing here? You indicated you'd been brought here
against your will.''

It occurred to him he was way out of his depth here. Here the
SID Team had been insisting all along on their expertise in police matters versus the Guardians' pronouncedly amateur status,
and here there was the real police work to be done—questioning
a witness—and none of them wanted to be anywhere near. Life
was a pretty peculiar critter, however much he preferred it to
the alternatives.

She was twisting the tissue Sloan had given her into little
minarets. ''I was kidnapped. My mom and I lived in Cheyenne,

Wyoming. We got out just ahead of the fallout . . . at least, I did. She stayed behind to help these old people we knew."

She shook her head and threw the tissue down. "When she finally came out she'd already picked up a lot of rads. She lasted about two weeks in the refugee camp. There was nothing the Red Cross people could do. I stayed there a month or two and then McKendree's people raided the place, looking for medical supplies. They decided to just take me along."

Sloan sat back in his own chair. He felt a little less bad about last night's slaughter.

"You seem pretty calm about what happened to your mom," McKay remarked.

McKay! Sloan mouthed. The girl looked squarely up at the big man.

"After a while you just get used to it, Mr. McKay. You get used to *anything*. People have to for life to go on, you know what I mean?"

"Yeah," he said, uncharacteristically quiet. "Yeah, I do." He'd lost what family he had left in the bombing of Pittsburgh. He'd been estranged from them, but they were all he'd had. Aside from Tommy Rogers's divorced wife and their two kids, who'd disappeared from his life four years before the War, they were the only family ties any Guardian had. That had been another selection criterion.

"What do you know about McKendree's assassination campaign?"

" 'Assassination campaign'?" She sounded incredulous. "I don't know what you're talking about."

"McKendree and his goons've been offing leaders in all kinds of ethnic settlements around Wyoming and neighboring states," McKay said.

She laughed, a musical adolescent sound, ringing with adolescent malice. The two men stared at her.

"I'm sorry if I shocked you," she said. "But c'mon. Don't be silly. The White Action! people liked to dress up and play soldier and carry on about how they were the last hope of the white race. But actually *do* something? Nope. McKendree was the only one with any real—what's the word? Initiative. And even he'd rather appear on talk shows and that kind of stuff. But running around killing people . . . no. Not their style. They might talk about it, they were always talking about great crusades and purifying the race and all. But talk's all they had in them.''

"Not entirely," Sam said. "They put up a pretty good fight last night.''

She shrugged. "Defending their homes, I guess. But Mc-Kendree never did anything like what you're talking about.''

"We have quite convincing evidence that he did," Sam said, more stiffly than he liked to think himself capable of.

"He seems to have done all right kidnapping you," McKay said.

"That was then. See, life after the Holocaust taught the White Action! people one thing: in the real world, when there aren't like police around and stuff to tell them they can't, people shoot back. The police are there to protect the criminals as much as anything. McKendree even said that, but I think deep down he realized he was one of the ones being protected that way.''

"Why are you defending him?''

"I'm not defending him, mister!'' she flared at McKay, starting half out of her chair. "I hate the son of a bitch. He *used* me!''

McKay held up a hand. He always had trouble dealing with angry women. You couldn't just shoot them.

"Hey, hey now, simmer down. I'm sorry. Besides, you ain't gotta worry about him anymore. He's dead.''

For a moment her face went totally blank. It was so devoid of expression it was impossible to recognize her as the animated adolescent girl of moments before.

"What are you talking about?''

McKay jerked his head up at the top of the hill, visible out the kitchen window. "He blew himself up with all the other looney tunes.''

She was shaking her head vigorously. "I don't know where you got your information, mister," she said, "but it's all wet.

"McKendree left the compound two weeks ago and hasn't been back since.''

CHAPTER
SIXTEEN ───────────────

"Incredible," Nicholas Brant intoned.

It was a pity, Sam thought, that Brant hadn't had his heyday back in the twenties or thirties, when radio was king. It was a radio voice, sonorous and beautiful and deep. It was wasted on the sensibilities of the Television Age.

Besides, if Brant had been in his prime seventy years ago it was most unlikely he'd still be around to descend on their case *now*.

"You allowed McKendree to slip through your fingers. A fugitive as dangerous as any of the twentieth century. Incredible."

"Listen, Doc," McKay said, "don't you think you're layin' it on a little damn thick? He split outta here two weeks ago. Our fingers were still back in Chicago then."

"Excuses, Lieutenant? I expected better of you. Perhaps that was unwise. Besides, how authoritative is your source? What reason do you have to believe his assertion that McKendree was away from the settlement, or how long he has been absent?"

"It's a *she*," Sloan said. All four of them were tied into the circuit, connected via milliwatt transmitter to a satellite and from there to JFK City. "Her information has been quite detailed. Also correct, to the rather severe limits of our ability to test it."

Today's sun made it seem last night's cold rain had been a

mere figment. It beat on Mobile One's upper surfaces like hammers. Sloan sat in the ESO's chair, McKay in the driver's seat. Casey and Tom were flaked out either side of the open side hatch. Sam didn't know if it was cooler there. Personally, he felt like hanging his tongue out and panting.

"What about corroboration? Do any other witnesses confirm these claims?"

"There ain't any other witnesses, Doctor," McKay said. "They all either died in the fight or blew themselves up."

"How convenient." They could feel him cogitating across a couple of hundred klicks. A man with a forehead like that would naturally have a hell of a cogitate to him.

"Very well," he finally said, as if giving a spoiled child permission to buy a hamster. *"But send the girl along to JFK City at once for further questioning. Any clue she can provide as to McKendree's whereabouts will be invaluable."*

"No, please!" a voice cried. "You can't!"

"I beg your pardon?"

"You got it, Doc," McKay said, swiveling his heavy body in the chair. "What the fuck, over?"

Jessica Turner was scrambling in through the open hatch, banging her bare knees on the frame. "Don't let them take me, *please.*"

Casey was scooting back away from her as if afraid she might bite him. Tom took her by the arm, gently but decisively: controlling the situation. She briefly tried to pull away, gave up.

"Don't be afraid, honey," Sloan said soothingly. "They only want to ask you some questions."

"What's she doing here?" McKay asked.

"I was listening outside. I heard him say I had to go to JFK City."

"Jesus, is all this going out over the airwaves?" McKay's voice said in Sloan's ear.

"Of course not," he replied the same way. He had killed the transmit function almost immediately.

"Weren't you supposed to be locked in the house for safe-keeping?" McKay asked the girl.

She crossed her arms under her little pointy breasts and stuck out her lower lip. "She knows her way around the place, McKay," Sloan said.

Brant's voice was sputtering out of the console speaker like basso static—Sloan had had the presence of mind to pot down the volume too.

"Why are we debating this?" McKay demanded. "The kid's going to Kennedy City. What's the big?"

"Why don't we hear why she doesn't want to go, man?" Casey asked.

"They'll kill me," Jessica said firmly.

"Of course they won't kill you," Sloan said exasperatedly. "They're the police."

"That's what I mean. They hate everybody here."

"But you were a prisoner here. They're not going to blame you."

"They weren't stopping to ask a lot of questions last night. And they were all ready to kill me this morning."

"That was a misunderstanding."

She shook her head. "McKendree always talked about them. They're SID, aren't they? The governor's death squad."

"You can't believe that," Sloan said. "Surely you didn't believe anything McKendree told you?"

"I didn't believe everything. But these guys act just the way McKendree said they would. They don't *care* I was a captive here. I'm just another White Action! creep to them. They'll kill me."

"Oh, bullshit," McKay said. He turned the volume back up on their satellite link.

"—mand to know what's going on."

"Nothing, Doctor. Our, uh, subject seems to be reluctant to go. No big deal."

Sam was looking worried. *"Maybe we should think about this,"* he subvocalized. *"She seems awfully emphatic."*

"Oh, Jesus."

"You are under no circumstances to try to withhold the subject. This is much too important."

McKay opened his mouth, stopped, frowned. "How's that again, Doc?"

"I order you to surrender the prisoner at once. You are not equipped to deal with the situation."

"Now, just a God damned minute, Brant. She's in federal custody."

"Are you going to try pulling technicalities on us, McKay?

We aren't prepared to accept business-as-usual obstructionism from the federal government."

"Business as—? Listen, bud, we played point for the attack last night all by our lonesomes while your Team was playing Babes in the Woods. Is that what you call obstructionism?"

"Quit trying to cloud the issue with irrelevancies. Trying to lay off blame on an elite unit the death of one of whose members has already been caused by your lackadaisical approach—"

The tirade stopped in midsentence. McKay studied the white-blond hairs on the back of the hand that had cut the satellite connection.

"Okay, kid," he said, not looking away, "you just bought yourself a ticket. But it ain't gonna be a comfortable ride."

"You're crazy, McKay."

"Didn't you say that already this week, Sloan? I'm gonna start rationing you."

"I'm serious. We can't drag a child around with us into God alone knows what kind of danger. Not to mention the fact that you've alienated the governor's special adviser."

"Fuck him. Special advisers give me a pain. And how does some eco-freak writer wind up being head of the highway patrol anyway?"

"I'm sure Governor Greenwell finds him the most qualified man for the post."

"Yeah. I just bet he does. He'd probably name Ronald McDonald secretary of agriculture if he could catch him."

"Get serious, McKay."

"Okay. I'm serious. Now what?"

"Never mind. I'm going back in the car."

"What? Inside? It's cold as a taxman's heart, the stars look like pinholes in cheap construction paper, and there are gnats crawling up my nose. How can you turn your back on all these glories of nature?"

"Billy."

He knew the soft voice in his bones, but there were reflexes that ran deeper than that. He came awake with his pistol in hand, cocked and locked.

The only light in Mobile One was the gentle glow of pilots from the consoles up front. Their faint illumination was enough for him to make out the blocklike form of Tom Rogers, squatting a safe distance from McKay's air mattress, beside the turret root.

He let in the hammer with his thumb and lay back with his forearm over his eyes. "What you got, Tom?"

"Word came through from Kennedy City. Sam took it on the portable, inside the house."

"So did Brant get a writ of habeas corpus sayin' we got to ship him that bimbette he's got the hots for?"

"Didn't say. Highway patrol intelligence turned up some fresh leads. They think they know where McKendree's gone."

McKay sat up. Sleep was suddenly the last thing on his mind. "Then what are we waiting for? That puke's overdue for the ass kicking of his life."

"The fools did poorly with the weapons we provided them."

"Lucky we had a fallback position."

"Fortune had nothing to do with it. It was planning. Proper planning removes the need to rely on luck."

"What about the girl?"

"A complication. No more. Another testimony to the efficacy of planning. We can adjust to this unexpected turn of fate."

"Then there's McKendree. What if they find him?"

"They won't. Of that I can assure you."

CHAPTER
SEVENTEEN

There's a story that if you stab a sentry in the kidneys it hurts too bad to scream.

Billy McKay knew it never hurt too bad to scream.

Stew Jeffcoat threw his arm like a titanium band around the sentry's throat and jammed the knife deep into his kidneys. McKay could see the scream trying to break out, through the pores on the man's rain-soaked face, could see his every muscle stretch to the breaking point. But Jeffcoat's arm cut off his air.

"Quit fucking around!" he hissed.

Stew withdrew the Arkansas toothpick with a sound like stepping in one of the innumerable puddles the storm was laying down around the forest, whipped the red-dripping blade up, punched it through the sentry's throat, right to left, and slashed it out forward in a black gusher of blood. He held the sentry then, crotch pressed to cammie-clad buttocks, while he jerked and thrashed and his racing heart pumped the blood out of him. When he was spent Jeffcoat let the man drop, and gave McKay a slasher's grin.

"Jesus," McKay said. He half-raised his MP5 with integral silencer, then shrugged and followed Jeffcoat down the short, steep slope through a stand of skinny second-growth trees.

A retreater's earth-sheltered cabin dozed at the foot of the slope. The rain dripping from furry boughs overhead would have eaten the sound the encirclement made, if the men in it had made any. These Team troopies knew their shit; McKay had to grant them that. No matter what assholes they were otherwise.

He hunkered down in semidarkness, poised above the grass-grown deck that formed the roof of the earth-sheltered cabin. The interval between sunset and full night, like the false dawn before actual sunrise, was the ideal time to attack. Eyes never adjusted to twilight quite so well as full dark or light. Proportions and perceptions were thrown way off—an ideal cloak for attackers.

It was needed. There wasn't much cover provided by the skinny trees, and none of the scrub-oak kind of undergrowth you sometimes got in forests around here. McKay could make out the others filtering down to their positions: Lew, Alex, Dozier, and Tom Rogers, silhouettes broken by forest camo, faces daubed black and green and brown. Casey and Sam were back at the car, three klicks down a twisty goat track you couldn't call a *road*, ready to come provide heavy fire support at need and meantime making sure young Jessica didn't blow anything up. She was a real sharp kid, with too many hormones seething around in her to be real docile.

How'd I ever let her talk me into letting her come along? he wondered, waiting for the word that his companions were positioned. He knew damn well it hadn't been Jessica who'd talked him into it at all; it was that stuffed-up asshole Brant, trying to boss him around. That's what he'd tell Doctor J when he called to gnaw on McKay's ass for compromising the mission by dragging a teenybopper with them. He couldn't just let Brant boss him around as if the federal government was subordinate to the state of fucking Wyoming, could he?

"We're ready, Billy," came word from Rogers.

The sun had long since done a disappearing act behind the mountains on the far side of the valley. The gold last light that had turned the treetops on like light bulbs when they began working their way down the baby mountain had drained all the way up the tops of the peaks now. It was that still time of evening that just held its breath and waited for something to happen.

McKay was ready to oblige.

"Going," he subvocalized. He nodded to Stew and started down the slope in a crouch, slipping on the carpet of wet ponderosa pine needles, skinny and long and three to a cluster.

The trees ran out about ten meters from the end of a meter-and-a-half drop-off at the foot of the slope. McKay skidded to the verge of the minicliff, paused, looked at the house as if his eyes were going to turn to X-ray lasers and drill right through the log walls.

The rain was diminishing. This place went in a lot for the kind of defense-by-inconspicuousness that had been unavailable to White Action! at their stronghold on the former Coleman ranch by reason of sheer size. From the air the house and its few outbuildings, also concealed under earth mounds, would look like nothing but terrain features. With smoke catalyzers on their fireplaces and small shuttered windows holding in the light, there was little to betray the retreaters' presence except the cultivated patches nearby.

An ideal backup burrow for a fox like McKendree to go to ground in.

McKay dropped to the level, slipping a little in the wet red mud. He'd always thought Wyoming was supposed to be like a desert. He hated when nature screwed him up like that.

He moved forward to the mound that concealed a storage shed. Human nature had had its way here. For all the cunning and effort that had gone into that place, its occupants had gotten lazy. There was a tractor parked next to the shed, ignoring a garage shaped like an earth-covered Quonset hut on the other side of the yard. Poor security. Also tough on the machine, McKay figured. From the way the rain beaded on the dark green paint it looked as if the tractor was generally kept in pretty good repair.

He peered around the front of the shed. Tom was on the roof, walking forward with his own silenced MP5 cradled in his arms. McKay was just starting forward when the cabin's front door opened.

Hastily he dodged back out of sight. Footsteps followed him, splashes getting closer. *Great. Now they think about their fucking tractor.*

The tractor was parked on the side away from the house. McKay made himself small between it and the earthen mound.

A man wearing a rainslick open over work shirt and jeans came trucking around the corner. A low gleam spun in McKay's peripheral vision, and Stew's big knife planted itself in the man's sternum.

If this had been the movies that would've been it: *bang*, he'd have dropped into the mud without a sound.

But a single knife wound is seldom enough to kill a full-grown man. And almost never enough to take him down at once. Even a knife that big. A man's chest, as Yellow Bull had said, is mostly air.

The blade's impact did take the air out of him. But he drew a long black cowboy gun from a hip holster and triggered two shots, loud as the mountain cracking open.

"Fuck," McKay said, and shot him. Short burst, very quiet: the H&K was a special-production antiterrorist model chambered and barreled for .45 ACP. No supersonic crack, plus lots of takedown power.

It took him down. Then a buddy came busting out the door firing an M16 full-auto from the hip.

Tom was on top of the situation, as usual—right above the door. He gave the man—boy—three quick quiet ones to the center of mass. The survivalist went down, moaning and rolling side to side in the muck.

"You stupid fuck," McKay told Stew, who'd slipped up next to him, grinning at him with slack blue lips and holding a mini-Uzi with a full thirty-two-round box mag stuck up its butt. At the same instant firing blazed out from three sides of the cabin, flattening his words.

McKay just stayed where he was. The survivalists were shooting blind. *Let 'em have their Mad Minute. Plenty of time to move when they run out of ammo.*

Which they duly did, and more or less at once. McKay swung around the front of the shed, MP shouldered. As he expected, Tom was making an arm over the end of the roof to bounce a CS can off the cement stoop inside the burrow. He followed it with CN-DM, nausea gas. Nothing like burning blind eyes and the projectile pukes to take the polish off a would-be Rambo.

White smoke and gagging sounds rolled out the open door of the cabin. McKay sidled back so he could cover the entrance without exposing more of himself than necessary. This battle was over, as far as he was concerned.

A man wearing blue coveralls staggered out, with one hand held over his mouth, vomit dripping between the fingers, waving his other arm in the air. Three more men and two women stumbled out on his heels, disarmed and barely able to walk.

"Yee-ha!" With a rebel yell Stew Jeffcoat bounced around the corner and blazed off the whole magazine into them in one single orgasm of fire. At the same time Alex and the Dozer cut loose

from the far slope forty meters off, Dozier with a SAW, Barka with his beloved Beretta SMG. Polidor joined in from the roof with his CAR-15.

The survivalists screamed as bullets sleeted through their bodies like high-energy particles. One woman stayed on her knees for a few seconds, holding up her hands as if pleading, and then the left side of her face blew out in a black spray of blood and brains.

"What the hell do you think you're doing, you murderous son of a bitch?" McKay screamed. He grabbed Stew by one skinny wrist and swung him against the tractor's gleaming side as if he were a Cabbage Patch Kid. *"We were supposed to get some goddam prisoners!"*

Jeffcoat just laughed at him. It took every gram of self-control he had to keep from smashing that pale gloating face.

All they found were bodies. Two of the survivalists were still breathing when the firing stopped. They stopped too in a matter of minutes.

The house ran ten meters back into the mountain. A cement-lined passageway ran from a closet in the rear to an opening concealed in a cluster of rocks twenty-five meters upslope. Both doors were open.

"You dumb bastards," McKay said, coming into what had been the living room. The windows were open wide; the black-pepper sting of tear gas still filled the air. He dropped on a heavy woodblock sofa. "Why'd you have to go and shoot everybody?"

"We don't take chances," Dozier said, very aggressive.

"Well, while you were making sure a half dozen unarmed people who were puking their guts out didn't get the drop on you, our man McKendree ran right out the back door. No wonder you fuckers lost the war on drugs."

"We were seeing the light at the end of the tunnel!"

McKay felt very tired. "It was a subway train," he said. "Coming the other way."

"You had to kill all those people?" Jessica Turner asked, long-almond eyes wide in disbelief. She sat dangling her long legs, now encased in blue jeans salvaged from the White Action! settlement, out the open hatch of Mobile One. She had a Levi jacket and her hair in braids.

The rain had stopped. The evening was warmer than you'd expect. The Guardians and the girl were finishing a meal of freeze-dried rats out in the car, which Casey had threaded painfully up the road. The highway patrolmen, who'd taken the house as a bivouac, were chowing down on the perishable-type foodstuffs. "No point lettin' it go to waste," Lew Polidor pointed out.

"Sergeant Barka and his men made a judgment call," Sam said measuredly, stirring his chicken kiev with a plastic fork. "Maybe they reacted a bit . . . drastically."

"You havin' second thoughts, navy boy?" McKay asked. He was outside leaning against the hull, smoking a cigar and gazing up into the trees.

Sloan chewed his lip and said nothing.

"I can't see why you came here in the first place," Jessica said. "If you're not going to eat that, can I have it, Commander Sloan?"

"Huh? Oh, sure." He passed her his tray from where he sat with his back to the turret root. "We came here because it was reported that McKendree was staying here. And call me Sam."

She frowned at him. "What would he be doing here?"

"Reports said these were, like, major friends of his," Casey said.

She laughed disbelievingly. "McKendree didn't know these people from the pope."

"How the fu— How do you know all this?" McKay asked. Jessica's presence was imposing certain monastic restraints on their habits. "Did McKendree talk all his social contacts over with you?"

She blinked, hugged thin arms about her knees, and looked pointedly at the ground. "Some people talk a lot in bed. You know?" she said after a moment.

"I think I'll take a turn around the perimeter," Tom Rogers said into the sudden glaring silence. He picked up his Galil Short Assault Rifle and slipped out, merging instantly with the night.

"So, ah, what do you want to do when you grow up?" Sloan asked, thinking it was time to change the subject.

Jessica slowly shook her head. "My mother was a stewardess," she said in a faraway voice. "I could never get into that."

"A stewardess?" McKay asked. "A flight attendant? In Cheyenne, Wyoming?"

"She used to commute to Denver. Stapleton. She was gone a

lot.'' She twisted the end of a braid around her finger. ''She was studying to be a doctor, though.''

''So what do you wanna be?'' McKay asked.

''A quantum physicist.''

''It figures.''

McKay was wakened by fists pounding on the hull. He disentangled himself groggily from the bodies in sleeping bags piled on top of each other on the rubber-matted deck. A V-450 was designed to carry a squad, but that was sitting up, and anyway a lot of interior space was eaten by conformal cargo lockers.

He pulled his M60 from its brackets and shot the action. It made a lot of noise. He wasn't going to be the only one awake at whatever godforsaken hour this was. As a token of solidarity or some damn thing the Guardians had been splitting watches with the SID boys.

Jessica sat up from between Tom and Sam and blinked at him, rubbing her eyes. They all felt a little strange about having her sleep right next to them—even McKay, who wasn't exactly Phil Donahue. But she claimed she didn't mind, that nobody had to spread his bag on the top deck or try to rack out in the turret or anything.

The pounding came again. Somebody was shouting out there. Must be serious shit. McKay opened the armored shutter over the hatch vision block.

Lew Polidor was outside in gray postdawn cloudy-morning light. He stuck his sheet-white face right up against the block and screamed at McKay to open up.

''Huh,'' McKay grunted. He opened the hatch.

''—Stew!'' Lew was shouting. He sprayed saliva in McKay's face.

McKay scratched the back of his neck with his left hand, holding the rear pistol grip of the MG with his unassisted right and pretending it wasn't a strain. Fucker weighed twenty pounds.

''He took over watch about four.'' He stopped, frowned, checked back over his shoulder, then looked at the watch strapped to his brawny wrist. ''Hey, I'll be damned, he was supposed to wake Sloan at 0600. Gotta be later than that now—''

''He's gone!''

CHAPTER
EIGHTEEN

It didn't take long to find him. He hadn't gone far. And he wouldn't be going any farther.

McKay took the first cigar of the morning unlit from his lips. "Shit," he said. Jessica gasped and clung to Sam Sloan, who absently hugged her to him.

"Oh, my God," choked Lew Polidor. *"Stew!"* He dropped to his knees, vomit spilling over his lower lip.

Stew Jeffcoat had been an artist with a blade. So was whoever had strung him up by his heels from a tree with a gag in his mouth, expertly worked him over, and finally—mercifully—slit his throat.

"He who lives by the sword," McKay said, "dies by it. What the fuck?" He scratched a match live with a thumbnail and lit his smoke.

The Guardians endured with hardly a murmur Nicholas Brant's tongue-lashing for letting McKendree slip through their fingers again.

They had it coming. There was no getting around the fact: McKendree was fully as dangerous as Brant and SID had said all along.

"All right, Dr. Brant," Billy McKay said, when the tirade

finally ran down. "You made your point. From here on in we're really gonna *bear down*."

Flames rolled out of the windows of the trailer, bright beneath the wide lead-colored sky. The thin-gauge walls were already beginning to glow and buckle in places. They were already sieved from a couple of hundred assorted rounds of 5.56, 7.62, and .50 caliber, not to mention three much bigger holes just to the left of the doorway with its built-up wooden porch—the railing burning now, whipping flames like the strands of brightly colored plastic pennons they used to put up around filling stations and used-car lots.

McKay moved cautiously forward alongside the cattle chute. The sodbusters had put up a good fight. Too good for their own good.

Movement to the left—he spun, whipping up the chopped Maremont by fore and aft pistol grips like the world's biggest tommy gun.

—Glint of dull hard-hearted light on blued steel. His stomach did a flip-flop and he turned and just sat down hard.

A blast of double-aught splintered the top plank of the chute a centimeter above his flattop. A heartbeat later another charge blew out the whole middle of the thick board, leaving halves connected by the merest sliver at the bottom.

McKay's photoflash impression was of a big side-by-side pointing at his face like a pair of culvert pipes. That meant the other guy was empty—in case McKay wanted to bet his life on the split-second identification's accuracy, on the other guy not having a cowboy pistol for backup, on his being alone.

But there was a better way: cheat. The hard lessons the pursuit of McKendree had taught them left them in no mood for Marquis of Queensberry rules.

He scoonched his ass around in dried cow shit deposited over years in deep drifts. Bracing his boots against the hard dirt underneath, he clamped the black steel butt of the M60 between elbow and ribs, aimed the muzzle brake at the base of the chute, and cut loose a burst.

No matter how strong you were—and Billy McKay was *real* strong—a 7.62-millimeter machine gun was going to climb on full auto. That's just the way they are. A good gunner takes advantage of that.

McKay was good. He fired in quick spurts, three shots, four, five, four, letting the muzzle come up naturally, letting gravity pull it down, not as far as before, firing again.

He burned half of the fifty-round belt coiled inside the plastic half-moon-shaped ammo box hung on the receiver's side. Somewhere in the middle of it he heard a high-pitched scream.

He picked himself up, threw himself backward against the splintered chute, the barrel of the M60 high. He felt the heat of it wash across his face. He waited a moment while his hearing returned. Even the pop-'em-in-and-forget-'em plugs the Guardians wore at all times on duty could only take so much of the sting out of the big machine gun's voice.

Nothing. Just the wind sighing round and about off the endless-seeming prairie, and the constant low chant of the flames.

He snapped around, MG leveled. Nothing. He moved forward, boots sinking soundlessly into the fossilized manure, then pivoted around the other corner.

She had been young. Maybe Jessie's age. She looked like she'd stepped in front of a tractor rig that was ignoring the hell out of the federally mandated speed limit. The broken-open shotgun lay by her side, barrel twisted, stock shattered, two fat fresh shells halfway inside.

"*Problems, Billy?*" Tom Rogers said over the communicator.

"Nope," he returned, and started toward the flaming trailer.

"*You communist bastards can kill my friends. But the great white race is awakening at last. More and more defenders will rise up from the earth like dragons' teeth to crush you for your treachery.*

"*You can kill me, too, but my blood will fertilize the purple mountains and fruited plains of this great nation, and more and more avengers of the endangered white species will spring forth where it flows.*

"*You can kill me, pigs, for all the good it will do you.*

"*But first you have to catch me. This is McKendree.*"

The bulldozer's engine growled to a crescendo. Sloan popped onto his knees behind the plastic drums and fired a long burst. The copper-jacketed 5.56 slugs didn't even raise sparks as they ricocheted harmlessly off the blade.

"Jesus," he said. "How do I get in these situations?"

He dropped like a prairie dog down its hole. Choking on white limestone dust he pushed open the trombone-slide receiver of the M203 slung under the barrel of his Galil SAR, popped in a fat grenade with the green body and gold head that signified an HEDP round. It was meant to take out an armored personnel carrier. *Let's see how it works on a bulldozer.*

He came up. The dozer was twenty-odd meters away, not moving fast. It didn't need to. He fired for the dead center of the blade.

The round went off with the characteristic high *crack*! and eye-hurting flash of a shaped charge. The big engine never missed a beat.

He sat down with his back to the blue plastic barrels. "Shit," he said. "Shit, shit, shit." He seldom used vulgarity, and tended to make the most of occasions when he did.

He knew exactly what had happened. The jet of vaporized metal spat out by a shaped charge dissipated with shocking quickness in open air. He had just copper-plated the mesh over the bulldozer's radiator.

He slithered down to the end of the row of barrels, took a cautious three-second look. It turned out to be a lot shorter than three seconds. The two bastards in the cab were reading his mind; one of them had a nasty BM-59, an Italian clone of the M14 with a folding metal paratrooper stock, and it was pointed right at the bridge of Sam's nose. Synaptic delay was the only thing that kept his brainpan from being evacuated by the thunder-stutter burst of 7.62 that sent the end barrels flying as he scrambled madly back for the center of the row.

The outsized blade was protecting him and his enemies alike. With it interposed neither side could see or shoot the other directly. On the other hand, in a matter of moments that was going to be academic. The snorting monster would crush him beneath its caterpillar treads or flush him into the open.

The crackle of gunfire to either side told him his buddies had problems of their own. *You're a Guardian,* he told himself. *You work it out.*

If his damned grenades were going to be any use they'd better pan out in a hurry; a few heartbeats and the beast was going to be inside the ten-meter minimum range at which the projectiles would arm.

Hurriedly he jacked in a white phosphorus round. If he put

that into the blade he'd be in a world of hurt, with the white starfish tentacles of smoke drawn by viciously burning metal flakes reaching right back at *him*. It would be one quick way to find out if the heavy-sounding liquid stored in the drums was still, as the cracked and weathered legends on their sides said, INFLAMMABLE.

But Mr. and Mrs. Robert Sloan of Stone County, Missouri, hadn't raised any sons who weren't resourceful. Sloan aimed just past the right end of the blade and fired again.

The round blew on the ground just beside the open-sided cab. Half a second later a man flew screaming from the heavy caterpillar, trailing threads of dense white smoke. He rolled and thrashed on the ground, tearing at his clothing.

His screams tore at Sloan's stomach; that was a hell of a way to die, like being eaten alive by burning soldier ants.

The dozer didn't veer. It came on, with a galaxy of tiny stars glowing along its right flank. The man's body had shielded his buddy from the phosphorus flake shower.

Great. The dozer blade loomed like a steel cliff. Time for one idea to half-bake—a good thing, since it was the kind of idea you'd throw away if it got to cook until it was done—time to jam one more round up the spout of the 203.

The blade hit the barrels with a thump of metal on plastic. Sam Sloan swarmed right up over the top of them, threw himself onto the blade, and clung like a monkey, hanging his face over like Kilroy.

He saw a startled face gaping at him through the polarized glass of the windscreen, saw a second assault rifle start to come up. He fired one-handed.

The face vanished in a sheet of granular white as the multiple-projectile round sugared the screen.

As any number of policemen have learned over the years, a buckshot charge will not go through a windshield, at least not an intact one. It bashes hell out of them, though, obscuring the vision of the man behind them, spoiling his aim, and allowing a hornet swarm of 5.56 bullets coming the other way in a hell of a hurry to sting the life right out of him.

"Who the fuck is Reuben McKendree?" the black-bearded man asked.

McKay's rock-solid right fist snapped his head around on a

neck like an oak trunk. The bearded man spat out blood and tooth fragments on the cement floor of the dispatcher's shack and glowered at him.

Sloan laid a hand on his leader's arm. "Take it easy, Billy."

He was aware that he was playing Mutt to McKay's Jeff—or was it the other way around?—but he was also quite sincere. He didn't have much taste for this kind of thing.

The shack was a building that was cinderblock to here and had been big glass windows up to *there*, except the windows were gone with the wind, even before the firefight. The roof was corrugated tin. A hot breeze whistled through, hardly slowing down on its way to the Yellowstone.

McKay massaged his fist. He was looking even less happy than a moment before. He might have busted a knuckle, to match the one on his other hand.

"Don't be such a bleeding-heart wimp," he rasped. "Don't you want to catch this McKendree fuck? You're the one who wants to wipe out all these right-wing assholes."

"Right-wing?" sputtered a man with lots of curly red hair spilling out from under a Detroit Tigers baseball cap. "*Right*-wing? I'm a card-carrying member of the Young People's Socialist Alliance! It's the Worker's Party you want. Those Trotskyite revisionist bastards are the next thing to fascists."

McKay looked at Sloan. Sloan, who wasn't good at reading McKay's looks except for the basics—lust, anger—couldn't read this one either.

"Radical politics makes strange bedfellows," he said.

A pig wandered past the shack, grunting to itself in apparent agitation. A large penful of them had gotten let loose somehow during the fight.

"What are you cement miners doing with all these guns, if you're so fucking innocent?" McKay asked. "You guys were all set up to take on the Eighth Guards Army."

"Cement *makers*," said the man with the baseball cap. "We're the forefront of a new heyday for industrial workers."

"Manufacturers," said the third captive tiredly. He was a middle-sized, predominantly colorless man, with thin blondish hair and bluish eyes, whose most outstanding characteristic was the outstanding sheen to his bald forehead. He wasn't tied. He hadn't been as cantankerous as his two buddies, and also wasn't as prepossessing as the other two, who were on the husky side.

If he wanted to try to make trouble, that was fine with both McKay and Sloan; *they* had guns. "We're cement *manufacturers*."

"*Fabricators*, then, if you want to get fancy. 'Manufacturers' makes us sound as if we're management."

"Shouldn't you be rooting for Cincinnati?" McKay asked him with unaccustomed blandness.

Red-beard blinked blankly at him. The one with the black beard just scowled. The blond one turned up a sour smile he obviously didn't want his buddies to see.

"To answer your question," he said, offering around a pack of cigarettes and drawing one himself, "what we do here is make cement."

"I'd think that'd be a pretty major industrial undertaking," Sloan said dubiously.

The blond man shrugged. "We work on a lot smaller scale than before the War, and we're much more labor-intensive, but we get by. The Romans made cement, and so can we."

"But we're slowly expanding," the man in the Tigers cap said. "We hope to get more and more of the plant functional again. There's a lot of demand for it, you know—comparatively, anyway. We send it out in exchange for the resources necessary to reclaim more and more of it."

"That sounds suspiciously like free enterprise," Sloan said.

The red-bearded man frowned, waved him off as if he were a mosquito. "Mere bourgeois obfuscation. Don't try to confuse the issue with word games, you running dog."

Sloan made a noise. " '*Running dog*'?" he subvocalized, outraged.

" '*Bourgeois obfuscation*'?" McKay came back. "*Hey, don't be too harsh on this dude. Sounds like your kind of guy.*"

"In any event," the blond man said, herding the conversation back to the point with the practiced air of a veteran sheepdog, "we have some very valuable equipment and assets here—fuel stocks, including a system we've designed for extracting methane from human and animal wastes, vehicles such as the bulldozer the commander did so much damage to."

"I'd think you'd be more concerned about the men we damaged," Sloan said.

"The blood of our comrades cries out for revenge," red-beard said.

"Oh, shut up," said the man with the black beard.

The blond man shrugged. He seemed tired. "Some of us have already died to preserve what we have here. We feel as if we're a part of the process of rebuilding America—"

"Along nonexploitative, nonimperialist lines."

"—in a small way. But we've had more than our share of marauders come through trying to help themselves to our gear. That whole *Road Warrior* trip, you know?" He grimaced. "At least you boys don't seem to be looters. More like straightforward killers."

Sloan cast a nervous look at McKay. It would probably be counterproductive if he ripped the blond man's arm off and beat him to death with it; he was the only one showing any signs of cooperating. After a week of savage battles in the seemingly endless hunt for McKendree, this was the first set of captives they'd come up with in any kind of shape to answer questions.

Of course, that may have had something to do with the fact that this was the first holdout camp they'd hit without having any of their Teammates along. But he didn't want to follow that path of thought too far.

McKay just puffed his cigar and grunted. That was the problem with him. You never could tell what was going to set him off.

"Now, exactly how long was McKendree here?" Sloan asked, hoping to get the conversation back on track. This was *supposed* to be an interrogation.

The blond man sighed. "All I know of Reuben McKendree is what I saw on TV. I remember a big thing on *60 Minutes*, just before the War, on how he used influence to beat some kind of federal rap."

McKay looked at him awhile, heavy face scowling through the blue smoke of his cigar. Then he turned to Sloan.

"We could bring in Tommy to work on these guys a little—"

"Come on, McKay!" he said, remembering his Good Cop role a beat late. "You can't do that. This is America!"

McKay laughed. "This is post-Holocaust America. You can't make an omelet without breakin' eggs, buddy boy." He shrugged. "But we got a fugitive to catch, so maybe we should just turn these campers and their friends over to the highway patrol and let them sort 'em out—"

"The highway patrol?" Black-beard spat red on grimy linoleum.

"Fascist swine," the Tigers fan said.

Blondie almost choked on his cigarette. He took it out, looked at it. "These things don't age so well. SID sent you, eh?"

McKay and Sloan looked at each other. "Yes," Sloan said guardedly.

The blond man laughed. "That explains a lot. They've been trying to take over here since right after the bombs fell. But they never had the balls."

"Come off that shit," McKay said. "Why would the cops wanna take you over?"

"Because they're under the sway of that eco-fascist Brant," the man with the red beard said. "They say we're damaging the environment and encouraging others to do likewise.

"But what they really want to do is set Greenwell aside and take over!"

CHAPTER
NINETEEN

"Yes, Dr. Brant," Billy McKay said. "We sure won't let him slip through our fingers this time. Thanks for the tip."

He tossed the microphone back at the portable radio they'd hauled out of Mobile One so they could enjoy the cool evening. For once it wasn't raining, though the rain had left the air sweet and clear. "Son of a bitch."

"I told you you were chasing shadows," said Jessica Turner, trudging up from the stream beside which they'd camped for the night. It was gorged with runoff from the violent storms in the mountains. She let down the plastic four-liter water bottle she'd been carrying with a thump. "Why do I have to do all this hewing wood and hauling water crap? You guys are real male chauvinists."

"You volunteered," Sloan said.

"You gotta do something to justify our hauling your skinny little butt around with us," McKay said. "We could always ship it to JFK City. That's what my man Nicholas wants us to do."

Sloan rolled his eyes at him. They weren't supposed to make any cracks around her that smacked of sexual innuendo. But what the fuck? Billy McKay didn't have any interest in screwing Jessica Turner, she was just a goddam *kid*. He had never in his life known anybody who *was* interested in screwing little kids, though God knew the pre-War media would have had you believing every third man in America had nothing on his mind but getting it up a three-year-old. If Jessica got the idea he had the hots for her, that was really her problem. In the meantime, talking like Mr. Rogers all the time was making him nuts.

Jessica showed no signs of reacting to his choice of words. She did react to the content.

"You can't!" she exclaimed, coming all over tearful. She threw herself down on one knee next to the fallen cottonwood on which McKay was sitting, grabbed his leg with strong little hands. "What did those people at the cement plant tell you? Those SID men are not one bit better than McKendree and his bunch."

A call to JFK City earlier in the day had gotten a highway patrol unit sent out from nearby Rock Springs to take charge of the twenty or so captives they'd grabbed at the cement works. Even McKay felt a certain sneaking relief that the detachment had been regular patrol, not Special Investigations.

"Billy," Tom Rogers said, staring into the little driftwood fire they'd made, "we need some information."

"That's all we get out of JFK City," McKay said. "Information. 'McKendree's here. No, he's there. No, you dumb fu— uh, clucks, you just missed him.' All the *time* we got information."

"And none of it ever pans out, man," Casey said.

Jessie was still weeping and clutching at McKay's pants leg. He jerked it away. "Knock it *off*, will you? Quit overacting. We ain't gonna send you back just yet. Unless you turn into too much of a pain."

Jessica sat up. "Thank you," she said in a perfectly level voice. Her eyes were miraculously dry.

"Tom doesn't mean that information," Sloan said helpfully. "He means—"

"When I need the help of some pointy-head Annapolis intellectual to figure out what Tom Rogers means, it'll be time to shoot me in the back of the head and roll me in a shallow grave." He stood up, stretched.

"We got some assets of our own in this part of the world," he said. "Time we made some use—"

He broke off. Tom had raised his head and was staring off into the night. There was something in his posture that set alarm bells jangling in McKay's head.

"What is it?" he asked quietly. He moved to where his M60 sat propped on a rock.

"Somebody's watching us," Tom said. If it hadn't been for their communicators they would never have heard him, though for once the wind had died to a mild sporadic breeze along the streambed.

Casey picked up his heavy-barreled rifle and melted into shadow, almost as deftly as Tom might have. Sam slipped into the car and up into the turret.

Jessica bit her lip. "What's happening?" she asked, her voice barely audible. "What does he see?"

"Nothing, exactly, Ms. Turner," Tom said. "It's more just a feeling. I've had it before, once or twice the last few days."

"Why didn't you mention that, Tom?" McKay subvocalized.

"Didn't want to make a fuss over nothin'."

McKay scowled. He had to buy Tommy's judgment as to what was and what was not worthwhile to call to his attention.

But he trusted Tom's hunches, more, maybe, than Tom did. In the field you acquired . . . instincts, call them, a heightened sensory awareness, a vast body of experience against which you could evaluate the impressions your senses gathered. McKay had them. But Tom had more than anyone he'd ever known.

"Is he psychic?" Jessie whispered.

"Probably," McKay said.

"A horse turd?" McKay said.

Squatting in the momentarily dry—at least not actively running water—bed of a creek that wound between swells of ground to feed into the watercourse by which they were camped, Tom Rogers raised his head.

"Fresh, Billy."

"Yeah. Even I can see that. What do we do about it?"

Tom shone a flashlight up the creek. Half-moon tracks were sunk in soft mud for maybe six meters.

"He rode that way, then found shale. No more tracks. He's good, Billy."

"Can you follow him?"

The light clicked off. Tom hunkered a spell in silence. "Somali might."

"Fuck." Somali trackers were the best in the world. Tom was good, but . . .

The short hairs stood up on the back of McKay's neck. They were used to being the unapproachable best in the league, like the '86 Mets taking on a bunch of A ball clubs. This was not the way it was supposed to be.

"Is it McKendree?" he asked.

"I don't think so."

"McKendree's been real good."

Rogers thought a little longer. That was the way he was. He seldom said much, never without having reason for it.

"McKendree's been keeping clear of us—"

"Leading us all over the damned state, you mean."

"Yeah. But he's got no *background*, Billy. He's a lumberjack who's been on a lot of talk shows. He's not SF, not Ranger trained, nothing like that."

"Maybe he's just naturally talented."

He felt the pressure of Rogers's eyes on him.

"A guy like that who's this good, to be able to just toy with us— I don't like it, Billy."

"But he's *been* toying with us, dammit! He dropped Girard with one fucking shot in the dark in Montana. He took Jeffcoat right out of the middle of us and all but skinned him out like a fucking deer. He's like the goddam Predator out of that movie."

"Somebody is, Billy."

McKay never got used to the feel of a honky-tonk in daytime.

He stepped through the doorway into stifling gloom a little warily, even with Sam Sloan right behind him. This was at worst likely to be neutral ground, too likely for him to come tramping through the door with his immense black M60 in his hands. But there had been too much spooky shit going down for his right hand to be able to get far from his .45.

For three days they'd managed to deflect JFK City's insistence that they follow up the latest lead on McKendree's whereabouts. A persistent transmission malfunction, they claimed, required requisition of transport for a trip to one of their secret caches. They had indeed requisitioned some extra civilian transport, a Kawasaki scrambler bike, using gold provided by Jake Morgenstern, which would have given paper-money fan Maggie Connoly fits. It was not, however, to travel to any caches—the locations of which McKay had cheerfully refused to so much as hint at, in the face of massive bluster from Nicholas Brant. Tom had a job he wanted to do that didn't need the whole crew.

Tom had split on the Kawasaki day before yesterday. The others continued what they'd actually been up to, traveling and talking to people they'd had contact with before, mainly during the phase of guerrilla warfare that preceded springing Jeff Mac-Gregor from the FSE-held Heartland complex. McKay had an uncomfortable feeling that's what they should have done right off the bat, instead of letting the locals razzle-dazzle them into hurtling all over looking for McKendree.

"May I buy you a drink, Lieutenant McKay?" a voice asked from the cavernous interior of Rosa's Cantina.

The day was sunny, for a wonder. McKay could feel the heat beating off the cracked asphalt of I-25 on his back. His eyes slowly adjusted.

The bar was much the way he remembered it from last year, cracked vinyl and dark wood paneling, a few sad strands of Christmas lights, dark at the moment, strung here and there in hopes of adding a festive air. Something was different about the place, but he couldn't put a finger on it.

He looked at Sam, who shrugged, then stared until a figure began to resolve out of the semidark. It was a man in a black frock coat, whose paunch was more impressive then his height, which was so-so. He had a bald dome of head rising out of a bush of long, curly, graying hair, one of your better beards, and round wire-rim spectacles perched on a great beak of nose. He had a hand-tooled c'boy kind of boot propped on the brass rail, and a slouch hat of the black and battered variety on the bar next to him.

"Who the hell are you?" McKay demanded.

"I'm Samuel Cohen, former Wyoming director of the American Civil Liberties Union. Is that Lieutenant Commander Sloan with you?"

The two Guardians had been drifting slowly into the bar, getting surrounded by the dim and the long-ingrained smell of sweat and smoke and beer. "It's okay, Lieutenant," a deep voice said from behind the bar. "He's good people."

McKay looked around. The broad smoked-glass mirror was still mostly covered by spiderweb cracks radiating from the bullet holes that had been put there when an Effsee hit team had tried to nail the Guardians last year. Standing in front of the mirror polishing a glass was a seven-foot giant in a white dress shirt with a red garter on his big right biceps.

"Lurch!" McKay exclaimed. He swapped bear hugs with the bartender, who got his name from a not-at-all fanciful resemblance to the Addams family's butler. The big man had to lean over the bar and couldn't get a proper grip, for which McKay's rib cage was grateful.

"What's happening?" Sloan asked, more prudently confining himself to shaking hands.

Lurch's eyes slid toward the front foyer. "This and that," he said cautiously.

Then Rosa herself came chugging out like a Mack tractor with huge breasts and a black moustache, which she plastered on each Guardian's face in turn while bestowing slightly damp hugs.

"It's so good to see you! When you left here, I thought I would never see you again, but then President MacGregor came on the radio and said that bad man Lowell was dead, and everything was all right."

"Well, things almost weren't all right, but we pulled it off," Sam Sloan said, dodging another kiss.

And then it hit McKay what was missing. "Where are your dancers? Or don't they come in during the day?"

Rosa looked at Lurch. "We don't have dancers anymore. Most of them are gone."

"Gone? Where?" Because Rosa's had been that historical inevitability, a by-God after-the-Holocaust topless bar.

"It was those bastards from SID," Rosa said. "They shut us down, said we were undermining morale and running a house of prostitution. Imagine, the Cantina a whorehouse!"

It wouldn't have been all that unusual an arrangement. But Rosa had refused to run her establishment as a brothel.

"They tried to rape Shiloh," Rosa said, wiping her hands compulsively on her apron. "When Lurch interfered they ran him in, made him go all the way to JFK City. I had to pay a big fine to get him out."

Shiloh was a long-legged blonde who'd had an eye for Casey, who was keeping an eye on Mobile One and Jessica out in the parking lot. "Who tried to rape her?" Sam asked.

"That Lieutenant Sawtelle, those two awful men, Doug and Slug or whatever they call themselves."

"Lew and Stew," Sam said, looking meaningfully at McKay.

"Stew won't be bothering anyone again," McKay said. "He sorta got hung up."

He turned to Cohen, who had been standing patiently, enduring being ignored.

"Now, what exactly brings you here?" McKay asked, laying an elbow on the bar.

"First, word got out that you've been asking questions about a man named Reuben McKendree. I was involved in some of his trials before the War; I know more than a little bit about him."

McKay accepted a tall mug of beer, the special scarfed stuff, chilled by an alcohol-driven compressor, from Lurch. He took a hearty slug.

"Ah, you remembered," he said. "Coors. The good stuff." Sam grimaced.

"What was the other reason you had for looking us up, Mr. Cohen?" Sam asked.

"Someone is murdering members of survivalist groups."

"Who's that?" McKay asked.

"You."

CHAPTER
TWENTY ─────────────────

For a moment the air in the bar seemed to have solidified, trapping them like flies in Lucite.

McKay let the mug fall from his lips. "Just what the hell do you mean by that?"

"What have you been doing the last two weeks?" Cohen asked blandly.

"None of your goddam—"

"Think about it."

"Now, hold on a minute here," Sam Sloan said. "You've obviously been hearing things, but they aren't true. Or only half-truths at best. We've been involved in several shoot-outs with groups suspected of harboring McKendree, who is a fugitive from justice with a record of extreme violence."

"Is that customary procedure for an investigation? To go in with guns blazing?"

"They shot first," McKay growled. But he was looking side-long at Sloan. They hadn't shot first at that semisubterranean cabin; the Team had. But in the half-dozen engagements since then the retreaters had cut loose at the first sign of Guardians.

"Word's been going around that you're squashing dissident settlements on behalf of the SID squad called the Team. Those gentlemen don't have that attractive a reputation to begin with.

You've left every such settlement you've been to a smoking ruin. Did you expect to be greeted with open arms?''

"They shot first," McKay repeated stubbornly.

Cohen shook his head. "In one, very limited sense I am relieved. You seem ingenuous in your denials that what you intend is mass murder. But it troubles me deeply that you didn't exercise better judgment—"

The veins in McKay's neck swelled, and his ears practically glowed red. Cohen cut him off before he could uncork an outburst.

"What makes you think McKendree has a record of violence? In normal circumstances that would be actionable, Lieutenant. Mr. McKendree has never been convicted of a major violent act. A couple of misdemeanor brawling raps do not convict a man of murder."

"We know all about the way he used some kind of undue influence to get out of that illegal-weapons indictment," Sloan said.

Cohen cocked an eyebrow. "Really? Frankly, I doubt you know anything about it at all, from the tone of your conversation."

"Listen, mister," McKay said, having simmered down to the point of coherence, "just what the hell business do you have horning in on this? And how do you *know* all this shit, anyway?''

"The Wyoming ACLU took an interest in the McKendree case, particularly after the federal indictment Commander Sloan refers to. Which *we* were instrumental in quashing. The federal court dismissed the case with prejudice because of lack of evidence. If there was undue influence it was exercised when the federal grand jury refused to act on evidence we presented— corroborated by the United States attorney for Wyoming—that the illegal munitions had been planted in Mr. McKendree's possession by agents of the Special Investigative Division of the Wyoming Highway Patrol. Under the command, I might add, of Lieutenant Tobias Sawtelle.''

"These are serious allegations, Lieutenant McKay." Nicholas Brant's voice, relayed via satellite from his ranch outside of JFK City, was dry as twigs snapping. "Not to mention ridiculous. I might remind you Lieutenant Sawtelle, whose record has been in all ways exemplary, with the DEA as well as with SID, was himself not indicted on the basis of the ACLU's wild accusations.''

McKay looked across the interior of Mobile One to Cohen, who offered a shrug, palms up. They were parked discreetly back of Rosa's in the slanting sunset light. A big rig had pulled into the side lot a few minutes ago; otherwise business seemed way off from a year ago.

"I might also add," Brant said, "that such details of McKendree's past career, or Lieutenant Sawtelle's for that matter, are completely without relevance. He is a criminal, and you are under orders from your own superiors to apprehend him. And he continues to release tapes taking credit for his crimes, which hardly seems a course an innocent man might choose.''

A pause, popping with a dust of static. "I suppose you received your hot tip from a gentleman named Cohen?''

Cohen's full-lipped mouth twisted in an ironic smile.

"Yeah," McKay said.

"There are things I suspect he's not telling you. He's not a well man. He's wanted himself in connection with two murders, in addition to innumerable counts of obstructing justice. You would really be doing him a favor as well as us if you were to hand him over to the nearest available Department of Public Safety station.''

Cohen laughed soundlessly.

"We'll get back to you on that, Doctor," McKay said. "Guardians out. So what's the story on this, Cohen?''

"Since the War I've supported myself by acting as arbitrator in disputes. I have achieved a certain amount of success at this. The state of Wyoming, or in any event Dr. Brant's SID, are quite jealous of their role as guardians of law. After all, they are seeking to replace the rule of law with the rule of sheer force—theirs.''

He shook his head. "If you wish to turn me over to the highway patrol, by all means do so. My conscience is clear. Yours might not remain so—for it would be naïve of me to expect to live to see trial. I would not be the first to fail to do so.''

"Aw, the hell with it," McKay said. "We're already holding out on Kennedy City." He jerked his head at Jessie, who sat with her back to the hull, staring over her bare knees with large dark eyes.

"Dr. Brant raised a good point," Sam said thoughtfully. "We

didn't just go racing off in pursuit of Reuben McKendree because the Wyoming authorities told us to. There's the little matter of those tapes."

"We got downloaded copies in memory," McKay said. "Play 'em for the man."

They listened as darkness gathered outside and the gruff yet powerful voice ranted about treachery, betrayal, of Jews and blacks and communists, of murder done and murder promised. Jessica turned and buried her head against McKay's ribs. He put his arm lightly around her shoulders, embarrassed as hell, afraid of crushing her.

When it was over Cohen sat on the fold-down stroking his beard. "It sounded like McKendree's voice, I can't deny that. It's not that easy a voice to forget."

"Well?" Sloan said. "What do you make of it, Mr. Cohen?"

"I am hard pressed to explain. However, I must point out that it is not unusual for activists—terrorists—to claim credit for acts they did not commit."

"Bleeding-heart bullshit."

Cohen turned hooded eyes to McKay. "It may be that I lacked the courage of my convictions, Lieutenant; that danger always exists when one changes one's mind. Things I have experienced since the fall of what we rather optimistically characterized as *civilization* have altered a number of beliefs that I thought I cherished. Nothing, however, has weakened my conviction that humans have rights, which must be fought for at all costs. It is possible that Reuben McKendree did all the things he stands accused of. That would be no reason for you to shoot him down like a dog on sight—nor does it justify gunning down a large number of people who you *suspect* are his friends, on no evidence at all save the word of an agency which has not proven itself exactly unbiased."

"I've always been a big fan of the ACLU, Mr. Cohen," Sam said, looking as earnest as Captain Kirk orating about why they were going to have to phaser the big papier-mâché tyrannosaur head to Cheese Doodle crumbs and boot the silver-haired aliens out of paradise so they could all die of famine and AIDS and whatnot. "But something is really bothering me. I mean, you *heard* the man, sir. He's a bigot. He hates your kind."

Cohen blinked, squeezed his eyes shut, shook his head as if

he had water in his ears. "What does that have to do with anything?"

"You seem to be an admirer of Dr. Brant's, Commander Sloan," Samuel Cohen said.

Sitting at a weathered picnic table behind the Cantina, next to Rosa's trailer, Sloan dabbed the last of the stew from the earthenware plate with the last piece of Rosa's famous corn bread. It struck McKay as tragic that a woman who once ran the finest tit bar in post–World War III America should have to be famous for her *corn bread*.

"Say, this is really very good. I'll have to compliment Rosa. Yes, Mr. Cohen. He did a lot of good work crusading to preserve our long-suffering environment. I find that admirable. Don't you?"

"Did you ever read his book, *Stemming the Tide*?"

"Can't say as I have."

"You might find it fascinating. If you were truly in sympathy with the goals of the Civil Liberties Union, I daresay you might also find it repugnant."

Sam frowned. "Why is that?"

"The premise was that immigration, at least from the Third World, should be completely banned. Further, he maintained that 'unassimilated' members of non-European ethnic groups should be isolated and, if possible, removed from American society."

Sam shrugged. "A lot of environmentalists wanted to close the Golden Door. The Mexican problem—"

"Was only a problem to racists, Commander. And Dr. Brant didn't confine himself to Mexicans. He specifically includes such groups as the Chinese and Vietnamese. Do you believe Chinese immigrants were in danger of swamping America?

"Dr. Brant also believes that only Europeans and Americans have shown any sign of environmental awareness, and puts forward the thesis that people in the developing countries are incapable of such awareness. He claims that in short order a world government will be—would have been—necessary in order to 'prune excess population' in the Third World.

"I defend his right to hold and express those views, Commander. But what he's advocating is genocide, and I do not admire that."

Casey was frowning. McKay kept almost forgetting that he knew how.

"That's pretty weird. Here Dr. Brant has us trying to chase down McKendree for killing all these leaders of ethnic colonies. And he, like, wants to do the same thing."

McKay was staring at Cohen with eyes like semaphore lamps. "Are you shitting me?"

"Why, no. Dr. Brant's views are a matter of public record. You might ask him for a copy of his book; I'm sure he'd be only too happy to give you one, with his compliments."

"Oh, wow," Casey said.

"But you just about lost me," Cohen said. "I understood that Mr. McKendree was being sought for multiple murders. I was unaware of any particular character to those murders."

"No," Sam said. "I won't believe it that Brant—no. You said so yourself, Mr. Cohen; we can't convict a man of bad acts because he has bad ideas."

Cohen frowned and pushed away his own plate. If he worked on it any more he'd be eating pottery. "I wasn't prosecuting anyone, Commander. I was merely engaging in the time-honoring practice of blackguarding somebody whose views I find reprehensible. As he gets to have those views, I reserve the right to express my opinion of them, loudly and often."

McKay took out a cigar and lit it. "I'm confused as hell," he said, blowing smoke and studying the red eye of the ember. "But as far as I'm concerned we're still hunting Big Rube McKendree. But, just for your sake, Mr. Cohen, I personally guarantee that he will be taken alive.

"*Unless* he endangers the lives of any Guardians or civilians. If he does that, I'll treat him like I would any man or woman, innocent, guilty, or with a note from his mommy: kill him like a fucking dog."

Jessica gasped. Her plate clattered into the gravel, didn't break. She covered her face with her hands and bolted into the car, sobbing.

"What the fuck got into her?" McKay asked the air.

"What about her story, Mr. Cohen?" Sam said, leaning forward across the table.

"What *is* her story?"

When they had told him he held up his hands. They showed calluses; McKay wondered how long they'd been there.

"That's quite horrifying. If McKendree is apprehended he should be tried for kidnap and rape, certainly. But he is not guilty until convicted."

"I still can't understand why you're so eager to go to bat for him, Mr. Cohen," Sam said.

"Nor can I understand your eagerness to proclaim him guilty. Or at least I *hope* I can't.

"I became interested in the White Action! case in the first place because I perceived similarities between the treatment accorded radical black activists in the late sixties and early seventies and that received by right-wing extremists in the eighties and nineties. In both cases a number were killed in confrontations with the authorities. It is true that in many instances those killed were in the process of committing a violent act themselves. Equally certainly, there were too many cases where evidence suggests they were killed out of hand.

"It offended me, Mr. Sloan, that people who claimed to be of my persuasion, the liberal persuasion, applauded the destruction of men and women simply because they were right-wing extremists, for the crime of disagreeing with them. It was difficult for me to tell them from the people they professed to despise."

Sam stood up and walked away from the table, into the night.

McKay rose. "I'm goin' inside to see what Rosa's got on tap," he said. "Don't anybody let the Big Bad Rube make off with them or nothin'."

"They're getting too close. They've run into that damned Jew."

"What can they know?"

"They must suspect something. Their behavior has been quite unsettling."

"They can't prove anything. No way."

"They don't need to prove anything. If they raise the wrong questions with the wrong parties—"

"No worries. They've served their purpose, right? It's time to move on to Stage Three anyway. It's all set up. So now we kill two birds with one stone."

"I leave it in your capable hands, Lieutenant Sawtelle. For our Mother's sake, don't let me down."

• • •

McKay howled at the halfway moon over the nearby town of Douglas and beat his hand on the top of the turret.

Startled outcries vibrated up from the innards of the great car. Casey had been awake when the call came through, reading an old *Wild Cards* comic. He had patched the call quietly through to McKay, who was on watch out under the infinite Wyoming stars. Cohen was sleeping in one of Rosa's guest rooms, and Sloan and Jessie had been snoozed out on the inflatable mattresses. Until real recently.

"My God, what is it?" he heard Sloan's sleepy voice exclaim. *"Are we under attack?"*

"Hell, no. But we got the fucker dead to rights."

"Brant?"

"McKendree! SID Intelligence finally got their dead heads out of their asses and did something constructive. They've quit fucking around finding out where he's been. Now they got a solid lead on where he's *going*.

"And we're gonna be there waiting for him!"

CHAPTER
TWENTY-ONE ─────────────

"This time," Samuel Cohen said, "why don't you try talking before you start killing?"

Hunched over the wheel, trying to find the twin-rut forest track in this poor excuse for light, McKay growled. For once the latest news update hadn't caught him asleep. On the other hand, since they had blown out of Rosa's within minutes of getting the word from JFK City, that meant he had gotten no sleep at all. It didn't help his disposition.

From Rosa's outside Douglas they had to swing east, then down, skirting the bow of the Laramie range, and back west again through the wide Platte watershed into the mountains. It was not low-risk territory. It was in one of those rare and specially favored regions of the earth that had been targeted for massive groundburst bombardment with nuclear weapons, the Warren AFB complex around Cheyenne.

Groundbursts were what produced radioactive fallout. As they had had pounded into them during Guardian training, *radioactivity* meant how fast an isotope decayed. The hotter the bad stuff was, the quicker it got used up. Which meant that two years after the bombing the worst fallout had faded into various less-active products of decay. Some of those, of course, were your noted bone-seekers, like cesium 137 and strontium 90. Long-term exposure to large amounts of them would boost your shot at leukemia, but they could be dealt with by expedients like testing suspect plants with Geiger counters and scraping off the top couple of centimeters of topsoil in contaminated areas. That was too much to ask of the whiny survivors in doom dramas like *The Day After*, but for a lot of people in the real world increased odds—not certainty—of leukemia down the line just didn't override the age-old desire to eat. The more daring had started filtering back into the Dead Zones around the missile farms within a couple of months after the bombs quit falling.

Of course, the resident or the casual visitor had to keep alert, and a film badge was better. There were occasional pockets of emitter-contaminated dust concentrated enough to be real dangerous if you stumbled into them.

It was the half hour before the sun actually got it up, a perfect time to attack if that's what they were going to do. That wasn't the idea. If Reuben McKendree saw immense black pillars of smoke climbing the sky from his intended destination, he would likely find another.

"Funny," said Sam from the turret. "Looks real dry hereabouts."

"Maybe it ain't *rained* so much around here. I mean, call me an ignorant city slicker, but that makes sense to *me*."

"The southeastern corner of the state's been quite dry this year," Cohen confirmed.

"How are we going to play this, Billy?" asked Casey, coming forward rubbing sleep and the overly long dark-blond hair McKay was always on him to get cut out of his eyes. *He'd* been racked out on a mattress in back all night, lucky bastard. But then, he did most of the driving, so it evened out.

"We drive right up," McKay said. "If they want to be reasonable, we talk, get everything worked out: *let us take McKendree when he comes or we'll kick your asses, drink your beer, and burn your damn huts down.* If they're like everybody else in the Equality State and shoot at us on sight, then we do all that anyway and probably have to take another crack at our friend Reuben farther down the line. Fair enough?"

"It has a certain simplicity to it," Cohen said, arranging his granny glasses on his nose.

"And don't go making me regret not leaving you in Douglas for the Staties to troll in."

Cohen blinked at him. "I'm not sure why you did."

"Neither am I," McKay said. "I'm mostly playing this by ear."

"Always the inspirational leader," Sam said. "Whoa, look up ahead."

Jessie came forward, tying her kinky hair back with somebody's OD rag. "Where are we?" she asked muzzily.

"There, basically," McKay said. There was your basic roadblock right in front of them, organic enough to satisfy even the environmentally conscious Team: a big dead tree with strong dry branches poking out like sea-urchin spines.

He braked. "Here goes nothing," he remarked, and popped the overhead hatch.

He stood up into cool pine-edged mountain morning air. *It's so fresh and pure you could just puke.*

"Good morning, there," he called. "Hello?" He tried to sound nonthreatening. It wasn't easy.

There was a pause, and a stir in the underbrush to either side of the track. It occurred to him he might have hung a Hard Corps IV armor vest on before sticking himself out the hatch. Oh, well, with his luck the bad guys would just shoot him in the head anyway.

There were two of them. McKay's first thought was that they were awfully small, dwarfed by the ancient bolt-action Czech Mausers they carried. *What, they got kids guarding the place?*

They started talking to him, then, in these funny high-pitched nasal voices. He realized they weren't kids at all.

"What the fuck, over?" he muttered. "They're *dinks*. This can't be right."

"*Billy?*" said Tom Rogers's voice in the middle of his skull. "*It's all set up. Come on ahead.*"

So somebody had tried to build a little mountain resort sort of thing in a private enclave in the Medicine Bow National Forest. There were all these half-timbered houses with high-pitched roofs in the middle of the woods with a stream running past them to the Platte, and they were all filled with wiry little Asians with singsong voices. It looked as if the North Vietnamese army had conquered the Land of Oz.

Ambient radiation was still enough higher than background that this place was off the list of the trendiest vacationers, but for frugal, hardworking Southeast Asian immigrants it was, basically, paradise. The original developers had had in mind lots of outdoor recreational things for their guests, in part to make up for the fact that this wasn't a ski basin. There had been tennis courts, riding stables, broad fields set aside for softball and golf.

Now cows grazed on the golf course, pigs quartered in the tennis courts, and the riding arena and exercise field were planted in neat little patches of beans and gene-tailored enhanced-protein maize that would grow damn near anywhere. This wasn't good rice country, which meant a change in diet for the settlers. But what they did get to grow had a better yield per man-hour than their traditional staple, even in a comparatively dry spring, and recently they'd actually been able to barter for rice being moved along I-25 by truckers and traders.

The kitchen was airy and cheery and immaculately clean, like a television vision of the perfect vacation home from McKay's sixties childhood. Only the lingering smell of alien spices challenged the gingerbread upper-middle-American profile.

Their host, Thoanh, had laid a square of white plastic on his kitchen table. Tom Rogers spread his discovery on the sheet in a shaft of slanting morning sunlight with the air of a magician fanning a deck of cards.

McKay stared at the debris. At first it looked like somebody's Walkman stereo had been run over by an eighteen-wheeler and dumped in an incinerator: some melted plastic, circuit boards, and twisted metal.

And then the pieces magically filled out and assembled themselves in his mind like a neat computer graphic by Industrial Light and Magic.

"Jumping Jesus on roller skates," he said. "Where did you find these?"

"Ruins of the White Castle."

"What is it, man?" Casey asked. He had on a Hooters tour cap today. Where he found them, Christ knew. McKay didn't even know where he *carried* them.

"Give me a break," McKay said. "You guys are supposed to be *Guardians*. Did you sleep through training?"

Jessie had picked up a random chunk and was turning it over in her fingers. "Gallium arsenide/gallium-aluminum arsenide superlattice semiconductor components. Wow. Radical stuff; EMP wouldn't *begin* to touch it."

"You weren't jivin' about that wanting-to-be-a-quantum-mechanic stuff, were you?" McKay said.

She looked at him with eyes narrowed to long slits. "No."

"Wait a minute," Sloan said, "what am I using for brains?"

"Good question," McKay and Jessica said at the same time. He raised an eyebrow at her.

"I can't resist a cheap joke," she explained.

"It's a radio-controlled command detonator," Sloan said.

"Congratulations. You win the all-expense-paid vacation in lovely Tierra del Fuego."

"Where did you say you found this?" Sam asked. He sank abruptly into a white vinyl and tubular aluminum dinette chair.

"White Castle," Tom said. "Had to dig around for almost two days."

Jessie Turner had sunk down to her knees. She had one cheek pressed to the Formica tabletop. Tears ran from her eyes to pool on the cool surface.

"Those people," she whispered. "Those poor, poor people."

"What's going on?" Casey asked. "What's everybody upset about?"

"Everyone is all right, yes?" said Thoanh, their host, bustling in from the living room to which he'd discreetly retired. He was five feet tall and wore a Caterpillar Tractor hat on his neat iron gray brush cut. A white tee shirt, khaki shorts, and cigarette dangling from thin-lipped mouth completed the outfit.

"Yeah, we're fine," McKay said with a wave of his hand. Rogers said something unintelligible. Thoanh bobbed his head in relief and vanished.

"So, like, I'm slow, all right?" Casey said, sounding peevish. "What's the matter?"

McKay snapped his fingers twice. The thoughts were coming quicker than he liked. "Jessica. Listen up, Sparky. Did you ever have a visitor at the Coleman place, looked like a dirty duffel bag, dark long hair with some gray in it, liked to fool around with explosives?"

She raised her head, wiping the corners of her eyes. "Greasy kind of guy?" He nodded. "Sounds like Dalton. He's been there off and on. Now that you mention it, he brought some antitank rockets and was showing people how to use them just a couple of weeks ago. Before that they'd just talked about the things and read manuals on how to use them and all that, but they never had any.''

Sloan looked McKay in the eye across the scatter of parts. *Dalton?* he mouthed.

And then he and Casey Wilson both said, *"Dooley!"*

McKay sat down with his arms folded over the back of a chair. "You know, we've gotten ourselves well and truly set up. Thomas, you have let me down. Your instincts never should have let you come here.''

Tom didn't say anything. He just went to the window and stood staring out past the plastic tub full of well water in the sink at the surrounding mountains. Excuses were not in his makeup.

Especially when there was no call to make them. "Shit," McKay said. "I'm sorry. We all walked into this with our eyes open, and I'm the one in charge.''

Samuel Cohen walked in the back door with his hat in his hand. "What a beautiful morning," he said. "What did Lieutenant Rogers learn?''

"Your man McKendree is off the hook," McKay said.

"But we're not," Tom Rogers said. He pointed out the window.

A gray ball of smoke was rolling into the sky perhaps a kilometer away across a wooded ridge. Another one followed it a few degrees to the right as a low rumble reached their ears and voices in the street began to chatter in consternation.

They ran outside. The houses in the refugee hamlet all had window boxes full of brightly colored flowers, giving the place a sort of jaunty retirement-home air. The *cracks* and smoke billows were marching around the place pretty much in order. Occasionally a gap appeared, but it was almost inevitably filled in a few beats late.

"Redundant firing systems on radio control," said Tom in that approving tone of voice he reserved for a job well done. Even if what was getting well done was his personal goose.

McKay estimated they were about a hundred meters apart, at a consistent radius of a kilometer. Sixty charges, then, incendiaries.

"They didn't just whip this up since we got here," he said. "They've been planning this party a long time. I think we got a last-minute invite.''

"I don't mean to intrude past my area of expertise," Cohen said, "but hadn't we better *do something*?"

Sloan's shoulders slumped. "What *can* we do? We're trapped."

"We ain't dead yet," McKay said. "Even with all kinda back-ups they couldn't have ringed us perfectly. Should we try to find a hole in the ring of fire?"

"Too dry," Sam said. "Even if it's clear now, by the time we reached it it probably wouldn't be. And if we guessed wrong that would be it."

Off at the riding stables the horses were beginning to whicker nervously, scenting smoke. *Now I'm never gonna get to see dink cowboys,* McKay thought.

"But the nearest trees are two hundred meters away," Cohen said. "Will the fire necessarily even reach us?"

"You don't understand," Sam said. "There're a lot of very hot-burning incendiaries going off almost at once, with plenty of dry underbrush for fuel. We're talking about ideal conditions for a firestorm. Dresden time."

He turned to Rogers. "Do I have the essentials, Tom?" Rogers nodded.

"Well, we sure as hell ain't gonna stand here and wait to get our eyeballs French fried. Casey, fire up the car. Shit, that wasn't a good choice of words, was it?"

Casey took off, scattering chickens picking for bugs in the flowerbed next to the house. Jessica clutched McKay's arm. "These *people*! You can't leave them! What about them?"

Actually, McKay was perfectly capable of leaving the locals to their own devices if that's what it took to keep his team intact and unkindled, but then, he was a cold motherfucker. But— "By now our good buddies from SID have dropped about twenty big trees across the one fucking road out of here. We can't get out that way, which means we can't just blow away. We're in this mess together."

Tom Rogers had a pinch of dirt from the flowerbed and tossed it in the air. "Wind out of the northwest," he said. "Yep. They're setting off additional charges that way."

"But wait—the fire blows with the wind, of course. Why are they setting off charges downwind?"

"Hammer and anvil, Sam," Tom said.

McKay was scratching at his chin, trying to think on his feet.

This wasn't so much different from a surprise attack. The key to command when it all hit the fan was to make decisions *now*. If any of them happened to be right, that was like an additional benefit.

"Who the hell knows about forest fires? Can we like knock down enough trees for a firebreak with One or something?"

"Take too long to do enough to make a difference, Billy," Casey said over the communicators. *"Besides, if there really is a firestorm, it'll jump any break we make."* California kid Casey knew that sort of thing in his marrow, the way he knew earthquakes, and had been pressed into brushfire-fighting detail a couple of times and volunteered a few more.

"Right. Tom, tell Thoanh to get his people on the road this second. They can carry what they can grab, but we leave any stragglers. Horses and four-wheel vehicles."

"What about the animals?" Jessica asked.

"They're gonna have to take their chances. If Thoanh's people wanna try to herd cows and pigs that's their damn business. We ain't stopping for livestock."

He gazed to the northwest, where tall orange flames were already beginning to leap up into the blue morning sky. "We got us some serious debts to pay. Payback's a mother."

CHAPTER
TWENTY-TWO ─────────────────

"Burn, baby, burn," Dooley said. His roots were in the sixties; he was older than he looked. Of course, he'd been something of a child prodigy, both as a blaster and as an *agent provocateur*. He'd lost his cherry as a Weather Underground cadreman, helping convince your more vocal black radical splinter groups to progress from the rhetoric-slinging stage to the bomb-throwing stage.

Of course, some of the high-explosive compounds he taught them to make were not exactly *stable* at the temperatures he had them working them, and some of the timing devices he gave them were preset to go off at a kind of surprising time—like, the instant they were fixed to explosive charges, say. The common late-sixties, early-seventies news stories about bomb factories suddenly wiping themselves off the map or would-be terrorists blowing themselves through the roofs of their VW bugs were generally the result of native clumsiness and stupidity. But not always.

Now he stood just meters from his latest masterpiece, this wall of lovely, lovely orange flame, and the heat on his sweat-soaked face was like a lover's touch. Dooley loved his work, and he was an artist.

The smell of gasoline and plastic-explosive residue filled his sinuses and veins like a blast of blue-flake. Using high explosives together with gasoline was an art form in itself—the explosives tended to blow out the fire, and while gasoline fumes were themselves high-explosive, they had to be contained, which wasn't practicable in the woods. Dooley's solution was a two-part package. A special gelled-fuel home brew of gasoline, medicinal alcohol, drain cleaner, and lanolin, splashed but not extinguished by a chunk of C-4, did nicely at getting the underbrush going. Hot-burning bags of improvised paraffin-sawdust incendiary fixed to the boles ignited the trees, which were tougher customers.

Instant firestorm. The best part was the Guardians would've guessed by now what fate had in store for them.

It was appropriate that their involvement as pawns in the big game of suppressing dissent and eradicating unassimilable ethnic populations should begin and end with a masterpiece of his. He smiled as he swigged his Bud longneck, and foam ran down into his beard.

Those poor dumb White Action! peckerwoods. They were so eager to have me look over their explosives, their pilfered dynamite and homemade Claymores. His credentials had been immaculate, of course. He had come highly recommended by the network of radical farm groups. Unlike his Teammates, he hadn't started out in drug enforcement. He had done some contract work for the DEA, arranging loud and terminal surprises for a couple of bush-league drug barons in Ecuador, and two domestic journalists who just couldn't bring themselves to buy the media party line that the war on drugs justified any means. One of the latter jobs had brought him into contact with Wyoming's newly formed SID. It was natural for him to take up with them when his original employers went abruptly out of business.

He was even ready to forgive the White Action! fools for not scragging the Guardians like they were supposed to. That had been the original idea; SID got to use the Guardians as a prop to build up the Rube McKendree threat—threat building was a lot tougher than it was before the War, when you had the media eager to promote any hysteria the government asked them to, but the deaths of four of America's most prominent post-Holocaust celebs should buy a lot of credibility for their boogeyman.

Then the stupid wool hats *missed*. And the rest of their rocketeers—four of the fuckers—had either jackrabbited or gotten offed. Christ. Even ghetto niggers and spoiled dumb rich white kids in 1969 had done better than that.

But it all worked out fine. The Guardians played the expanded role Sawtelle and Brant had cooked up for them to the hilt. That Brant was an uptight little turkey, but Dooley had to appreciate a fellow genius at work.

And now the Guardians were going to fry, heroically unable to save a village of seventy hapless Asians from arson. The unfortunate victims of Reuben McKendree's most monstrous crime yet. Even Forrie Smith would play that to jerk tears on his radio and TV networks, and he couldn't stand dinks any more than he could Guardians.

Beautiful. He raised the bottle in salute. He couldn't see through the flames at all, now. They were getting too close for comfort. He drained the longneck, tucked it in the ripstop bag slung from his shoulder. He hated litterbugs.

He turned and stopped. A man was standing in the brush thirty meters upslope from him.

"Who the hell are you?" he asked, angry at being startled, feeling soiled that his moment of private triumph had been seen by another. Not even his buddies, whom he was to rendezvous with two klicks upwind, had been privileged to see him consummate his act of fire.

Dooley moved closer, slowly but inexorably. He had a nasty little H&K P7 stuck in an inside-the-pants holster in back, under his photojournalist's vest. He hitched his thumbs into the belt at his hips, to have his hand handy to the piece without alarming the stranger.

"I am no one," the stranger said in a deep, guttural voice.

An Indian? He was a big motherfucker, dressed in dark green camouflage pants and jacket. Black hair hung over either shoulder in thick braids. His head was tilted forward, so that his face was shadowed by the brim of a black hat with the crown pushed up and a feather in the band. An eagle feather—Brant'd give him a bounty if he brought this coyote's hide in.

"What the hell do you want, Chief?" he asked, inching his right hand back toward the P7. The Indian looked unarmed except for a big Bowie in a buckskin sheath at his hip.

The Indian raised his head. Dooley froze.

The man's face was painted white. Mime white. The white of

a Kabuki performer's face. It changed him to something inhuman.

"I love you," the stranger said. "I want to help you."

His right hand came up. A highway flare fizzed into magenta life in it. He held it up for a moment as if he wanted Dooley to read the brand name or something. Then he threw it down by the toes of his black and green combat boots.

"What the fuck—?"

A sheet of flame *whooshed* up between him and Dooley. The dense, dry brush caught instantaneously. Beyond the Indian, Dooley saw the extra plastic jerry cans of gas he'd brought to insure that he built a good head of flame to sweep down on the former resort. They lay empty now on the forest mat. Seen through a curtain of heated orange air they seemed to dance.

"Have a nice day," the Indian said, looking into his terror-wide eyes. "Hello."

He turned and walked away, leaving Dooley alone with his screams.

With a *whoomp!* and a loud crackle the crown of a lordly ponderosa pine exploded in flames high over McKay's head. Riding shotgun on the turret of Mobile One, he stared up in openmouthed astonishment.

"What in the *hell*? We're not to the fire yet!"

"Treetopper, Billy," Casey said from the driver's seat. *"Crown fire. Moves a whole bunch quicker than, like, a regular fire. Doesn't threaten us unless it brings on the firestorm quicker."*

"Good news is everywhere." McKay looked ahead at the apparently unbroken Berlin wall of flame toward which they were sloshing along the bed of the stream, and figured that some days it didn't fucking pay to get out of bed. Even if you hadn't goddam *been* to bed.

His eyes were burning from the smoke beginning to congeal in the air along the creekbed. It went up his nose and down his throat like shards of broken glass. Soon it was going to be time to pull up the respirator mask slung around his neck. Some of the villagers had already dipped rags in the stream and tied them over their faces.

If there were an Olympic event in being refugees, the Vietnamese would be the team to beat for the gold, year in, year out. Thoanh's people were top-seeded survivors in general, with a heavy specialization in fleeing disaster. While the Guardians and cohorts had been discussing their plight, the immigrants had been moving quickly, purposefully, and on the whole calmly, as if they'd done this a dozen times before. They *had*.

Two vehicles groaned and churned up white and khaki foam in line behind Mobile One, an elderly Blazer and a beefy Suzuki pickup, piled high with important supplies: medicines, guns and ammunition, tents, chickens in cages, and an immensely fat brick-colored pig, lashed to the apex of the heap in the pickup bed. What few personal effects the villagers were bringing out they carried on heads or backs, trudging thigh-deep between vertically cut banks higher than the head of the tallest of them.

Several old women drove pigs along the stream with stripped-sapling withes. And McKay was getting his wish after all: three of the refugees were mounted, two men and a pretty teenaged girl with one eye, towing the other horses in prancing, eye-rolling strings behind them. The well-dressed Vietnamese cowboy or -girl was wearing shorts, tee shirt, baseball cap, and black high-topped sneakers this season, it seemed.

The whole exodus was being carried out with quiet professionalism. "I wish I was as calm as they *look*," Sloan remarked, sticking his head out the top hatch above the ESO seat.

"You'll be plenty calm when a big burning branch comes down and mashes your brains in. Get the hell inside and shut the door. Say, and while I think of it, toss me up a Fritz first." The Guardians carried army-issue Kevlar helmets with them, but almost never wore them. They were too cumbersome and cut down your hearing too much for special-duty troops. But now might be a good time to have one on.

"Fire's coming up," Casey reported.

From ahead came a frightened lowing of cows. As much of the village's stock as feasible had been chased into the stream ahead of Mobile One, which was shepherding them along like the world's biggest, best-armored collie dog. So far the beasts were more afraid of them than the flames on all sides.

"No shit?" McKay said, clamping his M60 between his knees while he fastened his helmet. "It ain't gonna get any better. Drive on, my man."

It was like the first ride they'd build when they opened a Disney World in hell. Tunnel o' Fire: *oh* yeah. With the brush alight at their bases all the trees were burning from the ground up, which meant they were going to burn hot for quite some time. And there was no telling how far it went—the breeze had been rising all morning, and was freshening noticeably.

Firestorm coming on? McKay glanced back along the ragtag procession. The sky was black behind, with the flames dancing stark against it, silhouetting a last glimpse of the peaked roofs of the defunct resort.

Mobile One entered the roaring corridor through the heart of the fire. The heat seemed to press in on all sides, as if he were in some sort of infernal pressure chamber.

He started coughing, thought to pull up his mask. The stinging sensation in his eyes diminished, and the rushing-wind noise of his breath began to compete with the voice of the fire.

They were in a vast cathedral of flame, soaring pillars that rose and closed into Gothic arches that blotted the sky above. Air currents darted along the banks like frightened animals, stirring up clouds of the forest-floor trash, which flared into individual flakes of flame like burning snow when the wind swept them into the fire. The trees were burning and the brush was burning and the humus mat was burning and it seemed the soil itself, the very earth, was burning.

"These eco-freaks have fuck of a way of showing how they feel about Mother Earth. I guess you only hurt the one you love."

"Forest fires are part of the natural process, McKay," Sloan said.

"Yeah. So's Bambi getting eaten alive by wolves. So're the weak dying off. This is how your big hero Brant is building his brave new world."

He looked back along the column. Some of the Vietnamese were chattering excitedly, pointing and craning up into the nave of hell above.

Others dabbed their eyes with their face rags, bending as far as they dared without upsetting the loads they carried on heads or backs to splash cooling water in their eyes. The old lady swineherds were falling back; their charges were being difficult about entering the fire tunnel.

McKay couldn't really blame the damned things. On the other hand, he knew what was coming up behind, and they didn't.

He raised his mask and waved at the Blazer following immediately behind. Thoanh stuck his head out on its scrawny neck.

"Tell those people to let them pigs go if they won't come," he shouted.

"Pardon?"

"The pigs! Let 'em go!"

Thoanh bobbed his head and turned around to rattle out orders in Vietnamese. McKay practically leapt out of his skin as the Browning .50 woke up beneath him with an ear-shattering bellow. The vibration practically shook him off into the drink.

CHAPTER
TWENTY-THREE ————————————

"What the fuck do you idiots think you're doing!" His bellow was hopelessly garbled by his insectile mask, and was pretty inaudible inside the hull anyway, but the larynx mike got his point across.

"Sorry, Billy," Tom said from the turret. *"Some of the cows were trying to turn back. Had to get 'em headed the right way again."*

"Warn a body next time, for Jesus' sake. *Ooh,* shit."

"What, Billy?" Casey asked.

"Look for yourself. A fucking tree. That's why the damned cows were trying to turn around."

It was a big mother, as fat as these ponderosas ever got, fallen long enough since to have become embedded in the bank. The cows could just get under it—he had the impression they were too fucking stupid to duck beneath it if it were lower—but seeing it ahead had spooked some of them.

Mobile One's huge diesel developed torque to spare, and they probably could have bashed through the son of bitch, except it just cleared the upper deck, and McKay did not want to see just how well seated the turret was.

"Fuck. Now we gotta ditch the vehicles."

"Let me out, Billy?"

"Sure, Tom." He sat there a moment, feeling the sweat pouring off of every square inch of his body except maybe the soles of his feet, thinking how he was getting hotter now than he had in the midst of his own man-made inferno in Sauget. Only then he'd had his neat asbestos suit—

"Billy."

"Oh. Sorry." He shifted to the deck aft of the turret so Tom could get out the top hatch.

The former Green Beret came swarming out with strap charges over either shoulder. They consisted of little nylon pouches of Composition C-4 sewn into a kind of belt and linked with det cord. They were standard antiterrorist gear, a quick and dirty way to get through obstacles such as doors, walls, and floors.

—Or trees. Tom set the fuse on each to command-detonation and looped them over the log, a half meter or so inward from either bank. Then he came sloshing back to stand behind the car, yelling and gesturing for the people to get back and *down*.

The heads of Thoanh and his driver vanished beneath the dashboard of the Blazer. "You too, Billy," Tom said.

"What? Oh." He ducked behind the one-man turret.

With the fire making movie-dinosaur noises on all directions, the multiple crack of the charges going didn't seem that loud to McKay. A few bits of debris fell into the water.

A squealing clamor from behind brought his head around in time to see the cowgirl's horse rear and go into the water on top of her with a colossal splash. He and Tom raced toward the rear of the column without even checking the outcome of Tom's handiwork.

One of the strings of horses had panicked and was racing back along the stream. The girl's mount fought to its feet, pulled bodily along by the nylon rope fastened to its saddle, and then was off and running to certain doom with its buddies.

The girl didn't come up. McKay and Tom bulldozed through frightened refugees and plunged into the mud-bloom in the water where she'd gone down.

McKay's hand found her first. She'd had the air knocked out of her, and from the way she came to life with a chilling shriek as he pulled her up by the ankle—it was what he'd grabbed—it was apparent her leg was broken.

"We gotta get her back to the car," Tom said. "I can't do anything for her here, and anyway we have to move."

The girl rode on McKay's back, her face white as paper and her black hair trailing down like seaweed, apologizing in endless broken English for having lost her string of horses. The other two cowboys were hurriedly untying the lead ropes from their own saddles. They'd hold the things in their hands from here on in.

As they walked forward an old lady toppled into the water. "Smoke and heat got to her," Tom reported, helping her up.

"Shit. Bring her. Tell 'em, anybody having trouble we can try to pile on Mobile One. But we ain't stopping from here on out."

Tom got the girl into the car where Jessie and Samuel Cohen could help him get an inflatable cast on her broken thigh. McKay swarmed up the back of the car and peered over the turret.

The treetrunk had been neatly severed—well, not *neatly*—at either end. The center section had dropped into the water and out of sight. At Casey's suggestion McKay dropped off again while Mobile One rumbled forward and trampled the trunk into the creek-bottom mud, far enough so the trucks behind could get over it.

He climbed up again, helped half a dozen children and old folks up onto the car. With all of them clinging like baby opossums to their mother's back, the V-450 grunted under way again.

McKay felt something strange. He couldn't identify it until he raised his mask again. There was a wind in his face, and while it was hot as a sirocco it was cool by comparison to what he'd been kidding himself he was getting used to breathing. He relayed the news to his buddies inside.

"Fire behind us is eating air so fast it's creating a vacuum and sucking air up the creek from in front of us," Sloan said. *"Or at least that seems likely."*

"That means a firestorm's about to start, right?"

"Or has already started," Casey said.

"Great. All we need—"

A branch broke away from high overhead and fell blazing into the stream just in front of the car with a demonic hiss of steam. An old lady with a seamed parchment face screamed in alarm, lost her grip, and slipped into the water.

McKay slipped down the side of the turret to help her. Two lagging cows were caught on this side of the burning bough. They came bellowing back along the right side of the car. The one in the lead caught the old lady with a shoulder as her outstretched fingertips touched McKay's and she fell right under the hooves of the second. The water boiled briefly red.

Cursing, McKay snatched his machine gun off the tip of the turret, braced its butt against the armorplate, and fired a burst. Thoanh and his driver dived below the dash again as huge gouts of water fountained up in front of the Blazer.

The second burst knocked the two cows down as they stampeded past the Blazer, seconds before they would have burst in among refugees trapped between walls of earth and fire.

"Can't we pick up the pace?" he demanded, clambering back on top. A steady hail of flaming junk was falling from above now. The fiery tunnel ahead of them seemed to have no end.

Came a howling, climbing to a demon shriek. The wind in their faces rose to a gale. The flames to either side seemed to reach inward for them like demon claws, only to be sucked back and away by the furious wind.

"Firestorm!" Casey yelled, and even vibrating in his skull the words barely won out over the wind from hell.

—Or *into* hell. McKay looked back above the bent heads of the refugees. The tunnel seemed to be collapsing behind them. He hoped it was illusion.

A shrieking, protracted crack. McKay turned to see a hundred-foot ponderosa on the bank right beside Mobile One, burning along its entire length, falling in what seemed slow motion. He yelled at the refugees to clear the car's decks.

But the wind had the tree. It missed the V-450 and the Blazer, and slammed down on the cab of the Suzi pickup. Instantly the truck was engulfed in flames.

McKay stood up to wave at the people wading behind and beside the truck to drop everything and run like hell. The wind grabbed him and pitched him ass over teakettle into the muddy water behind the car's square tail.

McKay's yell echoed from the speakers inside the car and inside his buddies' heads. Casey was bent over the wheel, peering into the inferno ahead. Tom was finishing the work of immobilizing the injured girl's leg. It took Sam Sloan about half a second to realize that he was the one not doing anything real constructive. Who the hell was he going to talk to, Smokey the Bear?

He came out of his seat, threw open the side hatch, and promptly fell in the water himself as the wind hit him.

He managed to keep his head up. Through the flames of the burning tree he saw a stick-thin Vietnamese shinny up the mound of baggage piled on the back of the trapped pickup, slashing at the bindings with a big knife. Squealing in terror the enormous pig leapt into the water.

Then the wind plucked the man off the baggage pile and whipped him away back along the creek.

He saw McKay's bullet-shaped head pop out of the water right in front of the Blazer's front bumper. He yelled a warning to Thoanh and his driver, who were already craning forward looking for McKay, and ran back to help haul him sputtering to his feet.

McKay came up spewing water like something from an old Warner Brothers cartoon. "Fuck," he sputtered, "that *wind*! I never seen anything like it." He reeled for Mobile One, dragging his M60 stubbornly by the strap.

One of the riders was fighting for control of his horse, which was rearing up out of the water right in front of the truck with the blazing tree across it. A little girl was clipped by a flying forehoof and vanished in the surging water.

Horse and rider lost it at the same time. With the impulse that sends horses running back into a burning barn the animal lunged abruptly for the bank, scrabbling furiously at a place where the cut had partially collapsed. The rider, bareheaded now, stayed with it, still fighting for control.

It was a mistake. The horse gained the top of the bank.

He and his rider simply burst into flame. *Bang*, like that.

McKay and Sloan stared. It was like something from a Spielberg movie, horrible and surreal. The inrush of air sucked toward the center of the firestorm had whipped the flames to either side of the creek to an incredible temperature.

The screams pierced walls of noise and shock. "Aw, fuck. Fuck no," McKay said. He brought the Maremont up at his hip, worked the bolt, hosed the burning horse and rider as they thrashed together in a final awful dance on the burning bank.

The Suzuki's gas tank blew, blocking the stream with a blossom of flaming gasoline. The people caught behind cried out in terror. An old woman screamed and tried to hurl herself back, stretching her arm as if she could somehow pull a loved one through the wall of fire. A young woman in a UCLA sweatshirt restrained her.

McKay pounded on the rear armor of Mobile One. "*Move,* dammit. We got to *keep moving!*"

A forest fire can move faster than a man can run, depending on wind and fuel. A firestorm cannot.

A firestorm is a self-limiting system. It creates its own weather; all winds rush in toward the center, where the fire is hottest, greediest. It squats in one place, gradually feeding upon itself, burning until nothing remotely inflammable remains.

On that morning the northwest wind was blowing at about fifteen kilometers per hour, gusting past twenty. As slowly as Mobile One was forced to move along the sole available escape route, they could probably not have outrun a forest fire, even if they left the refugees to their fates.

But they finally reached the point at which the firestorm began to collapse upon itself, and so escaped.

"Fuck," Billy McKay said. "Fuck, fuck, fuck, fuck, *fuck. Fuck!*"

He should have been doing things like lying exhausted on the now-clear banks of the stream, breathing in huge lungfuls of blessedly cool air. Instead he gave the cleats of Mobile One's right front tire another mighty kick.

"*Ow!* Well, fuck." He decided he had probably broken his toe, steel reinforcement or no, and sat down in the water to contemplate the unfairness of life.

They had come through the fire. Some of them, anyway. The Guardians, Jessica Turner, Cohen, and perhaps thirty-five of the Vietnamese, most of whom had had nothing but wet rags and their own determination to pull them through.

Mobile One had served nobly. It had forged determinedly up the stream, protecting the Guardians and as many refugees as they'd been able to cram inside with the filters of its NBC system. It had led the way beyond the burnt-out fringe of the contracting firestorm, out of the forest to the plain, beyond the zone of lethal winds.

Then it coughed once, farted twice, and just died.

One string of horses had made it out. Thoanh had them hitched to the Blazer, which was blockaded in the stream by the moribund Mobile One. The bank was lower here, but the Blazer's engine wasn't up to extricating it unassisted.

"We're gonna, like, need parts, Billy," Casey's voice said from the dark interior of Mobile One. All the hatches stood wide open, airing out the smoke. The NBC filters would have cut almost all of it, but they'd kept opening the hatches during the run through the tunnel of fire.

"Don't tell me this, Casey. Give me some good news."

"We have to make a run to a cache."

"We have to go and make some people eat shit and die while they still think we're dead."

"No way. Not in Mobile One, man."

He was about to complain some more, but he noticed silence had set in. The refugees weren't chirping at the horses and each other. Even the Blazer's racing engine subsided to a grumpy mutter.

McKay looked up.

A man was standing at the top of a rise beside the creek. A tall man in camouflaged clothing, who wore a black hat with a feather in the band. He held the reins of a dun horse with a bridle padded in sheepskin. He was gazing at McKay with the imperturbability of a statue. His face was white, as if he'd started to make himself up like a clown and then forgotten to paint on the exaggerated features and apply the rubber-ball nose.

"And who the hell," McKay asked from the middle of the creek, "are you?"

"I have no name."

"Great," McKay said. "Just what I need. A cryptic Indian."

The newcomer turned his white-painted face toward the cloud of smoke that squatted above the former resort like a fire-giant from Norse mythology. Its howling voice was audible even here.

"The ones who did not start that fire were your friends. I helped one, gave him life; I have helped them before."

"Tom," McKay subvocalized, *"get out here, Tom. I've got an armed nutcase, and if I shoot him Sam Sloan and the lawyer are gonna claim he was out of season."*

There was a by-God cowboy Winchester in a scuffed leather scabbard tied to the front of the dun's saddle. But the long sealskin case rigged to the rear was the sort that would contain a finely tuned, high-powered, thoroughly modern rifle. There was a mother of a knife hung at the man's hip. The guy's weird speech and ensemble were nudging McKay toward a notion that made no kind of sense at all.

Tom and Sam both came out, and then Jessie Turner stuck her pigtailed head out, blinking in the sunlight.

"You shot my brother," the stranger said.

"I beg your fucking pardon," McKay said. "We've shot *lots* of people's brothers. You wanna refresh my memory?"

"Those men did not shoot him. That's why I did not kill them."

"I got it," Sam Sloan said. He snapped his fingers and hunkered down on his long runner's legs, which almost sat him in the water. "Took me a while, but I've got it."

"What the hell are you talking about?"

"Saying the opposite of what he means, painting his face white. A Crazy Dog Wishing to Die, Billy, like that old man said. A Plains warrior who's taken a holy vow to die on a quest, usually a mission of revenge, I think. Like a Contrary. Didn't you ever see *Little Big Man*?"

"No. Did you hit your head on something back there?"

"You are wrong," the tall man said.

"Yeah," McKay said, "that's what I reckoned. Sloan, maybe Tom oughta put you on sick call—"

"He is not Samuel Sloan. You are not William McKay. You did not speak to my brother."

"Oh, no. Don't say shit like that. I can't handle it today."

"I will not lead you to Reuben McKendree." Jessie gasped at the name. "You must not follow me."

He turned and led the horse down the far side of the hill.

CHAPTER
TWENTY-FOUR ———————————————

Nicholas Brant gazed out the window, which reached from the floor to the angled ceiling. The moon had sunk into the Bighorns half an hour ago. In the darkness was his ranch, if a man could be said to own a part of the land. He smiled at the prospect. It was like claiming to own a piece of the night.

In another sense all of Wyoming was soon to be his. In trust for the Mother, of course.

"It is a pity," he said, turning back to the mellow light of his study, "that our colleague cannot be here to accept our accolades for doing his job so well. Have you no idea what happened?"

The study was on the second floor. It was furnished in a Spartan, somewhat heavy style: dense, dark wooden furniture, chairs supplied with thin earth-tone cushions, a desk set against the wall with a computer discreetly tucked in an alcove beneath a shelf of books, more bookshelves occupying most of the wall space. There was a good deal of greenery in heavy wood planters, but no paintings, no photographs of Brant glad-handing celebrities, no personal effects. It was a room for a man who had little use for adornment, who liked his gratifications either more subtle or more elemental.

Toby Sawtelle shrugged. "Only to a point. He didn't make

the rendezvous. We went in to look for him, but the firestorm was kicking in, and the wind was dangerous.'' He shook his head. ''Whew. You can't imagine what one of those things is like.''

''Perhaps he'll join us yet,'' Brant said in a sudden glow of optimism. His speech was feathered at the edges; he was a trifle drunk.

''It's been two days, Doctor.''

Brant's mild euphoria vanished in a flare of irritation. He wasn't used to being contradicted. Still, he knew the need to treat his lieutenant circumspectly, as one might a pet leopard. He suppressed his annoyance.

''You believe he had a mishap?''

Sawtelle shrugged. He was wearing a uniform shirt, tan with epaulets, that set off his rangy build well.

''He was good at what he did. But he could be a touch on the careless side. He must have made some miscalculation that caught up with him.''

''Ah well.'' Brant sipped brandy from a snifter. ''Fortunately we have made no such mistakes. Everything is going better than we could possibly have hoped.''

Sawtelle frowned. ''I beg your pardon, sir. But what about Chip and Stew? What happened to them was not exactly . . . foreseen.''

Brant raised his big head, and for a moment a strange black light glittered in his eyes. ''It's our Mother's will that we succeed. Our plans are moving forward. Why cavil? Why raise incidental points?''

''My men aren't incidental points, Doctor.''

''Perhaps not. But they accepted the necessity of sacrifice. And we know too well how prominent a feature random violence is of post-Holocaust life. As if it weren't *before* the War.''

He crossed to an antique oaken sideboard, poured a brandy for the police lieutenant.

''Now, let us put all that behind us and drink to a new to-morrow!''

''Hey,'' Lew Polidor said. ''You guys know why women got legs, don't you?''

A field cricket trilled in the night not far away. The two troopers looked at each other under the brims of their Smokey the

Bear hats. They wore black uniforms, combat boots, slung M16s. Neither could see much of the other's face out here in the darkness along the wire, but the gesture was the important thing.

"I don't know, Lew," said Taylor, the one on the right, just a beat tardy. The skinny, high-strung man with the brown hair hanging in his eyes was just a patrolman, same as they were. But since Special Investigations came in before the One-Day War they'd had it drilled into them that any SID man outranked any regular highway patrol grunt. And any member of Brant's hand-picked Team outranked all the rest of SID. It would have been *Mr. Polidor*, but this one liked to pretend he was just one of the guys. "Why do women got legs?"

His buddy Buckhalter grinned into the shadow beneath his hatbrim, relieved he hadn't had to take the heat by responding. Out here on Brant's personal spread in the low Bighorns west of Kennedy City, a man didn't ask any questions at all. To the Team, *everybody* was a suspect. And even before the War happened suspects who didn't play nice with the Team had a tendency to disappear. The best thing to say to one of them was jack shit.

"So they don't leave a trail of slime!" Polidor jackknifed, slapping his skinny thighs, his slung CAR-15 bouncing around on his back.

Buckhalter convulsed. Taylor stood blinking and frowning. Buckhalter bent far over, forcing a laugh loud enough to stifle the crickets, and managed to get a hard elbow into his buddy just under the short ribs.

"*Uff,*" Taylor said. "What the fuc— Oh." And he started boffing it up too.

Polidor didn't notice anything. He finally got himself straightened out, dabbing at a corner of his eye.

"Yeah, women," he said, "if the sons of bitches didn't have pussies there'd be a bounty on 'em."

"Heh, heh," said Buckhalter. Taylor looked pained. *Mr.* Polidor was reminding them of something they didn't really need to be reminded of. Their unit had been rotated out here seventeen days ago, with four days to go before reassignment. Nicholas Brant's heart was still back in the late eighties, when sex, like anything else you did for yourself instead of for the government, was evil and whenever possible against the law. There were no women on the special adviser's ranch.

That probably didn't bother Polidor too much. Rumor around the tents that served the patrol detail as barracks said he and Stew Jeffcoat had been more than just clones. Polidor was even more keyed up than usual since his buddy's death—an additional reason to tread real light.

"Yeah, you can't live with 'em and you can't live without 'em. You boys keep sharp, now. Don't let any Guardians sneak up on you."

Both troopies laughed at that. "We ain't afraid of no ghosts," Taylor said, half-quoting Ray Parker, Jr. Polidor didn't get it.

Snugging his CAR against his back with a thumb in the sling, Polidor walked on along the eight-foot fence with the razor tape looped along the top, keeping close to the scrub oak and cedar that Brant had ordered planted along the inside of it. Brant resented the necessity of security measures like the fence, and didn't want to be reminded of it whenever he looked out the window. It spoiled the old state-of-nature feeling.

The two grunts stood flat-footed, watching him until he vanished into a fold of the rolling ground.

"Faggot," Taylor said.

They don't call 'em "grunts" for nothing, Lew Polidor said to himself, walking down into the hollow. Your average state patrolman had about the intellect of a turtle. You had to go down every hour or two, kick 'em in the ass and pinch 'em on the nose to keep them awake. Luckily for them he was an easygoing kind of guy, who preferred to use humor to sharpen them up. God knew you had to do something. If it wasn't for SID—and the Team—the bad guys would just overrun the damned state.

Good thing we're taking the initiative now. Best defense is a good offense. He liked the thought so much he rolled it around in his head a couple more times.

"Evening, Lew," a familiar voice said when he reached the foot of the low hill.

By reflex he nodded and skinned his teeth back from his lips, started to return the greeting. Then he recognized the voice.

A match flared, illuminating a heavy face with a broken nose and almost invisible eyebrows.

"You boys're getting a bit overconfident, ain't you?" asked Billy McKay around his cigar. "Walking guard-go with your piece slung? That shit's for grunts, not ee-lite killer squads."

Polidor's heart seemed to have expanded until it was crowding his stomach and pushing bile up his throat. "Yuh-you're *dead*!"

"Not me, big fella."

He came out of his stupor then, reaching back to pull his CAR into firing position. McKay was showing a pair of empty hands. Through some miracle he hadn't burned in the resort with the damned slant squatters, but Lew Polidor was just the man to set that right.

A heavy hand came over the top of his skull, clamped in the hair over his forehead, yanked his head back so hard his neck-bones creaked and stars exploded behind his eyes. His ex-buddy Stew Jeffcoat always liked to play with a sentry with his knife. The man behind him just laid the immense blade of a Bowie across Polidor's throat with the edge toward the thumb and laid him open with a single swipe that scraped bone.

Polidor's last scream gusted out through a severed windpipe in a geyser of blood. Blackness unfolded like a flower behind his eyes.

"One down," Billy McKay subvocalized. *"That's supposed to be a* Princeton *professor?"*

It was only about the two hundredth time he'd said it in the last two days. Some notions took longer than others to percolate through his thick skull. That was how Sam saw it, anyway.

One thing was certain: Sloan didn't really want to know what had elicited the remark.

"People are supposed to do crazy things after the Holocaust, Billy," Casey said. *"Didn't you ever rent videos?"*

McKay made a noise like a man trying to swallow a guinea pig. Sloan grinned briefly, then shifted his night glasses to his eyes and focused them on the main house.

Dr. Nicholas Brant hadn't done too poorly for himself. A sprawling ranch house with high clerestory windows facing away from Sloan's vantage point in a rocky outcrop at the foot of a forested slope, a riding stable complete with riding arena. Maybe a square kilometer of green mountain valley inside that decidedly inorganic razor wire. Brant had been a top-dollar lecturer before the War, as well as an author of numerous textbooks and popular works, and he'd always been ready to serve as paid consultant on economic affairs, especially for Senate subcommittees and blue-ribbon panels and the like. On the other hand, he might have simply expropriated his ranch in the southern end of the Bighorn range from some poor schmuck.

Steady, Sam, he told himself. *The man's personality doesn't affect the validity of his views. Don't throw over everything you believe because of one man's treachery.*

Well, maybe. But Brant's views had been those of the radical eco-activist elite, from the late seventies on. If you wanted to be considered politically correct, you had to admire them for their passion and conviction and carefully not make any parallels between what they preached and what the proprietors of the country between Poland and France preached between 1934 and 1945. It was a lot easier to maintain that kind of flip, hip indifference to consequence when you'd never smelled human meat burning as a result of those views being put into practice.

The man's a swine, he thought. *Fuck him and the horse he rode in on.*

That wasn't going to be easy. The horse Brant had ridden in on was a sexy little Aérospatiale SA.342 Gazelle chopper, the kind with the tail rotor shrouded to dampen torque, painted black with gold trim. It was parked on an apron on this side of the house. It and he were guarded by a squad of highway patrol regulars armed with M16s, quartered in two-man tents pitched in an oblong seventy meters north of the helipad.

There were also all six surviving members of the Team, who obviously were being rewarded for a job well done by a few days' well-earned R&R on the boss's spread. The Guardians had been keeping the place under surveillance since before dawn this morning, and had marked them all down. Their presence was going to make the strike a lot trickier—the SID killers were a different breed from the patrol grunts. But Sam Sloan was just as wolfishly happy to see them there as Billy McKay.

Got to watch that—you're starting to think like him. And maybe he was, but in a time and place like this that was probably survival-positive. And face it: would he have become a Guardian if he *really* believed all the world's problems could be solved by sweetness and light?

McKay announced he and Yellow Bull were moving in, north up the hollow toward the base of the rise on which the house sat. Tom was still working his deliberate way in from the west, trying to hit the house between chopper pad and DPS tents. The ground was open, virtually without cover, but Sloan didn't waste any time trying to spot him. The boys on the ground weren't going to see him, and they'd have a closer look.

Having sent out a prearranged signal over the portable satlink-capable radio, which he had charge of, Casey was lying up on a ridge virtually due north of the house, enabling him to cover it front and back. That meant he would be firing almost in the faces of McKay and Yellow Bull. Normally that was very bad practice. But then, normally you didn't have Casey Wilson on the trigger.

Light spilled out the front of the house. McKay, with Yellow Bull as his shadow, was moving up the road that entered the perimeter from the northeast and turned to run due south along the front of the house before veering west to the sizable garage. On their left was a two-meter earth bank at the base of the down-grade from the house, shielding them from observation from within. To the right the land opened past the tackhouse, stables, and riding arena into a wide meadow.

The horses were whickering nervously as they got close. To McKay they might as well have been announcing the intruders' presence with a megaphone, but Yellow Bull didn't seem both-ered. Billy McKay did not generally put a lot of stock in the opinions of amateurs, but he had grounds to make an exception in this case. The son of a bitch was well and truly over the top, but he had taken out four of the Team with only nominal assis-tance on the last, while the Guardians had yet to lay a glove on them.

Just past the garage McKay went up with his back against the cut, covering the door of the tackhouse with his .45. The Colt had an extra-long barrel dropped in, and a silencer screwed onto the threaded muzzle. They were going to play this quiet as long as possible.

Pressing into his back was the cold metal hardness of his Maremont. The strap was cutting his trapezius in half. At some point in the evening's entertainment the balloon would go up and silence would become academic. When that point arrived, McKay had some sentiments he felt could best be expressed with the M60.

Yellow Bull slipped up the drive, boots making no sound on the gravel for all his bulk. McKay would have been impressed, but he could do it too. Come to think of it, he was impressed

anyway. The Absaroka carried one of the Guardians' silenced
MP5s, part of what they'd brought along from Mobile One in
the Blazer they'd borrowed from Thoanh. He seemed to know
which end the bullets came out of.

The V-450 was still sitting in the stream next to where the
refugees had set up temporary shop. Sam Cohen had charge of
it and Jessie Turner, who had pitched a tantrum when she discovered she was to be left behind. McKay didn't think they were
going to steal anything.

Though the big portable satlink-capable radio had been one
of the items the Guardians brought along, Cohen also was serving as message central for the plan Rogers and Sloan had cooked
up. McKay had no idea how well it would pan out—not even all
of *Tom's* plans worked—but it had seemed worth his while to
restrain his natural impulse to go charging off to settle accounts
with Brant and his dog pack. At least for twenty-four hours.

Sam had carefully locked all computing and communications
functions beyond those necessary to play switchboard; no point
tempting their guests' curiosity. You'd have to be a hell of a
hacker to break that security. Cohen probably didn't come close,
though McKay wouldn't put it past young Jessica. But you could
never provide for everything.

Especially when you had to hustle to take optimum advantage
of being dead.

McKay counted seven, then wheeled and went up the drive
every bit as noiselessly as Yellow Bull had. The ex–Princeton
professor was lying on his belly covering the house. His back
was hunched by a light ruck like the Loco packs the Guardians
sometimes carried. McKay had no idea what was in it, and hadn't
asked. Yellow Bull wasn't exactly a talkative mother, and McKay
hated trying to untangle his backward speech when he did say
something.

They didn't need to talk much anyway, had said maybe half a
dozen words to each other since they'd started to infiltrate toward
the perimeter with the onset of full dark an hour after sunset.
They had just naturally fallen into a groove, where each seemed
to know the moves the other would make. It was like working
with Tom Rogers, or his buddies from his old RECON team. If
Yellow Bull had gotten this good merely by imitating the old
ways his brother always talked about, McKay couldn't see how
the Indians had ever managed to fucking lose.

For a full minute they lay side by side in the drive, making sure they hadn't attracted attention. No sign of activity from the house. The air hummed to the tune of the alcohol-fired generator behind the garage. McKay covered again while Yellow Bull ran to the end of the house. He joined him, hanging on to the butt of his M60 with his free hand to keep it from pounding his own butt to pieces. There were two large windows here, open to the cool air but screened, no light showing through either.

McKay locked eyes with Yellow Bull. McKay nodded. The Absaroka shook his head. Then he drew that young sword and opened the screen with two slashes, a horizontal one high, a vertical down the side.

McKay unslung the Maremont, slid it through, quietly propped it against the frame. Holding the .45, he climbed gingerly through.

It was a bedroom. Their ears had already told them it was unoccupied, but he squatted there in darkness, breathing very quietly, a long moment, before moving to the bed to make sure he was alone.

He moved to the door, pressed an ear against it. A radio was playing somewhere. A young man's voice was speaking in somber, measured tones.

He grinned. That was the multi-megabuck voice of broadcast boy-wonder evangelist Nathan Bedford Forrest Smith, king of Oklahoma and top theocrat of the Midwest, offering prerecorded condolences to the nation for the loss of the heroic Guardians and a village of innocent immigrants in yesterday's tragic forest fire. In all truth Reverend Forrie's only regret about their getting roasted was that he hadn't been on hand to turn the spit himself. But now that they were crispy critters he could eulogize the men he'd been consigning to hell via airwave a month ago, presumably trying to cement the détente the Morrigan crisis had forced him into with the godless regime in Washington.

It was probably a bad sign, but McKay had been listening to the speech since last night and it still gave him an incredible hoot.

He went back to the window, laid down the .45 on the hardwood floor, and started lengthening the M60's sling. It was Israeli-style, so that he could have the pistol in hand but the MG riding level at waist height for when things got serious.

Behind him the door opened. The light came on.

CHAPTER
TWENTY-FIVE —————————————————

Bubba Hughes stood there in his cammies. His satchel-sized right hand was wrapped around the carrying handle of an SAW, which had a box magazine in the well. He blinked.

"Wait a minute," he said slowly, frowning as if this were almost too much of a challenge for him. "You're dead!"

"Wrong again. Now, why don't you just put that thing down nice and—"

The old defensive-lineman aggressiveness kicked in. "Well," Bubba chortled, hiking his M249 up in the air, letting it fly free while he grabbed for the pistol grip, "we can take care of *that*—"

"Mine's bigger," McKay said. He yanked the strap with his left hand, flipped the Maremont up to bear. Bubba had his own, lighter piece in plenty of time, but he fumbled trying to get his finger in the trigger guard.

McKay squeezed his own trigger. The walls seemed to bulge to the hammering scream of the M60. Bubba was wearing his Kevlar vest, which was sufficient to stop stuff like pistol rounds or the soft, round-nose slugs a .30-30 like Eduardo Velez's cranked out.

It was sufficient to *slow down* the heavy 7.62 bullets coming out of the Maremont. That wasn't good enough. By the time the

Kevlar had stretched too far, given up the ghost, and parted before the sharp projectiles, the fabric had been driven clean into his rib cage and assorted vital organs. The Kevlar in back *was* enough to stop the bullets, absorbing the rest of the 60's fearsome muzzle energy.

Bubba went sailing back into the hall. He hit with a squish, and blood suddenly stained the armpits of his camo blouse and squirted out his collar. His big pale blue eyes met McKay's, did not comprehend, and so he died as he'd lived: without much of a clue.

The heavy barrel was pointing upward at quite an angle. McKay hitched it a few degrees higher and squeezed off three more. That had the desired effect: the bullets missed the bare dim light bulb hanging from the beamed ceiling, but the muzzle blast blew it out anyway.

McKay leaned his head back to the cut screen. "Come in, and move it. The party's started."

Nothing happened. McKay heard confused shouting, sprayed a quick five rounds mostly through the open door, splintering the right side of the frame. Just keeping the bad guys honest.

"Yellow Bull?" Still nothing. He stuck his head out into the night.

The Absaroka was gone.

Following their leader's conversations over their communicators, the Guardians didn't need to be told the party had started.

When he heard McKay say, *"Mine's bigger,"* Sloan triggered his M203 by reflex. Even as the weapon thudded it occurred to him that the boss Guardian was perfectly capable of making that kind of statement about something other than his machine gun. Fortunately for his peace of mind, the M60 was incredibly loud. The muffled clatter reached his ears just as the WP grenade was flashing off among the highway patrol tents with a brilliant white light.

The tents were a modern fireproof synthetic. Of course, *fireproof* didn't necessarily cover white phosphorus. Three tents blazed up anyway, and he knew the flakes were burning their way into maybe half a dozen others. From his point of view, the best thing was that he hadn't dusted any people with the hellish stuff. He felt a definite sympathy for the patrolmen, who were just following orders—and while that hadn't been much of a defense at Nuremberg, they were also engaged in nothing more evil than guarding a body the Guardians were real interested in harming.

In fact, he was being a real humanitarian. The unexpected and incredibly ferocious fire from heaven was going to give the patrol boys something other to do than get themselves killed trying to interfere with what was going on in the house.

Yeah, he thought wryly, *me and Mother Teresa.* He sent a tear gas grenade spinning through the night for the tent cluster, from which frantic voices were beginning to burst like a flock of quail.

Casey had been scanning the ranch with a pair of night glasses. The magic scope on his rifle had a scan function that gave him an enhanced-light view without narrowing the vision field the way a scope generally did, but it wasn't exactly efficient to try to track the heavy rifle all over the place. So he had used the binoculars to spot targets in advance, like the master sniper he was.

Now everybody with a weapon had a target painted on him except for his buddies—that was a distinct advantage to working in a four-man team: there was virtually no chance of confusing friend with enemy. Having an extra good guy on the ground didn't terrifically complicate things for a man with Casey's reflexes and eye.

The only targets available at the moment were two guards on the helicopter. He'd always liked the Gazelle. It was a real sweet little machine, almost as good as a real aircraft. The rifle was pointed toward it, propped on a rock on its bipod and stabilized by small sandbags. All Casey had to do was flow in behind it and weld his cheek to the fiberglass stock.

He didn't have to hunt around much to acquire a sentry, who had his M16 unslung and was looking real eager to kill something. Fortunately he was displaying his eagerness by posing like a pointer who's seen a pheasant auger into a bush. Casey was an artist with a sniper's rifle, but he wasn't a magician, and a six-hundred-meter shot at a target that was bobbing and dancing around at random was a matter of almost pure luck.

He had the trigger slack gathered without thinking about it. He never fired unconsciously in a situation like this: that was desperation shooting, not sniping. He let out half the breath he had drawn and broke the glass rod.

There was movement on the verge of his vision as recoil rode his barrel up. When the rifle came back down he disciplined himself to fix on and identify the target before he worked the bolt. A sniper's priorities tended to reverse those of a grunt in a firefight. Deliberation and precision were the keys. It was an odd martial art for a man who was used to throwing a fast and agile steel dart all over the sky with submillimeter twitches of a joystick, but Casey loved it in a way.

The mysterious figure was crouched next to the body of the man Casey had shot. It raised its head, and for a moment a featureless white blob of face fixed on Casey with an exactness that made his skin prickle. None of his teammates knew where he'd set up except in general; he'd picked his spot as the others dispersed to the positions from which they'd make their respective approaches.

I wonder what Yellow Bull's doing there? he thought as he withdrew his head for a wider look at the ranch. From his running commentary McKay obviously thought the Absaroka had run out on him.

Then he saw men running from the tents, which were now burning cheerfully, half-dressed and hastily armed. No time to speculate on their enigmatic ally now—

When he heard McKay's machine gun roaring inside the house, Tom Rogers sprinted the last thirty meters to the rear of the sprawling house. A one-story protrusion hid him from view of Casey, but Sam should still be able to see him. Not that he expected to need help.

He fetched up next to what he took to be the door to the kitchen or pantry. Only the screen was closed, and muggy cooking and cleaning smells were rolling out of it. He waited several heartbeats, leaning the small demo pack on his back against the wall, listening. Excited voices from inside, fearful speculation by the tone; nothing purposeful.

He took his hand off the stun grenade clipped to his left breast pocket. It might be possible to play this quietly.

He reached cautiously sideways, tested the door with infinite care. It wasn't latched. He whipped it open and pivoted through.

A short pantry passage, dark but for the light coming from the kitchen, such as it was. The voices were in there. Tom slipped to the end, paused.

"—going on," a voice was saying. "That was gunfire from the front of the house!"

"Where are those highway patrolmen?" another voice wondered in a theatrically husky whisper. "They're supposed to come if anything happens."

Tom stepped around the corner and aimed his Galil at the two young men crouched by the swinging doors that gave onto the rest of the house, listening in alarm to the confusion of shouts and shots. They wore casual civilian clothes and aprons, and appeared to be unarmed.

"Don't make any loud noises," he said softly, "and we'll all be happier."

They turned, faces strained, mouths open in almost comic shock. He gestured them back from the doors with the Galil's barrel. Hands behind necks, they moved over to stand in front of a large sink. The faucet dripped water; apparently Brant's generators ran pumps for well water.

Keeping the assault rifle aimed, Tom stepped across the tiled kitchen floor to the double doors, risked a three-second look. The brief corridor to the dining room was full of darkness. The fighting seemed to be elsewhere.

He heard the covert kiss of steel on wood. He spun around as the taller of the kitchen helpers lunged for him with a carving knife in hand.

There was no time for dancing. Tom fired a three-round burst. The youth shrieked as his apron blossomed red, fell down writhing and moaning on the tiles.

Tom shouldered open the sliding door and went. He'd lost his own element of surprise. Now the priority was to link up with McKay as soon as possible.

Back to the wall, McKay lobbed the stun grenade backward out the door. It clacked off the far wall and went off with the customary high-pitched bang.

Somebody yelled in surprise out in the hall. McKay stepped out. Three troopies had been moving on him. Two were pawing at their eyes; the third was raising a Remington riot pump and trying to blink back the big colored balloons of light that filled his eyes. McKay took them down with two side-to-side chainsaw sweeps of the M60.

He stepped over them, planting his cleated bootsoles carefully on the blood-slick floor. He quickly checked the doors along the corridor, thinking that this was why the lousy Indian was supposed to be backing him up. Fortunately all he had to do was try the knob. None of them was locked, which meant none was the one he wanted.

The hallway opened into a broad central room, open up to the slanted roof, with a second-story gallery running around three sides of it and a stairway with a polished rail climbing the far side. Billy McKay saw a dark hunched shape between the rails of the gallery above it, and ducked back just as the muzzle flash of a machine gun bloomed.

CHAPTER
TWENTY-SIX

"What do you mean, you can't send help?" Nicholas Brant screamed into the phone handset. It was a modified cellular phone, linked to satellite by the dish on the roof.

It died in his hands. He threw it across the room. "That sniveling coward Greenwell! He said he couldn't send reinforcements!" Kennedy City was less than an hour away by road.

Sawtelle stood by the door with his CAR-15 in his hands. "Why not?"

"He didn't say." Brant walked back and forth, clenching and unclenching his fists. "We'll have to get rid of him. He's outlived his usefulness. The pusillanimous fool!"

"Better stay away from the window, sir," Sawtelle cautioned. "You should have followed my advice and hardened the place."

"Was I supposed to live in a bunker like these swinish survivalists? You approved the measures we prepared. I—"

A quick knock on the door. Weapon ready, Sawtelle called for identification. Then he opened the door.

It was Alex Barka, bareheaded for once. "What's happening?" Brant demanded.

"We seem to be under attack by a sizable force. We've got incoming fire from grenade launchers, and the patrol tent camp is getting shot to hell."

"Yes, yes, but in the house? What's going on beneath us?"

The cowboy shrugged. "They're inside, boss. That's all I know."

Brant took a deep breath. "This will again teach me not to become too attached to my possessions. The time has come to move on."

He went to his desk, leaned over to flick open a protective cover, began to throw switches on the small panel within.

Sam was running low on grenades. He'd lugged in a case of them, assorted HEDP, WP, and tear gas, but they went pretty fast in a situation like this.

He was running out of targets anyway. Half a dozen forms lay strewn on the open ground between the tents and the house, dutiful types who had tried to rush to protect Brant, only to fall victim to Casey. The rest seemed content to fight the fires or stay out of sight, though a few were occasionally spraying the night with automatic fire.

Casey had just reported that he'd shot up the roof satlink-antenna array. It was mostly on general principles. It was unlikely any assistance would be coming out of JFK City tonight.

Sloan heard a series of dull pops beneath the random snarling of fire from the tents and the periodic jackhammer slam of McKay's machine gun inside the house. Clouds of dense white smoke were rolling out of the ground all around the two-story structure.

At first he wondered wildly about a sudden onset of vulcanism. But Yellowstone wasn't all that close, and as an old naval gunnery officer it didn't take him long to recognize a smoke screen from hidden pots when he saw one. Obviously Nicholas Brant wasn't above polluting the atmosphere in self-defense.

His support role had just been canceled. He wasn't going to fire blind with his friends down there.

"Casey," he yelled, jumping to his feet and hastily stuffing the last six grenades from the case into the empty pockets of his carrier vest, "hold position! I'm going in."

McKay crouched behind a planter and cursed under his breath. It was Dozier up there with his M249 SAW. He'd glimpsed enough to recognize the big black. He wondered what the hell he was doing with this bunch.

Unfortunately he wasn't getting to take more than glimpses,

and damned few of those. The Dozer was good at what he did, firing disciplined, precise bursts. The thick planking, dirt, and probable metal lining of the planter were enough to keep the 5.56 rounds away from him—thank Jesus Dozier didn't have an M60—but the Team man had definite fire superiority.

From where he crouched McKay couldn't see the front half of the atrium room, but he could see the rear. While he was wondering how the hell he was going to get out of this, a familiar head in a camouflaged boonie hat poked out of a hallway leading toward the back of the house.

"Tom, I've over here, hall to your right." The head ducked back from its three-second look, then emerged cautiously to peer at him.

Tom frowned. McKay jerked his thumb in what he hoped was the direction of the gallery above the stairs. Dozier caught the motion and helpfully fired, jarring the planter and sending a spray of splinters, rich black soil, and chopped fern bits flying. McKay made himself very small.

Several moments passed, or several weeks, depending on whether you were Billy McKay or not. Then Tom said, *"Give me a count, Billy, I'm ready to go."*

"Right." McKay got a good grip on the front and rear pistol grips of his M60, braced powerful legs.

"One—two—three!"

Tom stepped forward and hooked the stun grenade perfectly between the lathe-turned posts of the railing. Betrayed by reflex, Dozier flicked his eyes at it just as it went off.

McKay shot upright like a jack-in-the-box, trusting his life to Tom's aim. He started firing as soon as he was up, letting the recoil jack the weapon up, hoping the incredible blast and noise of the big machine gun at point-blank range would discombobulate Dozier if the stun bomb hadn't. The railing exploded into spinning splinters as he walked his fire up and into the other machine gunner.

Dozier rolled away from his piece. McKay brought the M60's butt to his shoulder, covered him, nodded to Tom. Tom raced bent over to the foot of the stairs, then doubled back and up them while McKay wished he'd hurry the hell up. Holding the damned Maremont like this made even *his* arms ache.

Rogers bent briefly over Dozier, then knelt just inside the corridor that gave off the gallery into either wing of the huge house.

"It's clear, Billy. Come ahead on."

"Thank God." McKay lowered the weapon till the sling took its weight. From his web belt he took a couple of firefight simulators, basically outsized strings of firecrackers. He activated ten-second-delay fuses and tossed them on the floor to complicate everybody's life.

Dozier lay with his back to a wall, glowering at McKay and trying to tear open the plastic wrapper of an emergency pressure bandage with white even teeth. He had taken at least one through the body. The camouflage pattern on his blouse was virtually drowned in red-black, and his right arm didn't seem to be doing him much good.

There was no time to finish him, and they could use at least one survivor of the Team to ask a few questions. He didn't seem to pose much threat right now anyway. He had no sidearm. If he had some kind of sneaky-pistol tucked away and wanted to make a play with it, more power to him.

"You go right," McKay said. "I'll take left."

The first door on the left opened into a big book-lined room. Peering in cautiously, McKay could see the lights were on, and they were brighter than any he had seen anywhere else in the house. *Brant, you little bastard.* He prepped a stun grenade, tossed it in, followed the report in with machine gun ready at the hip.

A *second* flash, exploding like a supernova, right in front of his eyes. Some clever bastard had averted his head when his stun bomb went, then popped off one of his own. McKay was temporarily blind and deaf, and probably permanently fucked.

He held the trigger down and threw himself sideways and back to where muscle-memory said the door was, practically propelling himself with the heavy weapon's recoil.

He ricocheted off the doorjamb, went lurching to the hard wooden floor of the hall, losing his grip on the MG. "You ain't getting away that easy," he heard the voice of Alex Barka say from a thousand miles away. His hearing was coming back quickly; the ear plugs had protected his ears. But he still could see jack shit. He clutched at himself with frantic fingers.

"I guess Dooley was a bigger fuckup than we realized," the SID man said from somewhere behind him. "I'll just have to finish what he started, I reckon."

McKay rolled something heavy toward the voice. Then he turned his face to where his knees were telling him the wall was, wrapped his hands around the back of his neck, and made himself the smallest ball possible.

He caught a break then. The Willie Peter grenade bounced into the doorway before going off, virtually between Barka's legs. The blast blew one of the highway patrolman's legs off at the hip and flung him in a flaming unconscious heap in the middle of Brant's study.

The doorway channeled blast and fragments so that McKay's back caught the brunt of the phosphorus, sparing his legs. A wasp hit the back of his left hand and drilled its stinger deep.

Biting back a gasp of pain he uncoiled, unslinging his Maremont, tearing his blouse off and throwing it down. He could feel the heat of a hundred metal pellets burning their way through his Kevlar vest. He tore it off his head and flung it away.

His vision was coming back, though he seemed to have pools of burning oil on his eyeballs. A Black & Decker drill was working its way through his hand, none too fast. He hauled out his Kabar knife and jabbed the tip into the back of his left hand.

The flake hadn't eaten too far in. The point hit it almost at once. The burning phosphorus welded itself to the knifetip, readily surrendered its grip on flesh.

"Need help, Billy?" He glanced down the hall. Tom was crouched halfway down the far corridor, covering him.

"I'm fine," he lied. He tried to bang the flake off against the wall. It clung stubbornly to the blade. "Fuck it," he said, and dropped the knife.

The hallway looked like the ceiling of one of those old-time movie theaters that had little lights all over black ceiling so it would look like a starry sky. There'd been one still open in Pittsburgh when he was a kid, he could never remember the name. It always used to freak him to come out of the theater and realize it was still daylight, when the ceiling had just convinced his senses it was night.

Of course, the stars in that old theater had been farther away, and they hadn't each drooled a strand of thick white smoke. Luckily there was nothing immediately inflammable on hand, but the paneling and framing were going to catch from the phosphorus, sooner or later. That was cool; he wasn't planning on spending a lot of time here.

He gave the study a quick glance. There wasn't much to be done for old Alex. The shock of his leg going had put him right

out, which was best for him and spared McKay having to listen
to a lot of howling. His nerves were just about shot.

"Billy," Tom said. He was almost able to hear his actual
voice, soft as it was and coming from twenty-odd meters away.
"I think I've found it."

"Great." He recovered his MG, which, shielded by his body,
had escaped the phosphorus, and reeled down the hall to where
Tom was fixing finger charges over the hinges of a closed door.
"Lemme set 'em off. You go keep an eye on the stairs."

Tom handed over the electrical hand detonator and moved to
take up position. McKay rapped on the door.

"Anybody in there, stand the hell back," he shouted. His
voice sounded muffled to himself, but if anyone was inside they
probably hadn't had the same kind of problems recently that he
had. He stood to one side and clacked the detonator.

The three explosions weren't loud, comparatively speaking.
He leveled his machine gun and kicked the door. The charges
had worked as advertised: the door swung inward and fell down
when he kicked it, rather than standing its ground and dumping
him on his ass. That had happened.

It was a bedroom with heavily barred windows. A burly man
dressed in jeans, boots, and a yellow tee shirt sat on the bed.
His hair and beard were long, black touched with gray, and
matted.

He was staring in complete incomprehension at the open door.
"Who the hell are you?"

"Your rescuers, God help us," McKay said. "Get a move on,
McKendree."

Shaking his head, the big man got to his feet.

Keeping him covered with the MG, McKay backed out into
the corridor. He looked to his right, to see someone standing
down at the far end of the hall, beyond the atrium: the lean,
clean, familiar figure of Toby Sawtelle, holding what looked like
an oblong box on his shoulder, pointed right at McKay.

Robert Dozier had crawled almost to the corridor. "Toby,
no!" he screamed.

"Fry, nigger," Sawtelle said.

"Tom, duck!" McKay yelled, and dove forward as smoke
gusted from the back of the box and a small missile snaked
toward him.

CHAPTER
TWENTY-SEVEN ─────────────

The rocket hit a planter at the atrium end of McKay's corridor. The hallway and part of the landing were instantly engulfed in a howling orange inferno.

Reuben McKendree stared in horror at the flames in the corridor, rolling through to lick at the top of the doorframe. "What was *that*?"

"M202 FLASH," McKay said in disgust. "What the army uses now instead of flamethrowers."

"I've heard of those."

"You have? Well, great. Then you know we are in serious shit. We can't just hold our breaths and run through this shit."

Over the hurricane rush of the flames he heard more whoosh-*whoomps*. There were four rockets in an M202 launcher, and Sawtelle was giving the house all of them. He went to the window and tugged on the bars.

McKendree laughed at them. "Think I haven't tried that?"

"Yeah. I guess you probably have. Give me a hand with this door."

"Why?"

"Because I'll fucking shoot you if you don't, you dumb son of a bitch. We want to keep the fire *out* and the air *in* as long as possible."

Which wasn't going to be very. They maneuvered the door back into place. Flames still licked lasciviously at the edges.

"I'm sure that'll help a lot," McKendree said sarcastically.

"Hey, I'm thinking about it."

McKendree sat on the bed. "I can't tell you how much that reassures me."

"Everybody's a fucking comedian. How'd they do those tapes? They make you do it?"

"What tapes?"

"All those death threats and shit."

"How do you know about those? They told me they had some shrink in to treat me for sociopathic tendencies, wanted to run a psychological stress evaluation on me. They had me read a bunch of psycho shit. I guess they thought it was like what I'd write, though anybody'd know the difference."

"Yeah." McKay was going over the room, which had nothing in it but a nightstand, a Bible, and a couple of copies of Brant's books. Nothing that suggested escape, anyway.

The window glass was open. McKay remembered there were times in fires when you were supposed to *close* the windows and others when you were supposed to *open* them. He couldn't remember which, but it stood to reason that if the window was shut that conflagration was going to eat all their air in a hell of a hurry, while it was going to get in at them sooner or later no matter what they did.

"I went ahead and read for the fuckers," McKendree was going on, as if McKay cared at this point. "They said there was a chance they'd let me go if they could treat me, get me straightened out. Well, I told them to go straight to hell and get in line to fuck their mothers. Then they said they wouldn't feed me if I didn't, so I said, what the hell, I'm way too strong for them to play games with my head, so why the hell not—"

"Shut the hell up."

"Billy? Billy, are you all right?"

"Hey, Tom, I'm just fine. Should be well done in just a few more minutes."

"Is McKendree there?"

"Yeah. Might as well invite all the highway patrol boys over; gonna be plenty of barbecue to go around."

"Sam's with me. We can get you out."

"How the hell are you gonna manage that? You can't get within twenty feet of the door, and the whole building's gonna go up before the incendiary burns out.''

''Trust *us*,'' Sloan's voice said. *''And whatever you do, don't stand in the northeast corner of the room.''*

He took a moment to take his bearings, then herded McKendree to the corner by the door, which was the southwest corner. McKendree looked doubtful about going and standing next to the door, which was starting to do some serious smoking of the kind that usually happens when wood's about to burst into flame, but then again McKay had all the guns, and a habit of talking to invisible people.

''Right, we are officially not in the northeast corner of the room. What's the punch—''

A geyser of incandescent gas blew right up through the floor.

''—line.''

''Shaped charge.''

''Yeah. I guessed that.'' He gestured at McKendree. ''After you. It's gonna be a tight fit, but that's better than being a pot roast.''

''Whuff,'' McKay said, as he dropped to the floor of the room below. ''Thought I was never gonna make it.''

''You could stand to lose a few pounds, McKay,'' Sloan said smugly. ''Get some more roadwork.''

''Fuck you very much.''

He was starting to say more when the sound of helicopter rotors beat through the wall.

''Fuck. *Brant.*''

They ran out, herding McKendree at gunpoint. Robert Dozier lay on his side by the wall, face the color of a long-dead campfire. He had managed to kick out the railing uprights splintered by McKay's bullets and roll through onto the stairs away from the flames. It hadn't done his internal hemorrhaging all the good in the universe. Tom Rogers stooped, swung him over a shoulder in a fireman's carry. The SID man groaned but managed not to cry out.

The atrium was in flames now, completely impassable. They went quickly out the way McKay had gotten in. The smoke pots were still burning. They left the injured captive by the wall and raced to the helipad.

It was empty. They ran on until the smoke thinned out, in

time to see the little Gazelle sweeping south, tilted gracefully forward on its big rotor.

McKay braced, pulled his M60 to his shoulder, pressed the trigger. Nothing happened. The feed belt had gotten twisted in the half-moon box in all the excitement.

"Shit. Casey, get some rounds in that thing."

"I've hit it twice, Billy. I'll do what I can." He sounded ready to cry in frustration. The idea of being unable to bring down a mere *helicopter* was agony for a man who'd splashed five MiGs in one mission.

But fragile as they are, helicopters aren't easy to bring down with single 7.62 shots, and when the thing leapt into the smoke it had already been in motion. Even as they watched it moved beyond even Casey's range, curving east out over the Bighorn foothills and plains beyond.

"Spread out, keep an eye out for highway patrol heroes and that ski bum fucker, the sniper."

"Dozier says he's gone to JFK City," Rogers said. "Toothache."

"Shit, shit, *shit*. We lost *three* of the bastards. That means we got to start all o—"

The Gazelle blew up. Just like that: a flash, and then a slow orange meteorite falling to the rolling land.

"I will be dipped in shit," McKay said.

"Billy, look!" Sloan gripped McKay's forearm and pointed south, toward the ridge from which he had infiltrated to the ranch's perimeter hours before.

A solitary figure stood, not quite silhouetted by the garish flame that seemed to light the prairie like a stage. He waved. They could make out no detail at almost a kilometer's range, but none of them had any doubt who it was.

Nor that he was holding in his other hand a radio-controlled command detonator.

"He's free," Sloan said. "If a Crazy Dog Wishing to Die fulfills his quest without dying, he's released from his vow, if I remember right."

"I wonder," Billy McKay said, "what the son of a bitch would've done if they'd actually *killed* his goddam brother."

EPILOGUE ──────────────────────────

There were Sikhs manning the roadblock at JFK City that morning, trim men with beards, turbans, and long black FN-FAL rifles. They waved the Guardians' borrowed Blazer through with triumphant yells.

A party of Spanish-looking guys on horseback passed them going the other way as they rolled for the Wooden Palace. Sloan nodded from behind the wheel to the leader, who solemnly nodded back.

"One of Velez's brothers-in-law, I'll bet," he said.

"Yeah," said McKay, stifling for the thousandth time the impulse to play with the dressing on the back of his much-abused left hand. The wound-healing accelerator, Tom had explained as he applied it, was something the late Dr. Nicholas Brant would have approved of wholeheartedly: one hundred percent natural and organic Arabian Sea catfish slime. McKay didn't want to know that. It *itched*.

The Team had made a few mistakes other than tangling with the Guardians. The "unassimilable" ethnic settlements they'd hit were the ones where they tended to keep most of the old ways. It was surprising how many immigrant groups held to notions of fanatical loyalty to the extended family, blood feuds, and all like that. It had taken twenty-four hours to arrange the peaceful seizure of JFK City—but only because it took a lot of radio and satlink back-and-forthing to work the details out. There had been *plenty* of cousins, brothers, friends, and whatnot of the Team's victims to volunteer.

And not just from immigrant groups. After they called Washington to present their superiors with a *fait accompli*, they had gotten a records check run on Frank Ed Yellow Bull's older brother. He wasn't exactly an amateur at the game he'd been playing. Back in the eighties he'd been in Special Forces, serving with the forerunner to SOG. His legendary exploits were as well known to Tom Rogers as the details of the Son Tay raid—under his game name of Spotted Rabbit, after the Absaroka culture-hero. He'd gotten the Princeton gig after retiring from SF.

The hefty four-wheeler stopped at the Kennedy City clinic, where a crew was standing by with a stretcher and a blood-replacement drip for Robert Dozier. Dozier was just barely hanging on to life. Tom Rogers had performed emergency field surgery on him by kerosene lamp the night before, after a personal call from Governor Greenwell—under coercion, of course—had convinced the remaining highway patrolmen to surrender.

McKay would have been just as happy to see the bastard bleed to death. Most of what he'd gasped out just confirmed what they knew or had guessed already. He himself had gotten turned on to eco-activism by a guest lecture by Brant at his college. He'd joined the highway patrol after a stint in the army. When before the War gubernatorial adviser Brant had talked his patron Greenwell into appointing him chief of a special organized-crime task force—in spite of his lack of law enforcement background—it had been a natural thing for the twice-decorated Patrolman Dozier to apply for membership on his handpicked Team.

It was occurring to Dozier, just a bit late, that he'd been accepted as a pure token. He had talked himself into overlooking the racist thrust of a lot of Brant's ideas—much of America had, pre-War. By the time the campaign against ethnic bands began, he was convinced his continued participation would convince Brant that blacks were capable of real environmental consciousness.

That convinced Billy McKay that Dozier was a silly son of a bitch who would be small loss. But his trial would be invaluable as a demonstration of how the MacGregor administration was reestablishing impartial law and order to a stricken nation.

It would also help secure their own tenuous legal position.

McKay had gone ahead and deputized the whole two hundred assorted friends and relations who had captured Kennedy City, in the name of the federal government. He hoped he was actually entitled to do that.

A contingent of Basques from Idaho guarded the Wooden Palace, big men with hard faces the color and texture of boot leather. The Team had certainly gone out of its way in a couple of senses to piss off the wrong sort of people.

Karl Greenwell came running down the steps to greet them as they de-assed the Blazer, his black lustrous hair in disarray. "This is an outrage!" he exclaimed as soon as he came in earshot. "I have already filed the strongest possible protest with Washington. I demand that you withdraw these, these *bandits* at once from—"

He finished toe to toe with McKay. The Guardian stuck a cigar between their faces and lit it.

"Justice, huh? Listen, dude, if we didn't have good testimony that you were just a patsy, I'd hold a drumhead court-martial and shoot you for treason. Or maybe accomplice to attempted genocide. I'm sure we'd find plenty of grounds."

He blew a noxious cloud into Greenwell's face. "We maybe still could, if you wanted to make a big enough issue of it. . . ."

The governor staggered away. His face had a distinctly greenish cast. *Some people just don't appreciate a fine cigar.*

A battered old Ford pickup truck, faded by the sun to a brick kind of color, was jouncing down the road from the direction opposite the way they'd come in. It wheezed to a stop twenty meters away. Samuel Cohen got out the driver's side. Jessica Turner came out the other.

She came flying straight for Reuben McKendree in an adolescent pinwheel of arms and legs.

"I hope she ain't got a knife," McKay subvocalized.

"Should we try to stop—" Sloan began, worried.

She hit McKendree in the chest at a full run and wrapped thin, strong arms around his neck.

"Daddy!" she screamed.

"The little bitch set us up," McKay said, kicking over a rock. Small white things scurried beneath it.

Blinking up into the high-noon sun on Kennedy City's outskirts, Samuel Cohen shook his furry head. "Not really. She was confused and scared."

"Of us?"

"In part. You came into the camp with all guns blazing. Of course, you had been shot at first—our friends on the Team having tipped off the denizens of the Coleman ranch that you were on your way to wipe them out. The same thing they told the inhabitants of the other retreats they sent you after."

McKay mashed up his face. That was not going to be one of his favorite recollections in old age. The Guardians had let themselves be used.

"You can understand why she might be reluctant to admit her relationship with McKendree. Then there is Jessie's complicated relationship with her father."

"Complicated? *Complicated?* She said she hated him, for Christ's sake. Said he *raped* her."

Cohen shrugged, spread his hands. A mounted patrol of Chinese-looking men in piratical red headbands swept by the base of the hill. They ignored the pair.

"She has a love-hate relationship with her father. He took her in before the War after her mother died. Jessica didn't resist—the State would have gotten her otherwise, and no doubt sent her to a reformatory until they could find a foster home, which most likely would have been never. But she hated him for abandoning her and her mother, and blamed him for her mother's death."

"He made her get radiation sickness?" McKay was completely adrift.

Cohen shook his head. "That was all fantasy. So was the rape part. Jessica told me the story while we waited for word from you, once she realized I knew most of it already. I was part of McKendree's defense team, after all, and learned more than a few details of the man's personal life.

"Her mother was an exotic dancer, an on-and-off girlfriend of McKendree's. As I said, she actually died before the War. Drug overdose, probably suicide. I'd say he loved her."

"Why the hell didn't he marry her and take her away to his White goddam Castle, then?"

Cohen looked at him strangely. "We're a very complex organism, Lieutenant. Sometimes I wonder if we'll ever understand ourselves, even if our science gets back on track in time."

"What are you talking about?"

"Serena Turner, Jessie's mother, was half-black, Lieutenant. Mulatto, they used to call it, though thankfully the term has largely passed from use."

He patted McKay's biceps. "Let's get back to the others. And you'd better close your mouth. You don't want a horsefly flying in."

"Lieutenant McKay," McKendree said, walking up to McKay with a peculiar bandy-legged biker strut as Cohen and he walked back to the palace, "I owe you a tremendous debt of gratitude and honor. Not just for my life but the life of my daughter."

There were the lives of all his buddies back at the Coleman ranch, many of which the Guardians had taken before the Team blew up the rest. But it was not convenient for McKendree to mention that right now. He was still in custody pending investigation of the recent events in the state of Wyoming, even though they had Dozier's testimony about the frame-up. Nobody was ready to take his total innocence for granted *quite* yet.

He stuck out a big hand. McKay looked at it as if it were some sort of Grade Z movie alien tentacle. Dripping slime.

McKendree gave a slight shrug and dropped his hand.

"It's an honor to meet you at last, Lieutenant. I've followed your career with interest since the *Parade* article."

McKay grunted.

"Yes, here is proof—blond, blue-eyed, Nordic living proof—of the evolutionary superiority of our mighty white Aryan race—"

McKay hit him. Straight right to the beard. Coldcocked him.

Jessica yelped and threw herself all over his prostrate form. McKay turned away so he could rub his knuckles without anybody seeing.

The Basques were roaring with laughter. Sloan materialized at McKay's shoulder.

"What on earth made you do that, McKay?"

McKay looked at him.

"You think I'm gonna let a two-bit pond-scum peckerwood son of a biker bitch like that get away with thinking he's every bit as good as me, just because he's *white*?"